Peter Bensley is an actor who [illegible] Australian productions. He and [illegible] children and live on Sydney's northern beaches. This is his first book.

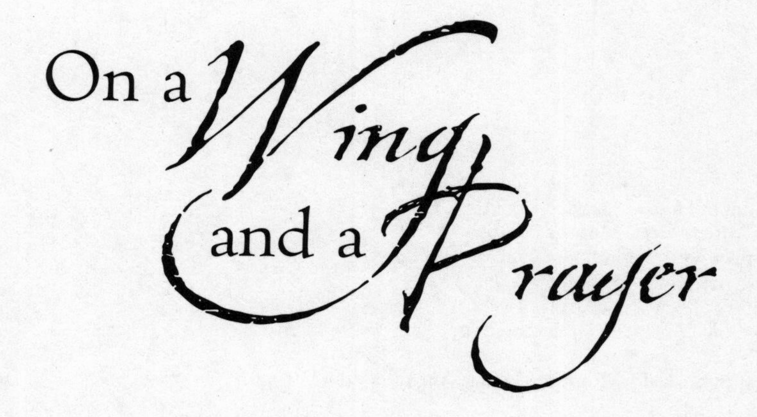

On a Wing and a Prayer

PETER BENSLEY

RANDOM HOUSE AUSTRALIA

Random House Australia Pty Ltd
20 Alfred Street, Milsons Point, NSW 2061
http://www.randomhouse.com.au

Sydney New York Toronto
London Auckland Johannesburg

First published by Random House Australia 2006

National Library of Australia
Cataloguing-in-Publication Entry

Bensley, Peter.
On a wing and a prayer.

ISBN 978 0 09183 235 3.
ISBN 0 091 83235 7.

I. Title.

A823.4

Cover and internal design by Darian Causby/www.highway51.com.au
Cover landscape image by photolibrary.com
Typeset by Midland Typesetters, Australia
Printed and bound by Griffin Press, Netley, South Australia

10 9 8 7 6 5 4 3 2 1

For Eric and Mary

Prologue

A black rubber face mask sucked tight against the Kid's skin as he took in a deep breath of oxygen. He could feel it filling his lungs, flooding his body with a sense of security that would last only as long as his breath. Goggles masked his eyes, and in turn, his sense of fear. He felt uncomfortable at this height. Vulnerable. Exposed.

With the throttle wide open, the Kid eased back on the stick. The Spitfire began climbing at two thousand feet a minute. He felt his body being pressed down into the single armour-plated seat of the aircraft and, just for a second, he thought about warm nights down by the park, and the peppercorns and willows that fish-tailed their leaves across the surface of the lake. But as he climbed higher into the night his lake turned to black; under-currents wrapped around his legs and dragged him down. He stole another breath as the aircraft buffeted its way deeper into the long bank of clouds. At twenty thousand feet he burst into the heavens, an insignificant speck among the stars.

It was a year and a half since he'd left England, a passenger skirting shipping lanes and air routes, a journey charted on Allied maps. He'd been among the first to be recalled to defend the homeland following the Japanese raids of February 1942. This was his first tour of duty. A routine patrol out of Darwin. It was a long way from the unforgiving skies of northern Europe. He'd made it. He'd survived the war. He was one of only a handful.

He concentrated on his breathing. Slowly, evenly. Treat every flight as your first – that's what he'd been told and that's how he'd stayed alive. Others had not been so lucky. He'd seen men incinerated, pulled from twisted wreckage with their skin festering. His thoughts sidetracked again, back to a time when flying was a passion. A dream held aloft by canvas and wood. He remembered how he'd discovered the curve in the earth and an ocean that reached beyond the horizon.

Night slid silently over the northern tip of Australia. A star fell across the aircraft canopy. He went to make a wish, but then it disappeared. He made one anyway. He wished he was home with Bernadette, their fingers entwined. He longed for the tender response of her lips, the prickling sensation of fingernails pulled gently across his skin. At twenty-seven thousand, he levelled off and hid with his thoughts of her, the two of them alone in the darkness.

Out of nowhere, a violent punch ripped them apart.

Tracer bullets pierced his aircraft, tearing deadly trails of lead and magnesium through the fuselage. He swore into his face mask, then kicked against the rudder bar. The Spitfire twisted violently, gravity rolling the skin across his face as the horizon lifted over the canopy.

'Break left! Break left!' His frantic voice confirmed his actions.

The scream of another aircraft filled the cockpit. Blood drained from his upper body. An eardrum burst. The shrill of the supercharged Merlin engine tore unimpeded through his head. He passed out. The under-currents of his childhood lake dragged him down. This was all wrong. This was not supposed to happen. He'd been caught out, drifting carelessly in his other life.

As the horizon levelled, blood pumped back through his arteries, redefining his features and bringing him back to life. He released the trigger guard and pushed the nose of his plane towards his assailant – a fleeing shadow. He too was alone, afraid, and worried about the moonlight on his wings and the red glow that trailed from his exhausts.

The night became a blackboard of probabilities; on it a mathematical equation ruled an imaginary line through his gun sight. For three seconds he held his opponent's life in his hands – a three-second burst of fire into his canopy, that's all it would take – but his thumb paused over the executioner's button . . .

Time slowed to the pace of a country town. The Kid steadied his right hand on the joystick by grasping it with his left. Three seconds turned to four, four to five.

Beads of sweat began to gather in the corners of his oxygen mask as he held the shadow in his sights for yet another, long second. Then, against his own instincts of survival, he broke hard and right. His body turned inside out as his aircraft rolled away into the night.

The smell of burning oil was permeating his oxygen mask. His breathing became laboured. He tapped the gauges, hoping the oil pressure might somehow right itself, but with each tap the needle dipped further. Falling engine revs accompanied a change in the whine of the engine – it was just a matter of time before it started choking back the heat, gasping for clean air. Nausea rose in his stomach as the altimeter needle began winding its way back down to earth.

He wasn't going to make it. Finally, it was his turn. The odds had been building for months. He deserved it. None of the others had – most of them were first-timers, rookies; for them it was just bad luck.

He broke the canopy seal and felt the heat searing past. He had to get out while he still had the height. Then, releasing his harness, he suddenly remembered his watch . . . How could he have forgotten it? It was his lucky charm, his return ticket. As a consequence, he was more than likely going to die. There was a time when he never thought about luck, but superstition and omens were now part of his life.

He pulled himself up in the seat, only to find his left leg had somehow got caught in the pedal housing. With every twist, it grew tighter, like the foot of a rabbit caught in a cruel trap. He thought about the fuel tank sitting between the cockpit and the engine. His burn rate had been low; the risk of fire was high.

A prayer. The one he tried to remember got all mixed up with another and then he started thinking about how he was still a virgin, and in a strange way he felt kind of pure, like a saint or some holy man, who'd go straight to heaven. But other images, of screaming men and body parts, blotted spilt blood over such pious thoughts.

He lowered the nose of the Spitfire and held his best glide speed. He'd cheated the last fifty miles, fifty to go. Eight more minutes to the Australian coast. Ahead, horizontal lines of white spray momentarily fluoresced before disappearing into the sea. A minute lasted three. Sea spray stung hard against the underbelly of the aircraft. He began skimming waves like a flat stone that he might once have skipped across the surface of his lake. He fought to stay conscious, for one last moment on the cusp of the earth. He looked up into the stars, then slumped forward in his seat. Dreamtime fingers of thermal air lifted the fighter plane over the sandbar and into Arnhem Land.

With dawn came resurrection. The early morning painted a steamy watercolour of greens and blues. It snared the East Alligator River flowing into the Arafura Sea, and the birds, in their thousands, on their mud-flat feeding grounds. A rising tide climbed the mangroves, then washed along a deep scar that ended abruptly at the fallen aircraft.

The Kid sat strapped in his seat, listening to the sound of his own breathing, the lapping of water, and the distant sound of the surf. He could have been anywhere – back home in Sydney, at the beach, feeling the sun penetrating his closed eyelids. Everything was still. There was no longer any rush. No panic. No pain. No terror. Nothing. It was over.

He lifted his goggles to reveal a round face carried over from childhood. 'The Kid', that's what everybody called him, and as a nickname it had stuck. Sandy hair, wet from the tropical humidity, was glued to his scalp. His eyes were set wide, like a hunter's, and were tainted by dark circles that came with the territory. In the northern hemisphere, every piece of bare skin had been covered; today he was in shorts, with flying boots that reached just below his knees.

His left foot felt loose somehow, disconnected, as if it were in its own warm bath; his socks, a wet hand towel. The frame of the cockpit floor had been ripped open and was twisted across his boot. Wiring and broken glass covered the floor pan. He reached under his seat for the carved-bone handle of his knife, with its buffalo and Indian motifs. He'd always wanted one as a kid, ever since he'd seen an ad on the back page of *Post* magazine. He slid the blade down the side of his leg and sliced back the leather uppers of his boot. Oil spewed freely from the seams, but his foot remained stuck.

Inside the cockpit door was 'the shoehorn', a small crowbar to be used at the pilot's discretion. He pulled it from its housing and placed it under the pedal bar, but the leverage needed to release his foot was too great.

Moisture condensed on his skin. Dried blood clotted his hearing. He pushed back in the seat and took in his surroundings. Mud and mangroves created a wall as impenetrable as any one might find around a prison; beyond that, a line of gums did a slow dance to the rising waves of heat. There would be no escape from his metallic island. He closed his eyes and slumped back into the seat. In some ways it almost came as a relief. It was all over. Thank Christ. An overwhelming tiredness suddenly consumed him. His head fell against his oxygen mask as he drifted into a semi-conscious state.

Evening brought with it the shrill of a tuppenny whistle, a songline that blew through the cockpit. It was night and he was still there, his foot still pinned to the plane.

The moonlight shone like a torch from the back verandah of his parents' house. Catching his eye, it was as reassuring as his mother's voice from the kitchen window. *You're not scared out there, are you, love? Why don't you come inside?*

He imagined driving over Sydney Harbour Bridge in his Uncle Neil's Riley, with the top down and the wind caressing his skin. He saw himself at the shop, making small talk with customers, with no sense of time. All that seemed to be a part of another life now. Through broken sleep he heard the sound of distant aircraft, distant voices, but nothing ever materialised.

The following day brought with it only more of the

same. To the south of his position, the Kid recognised a landmark – previously just a pilot's scribble on a guide map. From ground level, it appeared as a rocky outcrop that blistered out of the ground. That would be his objective, to make it to the rocky vantage point.

He tried to push back the cockpit flooring but the heat overwhelmed him. He would hide in the shadows of his jacket and try again in the cool of the evening. In half dreams he watched faraway thunderstorms vaporising through the bush and felt the hot wind drying his mouth from the inside out.

The screech of birds jolted him from a restless sleep. Their cries filled the landscape as they momentarily blotted out the sun and raced their shadows across the mangroves. Reality was beginning to blur. He thought he heard a low drone beneath the bird cries and chose to believe it was an aeroplane. He chose to believe it was Stainless, coming to save him.

Stainless sat in the back of the Catalina seaplane and thought about the lobsters he'd cooked on the beach. In some ways he resembled the crustacean he held in his hand, with his red hair and fair complexion ravaged by the sun, so much so that, as he turned the lobster over, its legs and his fingers became indistinguishable.

He'd set the cray pots the week before, dropped them from low altitude like mines into the sea, and now the opportunity had risen to 'do the rounds'. The Catalina's blister windows offered excellent visibility, and its ability to land on water made it a perfect aircraft for the job at hand. He flicked on the radio transmitter.

'Follow the estuary, Mort – might have more luck there.'

The Mortician mumbled something back from the pilot's seat, but it was lost to the sound of the radial engines.

Stainless was a man reinvented out of necessity. He was forty-two and, like the species of shellfish he was currently appraising in his hand, gifted with an uncanny ability to adapt to almost any given situation. He'd always been called Stainless, not that it was a reflection of his character in any way. At present the war was working well for him. With the arrival of the Yanks came a number of 'business opportunities'. A small but lucrative market had expanded into a moving shopfront of in-demand articles; this week it was crayfish.

'Look, there it is!' It was young Todd Davitt who spotted the plane first.

Stainless dropped the lobster back into the bucket and peered out of the blister window. There it was, all right, half submerged in the mangroves. They'd been sweeping an area of the sea to the north. If it hadn't been for the cray pots, he might have been missed altogether.

'Shit,' said Stainless. 'I spent half of last week getting that plane serviceable – and now look at it.' He turned to look at Todd. 'No respect for government property – whaddya reckon?'

Todd Davitt was sixteen or so and knew bugger all about anything, but that was a good point as far as

Stainless was concerned. As a mechanic's apprentice he wasn't all bad, the best thing about him was his ability to keep his mouth shut.

'Get us in closer, would ya, Mort?' Stainless called into the transmitter before looking back to Todd. 'He'll be all right. He's survived worse than that.'

The teenager nodded but said nothing.

'You ever been up to New Guinea, son?' Stainless asked. One thing the war had taught him was that life went on.

'No, sir.'

Sir. He liked that. That was a nice touch. 'Thinking of opening up an airline there. Commercial routes, along the Sepik River. New Guinea's up for grabs, Todd. It's the future, but now's when you've got to set it up . . .'

Todd had heard it all before, but took it all in just the same. *You gotta think big, son. There's a lotta opportunities out there* – that was where Stainless's spiels usually ended.

As the Catalina straightened out of its turn and lined up for a new approach over the crash site, Todd looked out of the window again. It would have been obvious to anyone down there that they were overhead. He willed an arm to wave from the Spitfire cockpit, but there was no sign of life.

Part One

Chapter One

Don Cameron didn't care much about how he looked or smelt. Any sense of vanity he may have had as a youth had gone. He'd shaved – that was a good sign. Quite often the outcome of the day simply depended on whether he could be bothered to shave. Never any aftershave, though. If needed, a bottle of meths waited behind bathroom-cabinet doors that had long since ceased to close. Alongside the meths bottle, mixtures sat in jars with handwritten labels such as *Black Ointment* and *Liver Oil*, together with used razors and small tubes of things that wormed out across brown-paper-covered shelves.

He dipped his fingers into a glass and fished out a set of upper dentures. He'd just turned seventy-seven. Maybe he was older than that. After all, it was the year . . . 1990-something. Was it 1995 perhaps, or 1997? He couldn't be sure. Maybe seventy-seven was just a number that stuck in his head. For that matter, maybe it had been somebody else's birthday.

The warmth from the two-bar heater radiated against the back of his legs. Keeping warm seemed harder than it used to be, and bathing every day no longer necessary. Routine was all that mattered and today was Thursday. Or was it Friday? He reached into the top pocket of his pyjamas and took out a small notebook. If it was Thursday, he had a driving lesson. That had been Paul's idea – 'It'll help you get your confidence back, Pop,' his son had told him. There was no test as such, nothing to pass or fail; just a 'top-up' lesson.

But if it was Friday, Tom Barton was coming over . . . Tom. He liked Tom. A dog man. Greyhounds. Three of them were buried in Don's back yard: 'Laddie', 'Zoom Boy' and . . . and . . . His memory was fading. He retrieved a pencil stub from the same top pocket and wrote the two names he remembered in his notebook.

They'd intended to bury the dogs in the grounds of Tom's Commission flat, but there'd been complaints, so they were now at rest alongside the fence that separated Don from his neighbour on the left-hand side of the terrace. Don thought about when he and Tom first met – it must've been a long time ago. At South Sydney Leagues maybe. He remembered sharing the winning ticket in a meat tray with someone who could well have been Tom.

The shrill of the kettle sent him out of the bathroom and down the stairs. The well-worn journey was a slow one, thanks in no small part to all his security precautions, as every door had a lock and every lock had a key. He shuffled his way past a colonnade of bundled papers that led to the hallway. High-wattage globes produced an unforgiving light; every metre or so, a wallpaper join had peeled back into a tight roll. At the end of the hallway was the kitchen, the room in which he spent most of his time.

An old fridge and a cooker shared valuable floor space with more recent additions. The old stove top was littered with tobacco tins overflowing with watch parts, magnifying eyepieces and miniature tools. Beyond the tins, yellowing stationery bore the name of a jewellery store. A window glimpsed out onto the neighbour's fence and the empty beer bottles that were stacked alongside. Through the pane of glass, a decade of sunlight had faded a kitchen dresser that contained fine crockery and porcelain, all of them long-stored wedding gifts that were always deemed too good for everyday use.

On the windowsill, pages of sheet music gathered dust under the painted skirt of a plaster ballerina. He paused for a moment, distracted. The rubber mould lay around somewhere. In the shed, maybe. He could still see Bernadette's hand mixing the colours then carefully following the pleats in the dancer's skirt with a fine brush. But that was a long time ago.

Over the fireplace a pendulum clock marked the passing of another hour with a slow chime; beside it, a calendar, courtesy of the local baker. With the pencil stub, Don marked off another day. What was left of it was Thursday.

The kitchen was empty again now, the sound of shuffling feet and jingling keys having disappeared into the hallway. At the foot of the stairs he began a conversation with himself. 'I should've said Friday. That would've been best . . . Put the order in for Friday.' It could have been a reference to the following day or a Friday long gone. 'Only time will tell,' he muttered to himself.

He rested against the bannister, gathered his thoughts in the folds of his dressing gown, then, step by step, took on the stairs.

The driving instructor deposited himself in the passenger seat of Don's car. He tightened his seat belt then looked across at the man beside him. The old man's skin loosely fitted over arms that stuck out of a short-sleeved shirt. He wore a hat and tie and was taking a long time to familiarise himself with the controls of the Volkswagen Beetle.

'I don't drive much anymore, just to Woolies,' Don mused, almost in explanation. He patted the steering wheel. 'But it's nice to know she's there.'

'There's a high-pitched noise somewhere,' said the instructor, looking around for the source.

'Hearing aid.' Don reached behind his ear and turned down the volume. 'You never get these things right. You always hear too much or too little.'

They set off and followed a road that took them past the city and down to Bondi Beach. Don tried to remember the last time he'd been down to this end of town. The buildings meant nothing, but the beach was familiar in a postcard kind of way. A street photographer had once taken a snap of him and his family, shoes in hand, fossicking among the rocks. The photograph had been framed at the time and placed on the mantelpiece.

'The piano.'

'The piano?' the instructor repeated, obviously confused.

'Yes, that's right. We had one. Well, we still do. In the lounge. My wife, you see, she plays. Well, not so much plays – she feels it, through the keys, into her fingers. And when you listen, you feel it . . .' He opened the palm of his hand and held it on his heart. 'Right here. We had to take the door off to get it in, the whole street turned up – it was a party. After all, it's not every day somebody gets a baby grand delivered to their house.'

'Indeed. Your wife, does she drive?'

'Oh yes. Yes. She's an excellent driver. She's got a brother, you know. He's very good too.' A long silence ensued as he tried to remember his name. He felt as if he was at a poker table picking up dud cards and trying to make a hand out of them. 'It's a gift. A God-given gift.' He waited for the lights to change, then returned to his hand. 'You should hear her play.' Sometimes he would make her a cup of tea, and just sit at his kitchen table and listen to her, the metronome clicking fast and slow to twice-a-week students. 'Paul could play too, he doesn't have his mother's ear, but he can play. Me, I just like to listen.'

'Right. Just to Woolies and back, you say?'

'That's right,' Don replied.

The driving instructor made a note on his papers then indicated they should perhaps head for the Woolworths car park.

It was a routine Paul Cameron had with his father. Every visit was the same, so today wasn't any different. But at least this time there was the driving lesson to discuss. A new conversation piece for the two of them.

He knew the street well. As an infant he'd been wrapped and carried like a loaf of white sliced down its asphalt footpath, and been wheeled in the pram past the shopfronts; years later, he'd ridden along it on his bicycle, with pegs attached to bits of cardboard rat-a-tatting through the spokes, and trudged, briefcase in hand, to the bus stop. He'd graduated from the local high school, and now, twenty years later, he taught there.

But today Knox Street looked different. Last week it had been punctuated by poplar trees with longitudinal roots that broke through the bitumen and buckled the gutters. This week, however, small shrubs on long stakes took their place. Shame, he thought. Now the street looked like any other. There was the obligatory corner shop and terrace houses. He felt for a key then knocked loudly on the front door of number 82.

'Bought you a present, Pop.' Paul greeted his father with a bouquet of biros. 'These'll keep you going for a while. Put a couple in each room maybe.' He closed the door and headed down the hall. 'Anything else you'd like?'

Don knew there was something, but he couldn't think what. He'd been forgetting everything lately. Simple everyday things. And his security was becoming obsessive. His fingers immediately began to explore his pockets . . . What did he do with his keys? What if he left them at the shop, or in the car? But he needed them to get in. Then again, he *was* in. They must be here somewhere . . . Best not tell Paul. There'd be no point in getting him all worried. Don emptied a pocket of a handkerchief in the hope the keys might fall to the ground, but nothing came of it.

'How's school?' he asked his son. That was always the first question.

'Good. Good.' That was always the first answer.

'Had to call the cops again last night,' Don continued. 'Bloody kids.'

'You must know 'em all by now.'

'The kids?'

'No, the cops.' Paul smiled. 'Just joking.' It was always the kids – kids rocking his roof, kids banging on his door. In his mind it was real enough, but there was never any tangible evidence. 'Don't worry about it, Pop. Everything's all right.' But Paul knew it wasn't. Noises in the yard or the laneway behind it or the sound of the telephone would inevitably lead to a panicked search for dressing gown and light switches. Aside from reassuring his father, there was little he could do. 'How's it going next door?'

'Perfectly good house and they're ruinin' it. That's how it's goin'. Enid'd be turning in her grave if she knew what was happening.' He wiped his nose with the handkerchief, then began a search of the other pocket.

'She's been dead for years, Pop. I don't think she'd be doing much turning. Progress, Pop. Real estate.' Paul walked out into the back yard he grew up in. He knew every spyhole in the fence, but now it was just a matter of popping his head over the palings. 'Looks all right. Pretty smart-looking kitchen. Lots of stainless steel. Bit of a sunroom happening there, too.'

'Doesn't get the sun there.' Don shook his head and shuffled back towards the house.

They sat in their usual seats, Don facing the window, Paul the fridge; between them a pot of tea. Paul passed his usual comment about the state of the place, and Don, as usual, agreed to clean up. Both of them knew it would never happen.

'Paul Kelly's playing the State Theatre next month.' Paul turned the page in his newspaper's gig guide. That could have been him. Bit late now. Twenty years too late, to be precise. He sat sipping his tea, thinking of what might've been. 'Council's cut the trees down,' he said. Maybe it wasn't too late. Lose some weight, get the old band back together – Stewie's still around and Clive's still got the amp.

'Yeah, 'bout time. All those leaves. A terrible mess.'

'Absolutely,' he replied. 'Couldn't agree more.'

Time ticked by, the fridge motor occasionally breaking the silence. Paul finished his tea and put his cup in the sink. 'Well, better be heading off, I suppose.' The empty pot was his usual exit cue. 'Give me a call if you want anything else.'

They headed down the hallway to the front door, where Don slipped the chain and pulled his cardigan tight across his chest.

'Electrical tape,' he said. He knew there was something. His keys would turn up, they always did, and he had it in mind to mark them with different colours. 'Different colours, but.'

'No worries, Pop. I'll get some from the hardware.' Paul said goodbye from the gate and wondered what had happened to the last lot he'd brought around.

He stood there out on the footpath and waited until Don was back inside the house. In some ways it was almost a relief – the door closing, his father safely on the inside, another weekly visit passing without incident. As Paul walked back along the street, the usual thoughts entered his head: *Must take Dad to the movies*; *Maybe we'll catch the next Swannies game together*. Last week he'd even mentioned giving the place a coat of paint, but Don had objected. It had been done quite recently, the old man assured him. Meaning within the last twenty years. By the time Paul reached the end of Knox Street, he'd realised that he'd completely forgotten to ask about the driving lesson. He was secretly hoping that Don might give up the car before he accidentally killed himself or someone else, which was why he'd suggested the lesson.

After closing the door and making sure to slip the chain across again, Don made his way back down the hallway, and back to silence. The terrace had been renovated in the 1950s and again in the early '70s, when a bathroom and toilet had been incorporated into the upstairs layout. But the original toilet still stood in the yard, and that was the one that Don preferred.

He sat there now, with the door open, his eyes wandering about the back yard. A lemon tree supported the garden shed and the obligatory grove of bamboo tunnelled under the back fence. At the rear of the house, shop fittings and wooden display cases lay decomposing.

The afternoon sun fell straight into his lap. He closed his eyes and felt the warmth penetrate his eyelids. His mind drifted away, to the imaginary sounds of the surf crashing against the shore, and the voices of his family. Paul was there, with his beloved surfboard and a couple of his mates. When might that have been, Don wondered, trying to pin a date on the moment – Paul must've been about sixteen or so, and he was born in 19 . . .

But there his thoughts stopped, struggling with the details. Dates were the worst, anything with numbers seemed impossible to retrieve. Names and numbers were all mixing together.

He sighed in resignation, then took refuge in the things he could remember. Drifting further now, he slipped the imaginary bolt in his mind . . . and there he was again, at the back of the shop, with Bernadette and that beautifully embroidered dress she had spent so much time making for what's-his-name's wedding. And then there was the watch, there was always the watch. It was a piece from the 1930s, quite common and of little value, but for the better part of his life it had obsessed him. It had led to sleepless nights, cold sweats and fits of depression that sometimes seemed to swallow him whole. Here were memories that could not be erased.

He once more removed the casing and gently placed it on the bench. Like a heartbeat, the tiny movement spun backwards and forwards. Backwards and forwards.

He couldn't be sure how long he'd been sitting there. The sun was moving closer to the horizon, lengthening the shadows in the yard. He felt a shiver and opened his eyes. A man stood before him, a mask covering his nose and mouth.

'You all right, mate?' he asked Don.

Don slowly nodded his head. Around him smoke swirled in tight eddies that sucked in leaves and ash and lifted them high into the air. Intense heat radiated against the toilet wall.

'Anybody else inside?'

Don stood up and looked over to the house. The window frame at the rear had just given in. Panes of glass smashed to the ground as the fire took in a deep breath of oxygen. He backed away, his head shaking from side to side, unable to believe that this was his house, that this was even happening at all.

The fireman repeated his question.

'No. No . . . just me.' Don's arthritic fingers fumbled with the tiny holes on his belt. He gripped his leg to steady a shaking hand.

Something exploded in the kitchen. Don looked up to see curtains billowing wildly, a frenzied maypole of burning fabric. His display cases buckled in the heat, leaves on his lemon tree shrivelled to ash. His whole world was on fire.

The man in the mask put his arm around Don's shoulder and forced him out towards the back gate. 'Is there anyone else inside?' he asked again. 'What about your wife?'

Confusion set in. Bernadette? Oh my God. He tried to think where he last saw her. By the piano maybe. Or in the lounge room dozing with a book, like she always did. Maybe she'd gone down to the shops . . . but she would have told him. She would've said so. And then there was Tom, maybe he was inside; he was planning to come over, wasn't he?

'You're certain there's no one inside?'

He shook his head and tried to speak but nothing came out.

At the front of the house, a crowd had gathered. Neighbours at first, then shopkeepers, then other curious passers-by. Three fire trucks blocked the roadway. Water flowed over the upstairs balcony and cut deep troughs in the dirt below. Flames shot out from under the corrugated-iron roof.

Don emerged from the rear lane, eyes darting between people, looking for anybody he knew. 'I was out the back, on the lavatory . . .' He kept saying it over and over, to anybody who cared to listen.

A policewoman finally guided him to one side. 'Do you have any relatives, any family we can contact for you?' she asked.

Paul was just here. Look for Paul. He must be still here. 'Paul. Did you see Paul?'

'Is he a relative?'

'Paul. My son Paul,' the old man stammered. He started to pick his way through the crowd; cut adrift as he wandered, listing from one group of onlookers to the next.

The policewoman caught up with Don and finally settled him in the gutter. 'Do you smoke, Don?' She repeated the question but received no reply. 'Mind your shoes,' she told him, but Don didn't hear a thing.

Water flowed over double stitching and hurried down the street. The fire destroying his house now turned on him, demanding his attention, as if it was pulling him into the flames. Linoleum peeled back through the decades. A cheap tin tray glowed intensely, then disappeared from sight. Boxes of sheet music and drawers of photographs rose high into the sky. He rocked forward over his haunches and felt his heart pounding against his knees. Voices closed in around him.

'Jeez, you were lucky, mate,' one of them said.

'It's the old wiring.'

He thought he'd had it rewired recently, and at considerable expense. Don leaned forward and closed his eyes against his knees, locking himself out of these surroundings. The keys. He suddenly remembered the keys. On the fridge. Where he always left them.

*

A quiet spliff in Prince Alfred Park before catching the bus home was the other routine Paul Cameron enjoyed after visiting his old man. He sat on a kids' merry-go-round now, with thoughts of the old band and marking Year 9 geography papers. A poet and public servant, that's how he saw himself.

He pushed himself off on a slow turn. His frame was thin but as he pushed further around the circle, a small pot belly came into being. On the top of his head, a bald patch at the back, combined with a receding hairline at the front, had shocked him into getting a number two cut, which was an unexpected improvement. A long-faded T-shirt carrying the slogan *Free Nelson Mandela* hung over his jeans.

Somewhere between realising that the band was not going to happen and accepting that teaching paid the rent, he noticed two fire engines rushing down Cleveland Street and turning into Pitt. It was then he saw the billowing clouds of black smoke rising from the direction of his dad's place. Must be the chicken shop, he thought, the one on Redfern Street. The kitchen must've caught alight.

Curious, he crossed back over Cleveland and retraced his steps towards the house. By the time he'd reached the lights on Redfern Street, he could see the police had cordoned off the block that included his father's house. Closer now, he turned into Knox, the street of his childhood. Then, at the sight of Don sitting in the gutter, he broke into a run.

'I was out the back, in the lavatory . . .' Don reached up for Paul's outstretched hand.

'It's okay, Pop.' Paul put his arm around Don's shoulder and drew his body close to his. 'Everything's going to be all right.' He repeated the words softly as he led the old man away through the crowd.

Chapter Two

Tom Barton had been working the lollypop outside Dawson Street Primary School in Surry Hills for the past five years. He'd seen families right through primary. The Watsons, the Nugents, the Johnsons – Tom knew them all. He was seventy when he first donned the orange plastic vest, and even now he still didn't look a day over sixty.

The crossing was not an easy one to monitor, as the road swept sharply to the left; a moment's indecision could have grave consequences. Then there were the blind spots, the corner fence and the Tuesday morning garbage collection. Local knowledge, that's what it was all about. People didn't realise.

Maybe it was time to move on, though. Not that there was anything to move on to. Five years of faithful service, and now he'd been put on notice. For what? Too old? Too slow? He almost hoped that a small child would fall in front of a wheel during his watch, so that he could carry out a suitably heroic rescue and prove his worth. Prove that he was indispensable.

He had rehearsed it a hundred times since being told he'd no longer be needed. Mrs Kirton would be driving the car, or even Deputy Principal Carmichael – yes, yes that would be perfect. A little water on the road perhaps, from the night before; not enough to be obvious, just enough to bring the oil out of the bitumen. Deputy Principal Carmichael's car would come around the corner just as little Skye Harrison set out on the crossing . . . Tom would swing the lollypop to the stop position and Carmichael would apply the brakes, but to the deputy principal's horror, his vehicle skids, sliding towards the crossing and little Skye. At this point Tom would sprint across the road, sweep the child up into his arms and execute a perfect parachute roll onto the footpath. Yes, he was well positioned to go out a hero.

He waved the Bardettas' Ford through with a smile for the twins in the back seat. Perhaps the sprint across the road might be asking a bit. And as for the parachute roll, well, that might need a rethink as well. He glanced at his watch. He was going to be late. Not that time had much relevance in his life, but he didn't want to let Don down.

Across the road, the school bell rang and a hundred school kids ran towards the crossing over Dawson Street. Tom took up his position and braced himself for the onslaught. As the first group arrived, he felt a drop of rain fall onto his hat, then another. Just enough to lift the oil from the bitumen.

*

A squall was building from the south. From where Don stood, he could see it quite clearly. As it approached the headland, it suddenly veered away, as if it had found a better place to cross further up. Water droplets began to appear on the floor of Paul's balcony. Don slid the door closed and returned to the lounge room.

The building contained six flats, two per floor, three floors high. It was red brick and tile, with no architectural features of any real interest. The front of the building, by accident, faced the sea.

'Sleep all right, Pop?' Paul's finger sat poised on the coffee-grinder switch.

'Yeah . . . well, you know.'

'No worries. I'll get something for you, from the chemist.'

The grinder screamed through Don's hearing aid and lingered there long after the coffee had been poured.

'So what do you think?' Paul asked.

'Think about what?'

'About tea . . . what I was just talking about.'

Tea? Don was still none the wiser. He returned to the window and looked out to Bondi Beach. How long had he been staying here? It couldn't have been more than a few days. They went to the house yesterday and they'd been back twice, he knew that much. The second floor was no longer sound and what had escaped the flames had been saturated by water. The lounge-room floor had collapsed under the weight of the piano. All that remained was the iron frame. The better part of the second day had been spent sifting through charred remains. A few small pieces that had escaped the heat were wrapped in a handkerchief and placed in his pocket.

'Never mind, Pop. We might check out the old hearing aid, eh?'

Don watched a drop of water slide down the outside of the window pane. Then he remembered the washing he'd left on the line.

'Tom rang again last night,' his son's voice called out. 'You looked pretty much asleep so I didn't bother you. He's taking you for a drive. Thought he'd be here by now. Said you had something organised for today, from ages ago.'

Don couldn't think what that could be. Something about his greyhounds maybe? No, that was too far back, surely. He looked down to the road and saw his own car, the blue Beetle, and wondered how long it had been sitting on the street. He was anxious now.

'Well, time to go,' Don said with a sense of urgency, breaking his silence at last.

'Go? Go where?'

'Home.'

'This is your home, Pop,' Paul told him, gently. 'For a while anyway.'

He knew that. It was just that every now and again he had to check. Just to be sure.

Paul studied his father at the window. Taken out of his environment, he looked like any other old bloke. He didn't seem as strong here as he had in the old house. Sun spots and blemishes were more pronounced, and his eyes were veiled in a cloudy film. Normally a green Onkaparinga covered pyjamas that were buttoned to the neck, but now Don's cardigan served as his dressing gown. Despite Paul's repeated offers, the old man preferred to wear his own clothes.

'I'll make an appointment with the optometrist this week,' he told Don. 'And I'll pick up some batteries for your hearing aid on the way home.' He almost missed his own cue. Glasses. Servo. Briefcase. Paul searched through the side pocket of his case. 'Try these for size, Pop.' He pulled out a pair of non-prescription lenses and handed them over to Don to try on. 'Ten bucks at the Shell.'

The fluorescent orange frames encircled the old man's eyes.

'Only ones they had left. They're all the go. They look like they might even glow in the dark! Maybe they'll work as a reading lamp. What do you think, Pop?'

Don directed his new-found sight to the window. What little dignity he had left disappeared with the frames. 'Better take an umbrella,' he said.

Paul didn't think he possessed one. He'd certainly never bought one. Umbrellas were the sort of things one just found. He rummaged around in a few obvious spots but came up with nothing. 'Must have left it at work. See you this arvo, Pop.'

The inside of the bus smelt musty. Perspiration mixed with damp clothing. Paul took a seat and thought about his old man. It had never occurred to him that Don was really old. Not until the last few days, anyway. Don had lived alone for the past ten years since Mum died, and Paul had never really given it a second thought. Now he was worried about leaving him alone for a day.

It was Bernadette's love of music that Paul had inherited, and music was the path he'd intended to follow. 'But you need something to fall back on, son,' was his father's more practical line. 'Everybody needs to know the time, so why not carry on with the business?'

Don was the last of his trade, and Paul the only child. It was never spoken of, but Bernadette's wish for other children was apparent, especially when the rellies arrived with their broods. Back then, it was either a 'plumbing' problem of Bernadette's or, as was the case with a lot of blokes who'd returned from the war, the fact that Don was 'still not quite right'.

So it was agreed that teaching would be the fallback position, which, as it turned out, was quite fortuitous. But there was still hope – the kitchen drawer full of his old songs was still a work in progress. And he was in the process of upgrading all the albums in his LP collection to CD format. Tim Buckley, Bob Dylan, the Stones . . .

Paul knew he'd have to ask for some time off work. Shouldn't be a problem, though, he figured. He'd been feeling pretty good this week, job-wise, after being 'headhunted' by another school. 'Headhunted', that was the term he'd used to inform his colleagues about being approached to head up a department. Which meant less teaching – a good thing in Paul's book.

As the bus crawled down Oxford Street, Paul caught his reflection in a shop window. He really needed to lose some weight. Smarten up his act. Get himself together.

Satisfied that he'd seen enough, he turned away from the shop window and looked around the bus. There didn't seem to be anyone on board that would fit his self-description: single, late thirties. If anything, it seemed to be full of happy young couples. He'd been close to being one half of a happy couple once himself, but it hadn't worked out with Michelle. She was too perfect, and it was too easy to look shabby next to someone who was perfect. Somebody with flaws might be the go. An ad in the personals perhaps: *Single male, well educated, living alone, seeks* . . . Seeks what, he wondered. . . . *seeks like-minded tragic*. He didn't even own a car, for Chrissakes.

He mentally put together his own school report. *Could do better . . . More concentration needed . . . Has the ability to do well.* He added that last bit to make himself feel better.

The rain was not going to ease up. It was school sports day and he had no alternative lessons prepared if the event had to be postponed. He began to put a lot of positive thought into the bus breaking down, but it didn't. If anything, it put on a turn of speed.

Don stared at the television. He was thinking of things he had to do, but came up with nothing. Only the weatherman spoke of an outside world. At least his face was familiar. Don was a part of someone else's life now. There were no memories here to keep him company. No keys. Nothing, nothing he could say was his.

'Ayyy, Don! It's me!' The voice at the door, and the accompanying sound of knuckles on cheap pine, took his thoughts from the TV screen and back to his unfamiliar surroundings.

Tom was late. He caught his breath, then started knocking again. For some reason the school assembly had been running late, and that meant an extra twenty minutes on the crossing. That was the other thing about the job – you had to be flexible.

Don finally negotiated the lock.

'Top glasses, mate. They're a class act.' Without waiting for a reply Tom guided him towards the landing. 'Come on, let's go. We're gonna be late.'

As they went downstairs, Don became anxious again. What were they going to be late for exactly? He held this thought until the two men arrived at Tom's Holden ute, which was parked just outside the entrance to the apartment building.

'Letter's still there,' Tom said, pointing to the glovebox as they climbed into the ute. 'Saw it the day before yesterday.'

The official-looking envelope, on the front of which the words *Public Trustee's Office* were displayed prominently along the top, had sat unopened on Don's kitchen table for a week or two. Surrounded by the items of paraphernalia on his old stove top, it had become a clean surface for the 'stuff' he'd accumulated in his day-to-day wanderings – some wood screws, a cup handle, the workings of a torch. Had it not been for Tom's insistence that Don go ahead and open it, it would have been lost in the fire a few days later. Inside the envelope they'd found a single sheet of headed notepaper. A lawyer's letter of some sort.

'Jeez, mate, it's an inheritance!' Tom had exclaimed. 'You've inherited something. You're gunna be rich! That's what happens to people. I mean, people not like us – *other* people. 'Cept now it's happened to you.'

In truth, it sparked curiosity more than any thoughts of material gain. The name of the deceased meant nothing to Don – a Robert Allan Steele, the letter said – but in accordance with the written instructions, the offices of Briggs & Tanner Realty had been contacted and an appointment was made for today, to view 'The Estate'. It was going to be an outing, something they could do together. A day out of the house.

'What's that address again, Don?' Tom pulled a street directory from under his seat and balanced it on the steering wheel. 'It was out west, wasn't it? Near Blacktown somewhere?'

'What?'

'The address on the letter. Never mind.' Tom settled back into his driving position, turned on the wireless and set off. It looked like a good hour's drive.

He wondered if he should bring up the subject of the fire again, but it had all been said. There had been lots of talk about how you never know what's around the corner, how it was all for the best, how lucky Don had been, how at least he still had his health, how fortunate he was to have his son Paul, how tomorrow was another day . . . There really wasn't much else one could say.

The wireless crackled to life.

'*Parrrradise-suuur-Mer*,' the laid-back voice of the announcer purred, covering the gentle sound of breaking waves. 'Seaside living. Yours for inspection. Why not take advantage of our no-obligation free flight to the Gold Coast?' Seagulls underpinned the words 'free' and 'flight'. 'Your dreams are our business . . .'

The waters of the Paradise-sur-Mer plunge pool lapped against Tom's body. For a man of his age, he was still in pretty good nick. His hair helped – he'd been blessed with an abundance of it; a neat part anchored a grey wave at the front. He imagined himself in shorts and a Hawaiian shirt, lying in a deckchair, beside him a cold beer marked his place in a track guide –

'HEY, DICKHEAD! HOW MANY LANES DO YOU WANT?!'

At the fellow motorist's suggestion, Tom veered away from the plunge pool and back onto the road. 'Dickhead yourself, dickhead!' he hollered in response, before turning to his passenger for support. 'Some people think they own the roads, eh Don? Could've caused a shocking accident. Just goes to show, you never know what's around the corner. Isn't that right, Don?'

Don sighed in agreement. 'Apparently.' He leant back against the headrest and closed his eyes.

*

They pulled up outside a building that had started life as a small iron foundry but hadn't survived the Depression.

Tom wound down the window and reached outside for the door handle. By the time Don had got out of the ute, Tom was already investigating the yard.

'Mr Cameron, is it?' The woman's voice came from behind them and caught both men unawares. 'I'm Kylie Hogan, from Briggs & Tanner Realty. I'm dealing with the estate.'

Tom had figured the voice on the phone to be that of a much older woman, and was surprised to see someone who, he thought, should still be at school. 'Um . . . well, I'm Mr Barton – Tom,' he replied. 'We spoke on the phone. Hope you haven't been waiting long,' he added. 'Got caught in the rain.'

'No worries,' she said, noticing now the second old man as he headed over from the car park. *Bummer* was what she thought. The guys in the office had made Tom out to be a major spunk, but he looked like an older version of her Uncle Herb: a man in a hurry but going nowhere. As for Mr Cameron, he looked like he was about to cark it.

'Is there a toilet?' Don asked.

'I dunno. Out the back maybe.' Not waiting for a response, she unlocked the gate and strode into the yard. 'I'm told Mr Cameron has been willed the contents of this building.'

'I believe that to be so,' Tom replied for him. 'Bit like opening Tutan what's-his-name's tomb, eh?'

'That could be aiming a bit high.' She put a key into the door lock.

The main door to the factory swung open. The only source of light came from a bank of windows high on the eastern side, which normally would have brightened the room up, but, due to the weather, the natural light was now considerably diminished.

They stepped inside, followed at a distance by Don, who was more interested in finding that toilet than discovering what the building housed. In front of them, boxes of tools lay dormant on wooden workbenches. To the side, sheet metal had been stacked against a press, ready for the next step in a production line that had ceased well over half a century ago. The other side of the building fell into half shadows. A tarpaulin fabricated a precipitous landscape that lay beyond.

'Are there any lights?'

'The electricity's been disconnected,' Ms Hogan replied. 'The owner of the building is selling up – the place has to be vacated by the end of the month.'

Tom took in what he could of the floor space and size of the building. 'Selling up, eh? Well, it would be worth a bit, I imagine.'

'Yep, good location, close to transport.' She reached into a plastic folder, pulled out a few sheets of A4 paper and made to hand them to Don, but found no interest there. She turned back to Tom. 'Maybe you could see that he gets the paperwork,' she said and thrust it into his hand.

Kylie Hogan figured her part in the proceedings was over. Besides, the place was giving her the creeps. 'Right, just fix the padlocks when you leave, and let the office know when you next need the keys, okay? See ya.' Her boss wouldn't have approved of such a lax attitude to property security, but it didn't matter to her a whole lot whether she kept this job or not. Ripples of water washed over rain-drenched Doc Martens as she headed towards the door.

Tom crossed over to the tarpaulin. On closer inspection, it appeared to be in such an advanced state of decay that it was difficult to tell where the tarp ended and the floor began. Lifting an edge, Tom opened a fissure that quickly spread to its weakest points and gathered momentum as the weight of the canvas pulled against it. Finally the tarp fell away in an ever-expanding cloud of dust to reveal an emporium of old war surplus.

Don stood stock-still at the sight of it all. Then, pushing the orange fluoros back on his nose, he pointed to the other side of the room. 'There it is,' he said. 'Had to be one somewhere.' He stumbled over rotting parachutes until the way was clear to the toilet.

Through the louvres of the dank room, he could see Tom wading through the dust. He watched his friend working the mound as a seagull would a tip. Rubbish, Don thought, utter rubbish. Nothing good will ever come from this stuff; nothing ever did.

An inner voice seemed to be clamouring for his attention: *Leave it. The war, the past* . . . But once he'd left the toilet area and headed back towards the pile of surplus, his eyes wandered over the items, searching them out for their practical qualities. They came to rest on some handy-looking workbenches. He pictured a couple of them in his back yard. Some of those tools didn't look half bad either. As he crossed the floor, he stretched out his cardigan and began placing things in a pouch made by the fold. Bits of wire, an old handsaw, the end of a mallet . . .

'What about this?' Tom shouted from deeper within the mound. He was holding a compass in the air. 'Looks pretty genuine. Might even be worth something.'

Don didn't answer, but now that he'd looked over to where Tom was standing, it was the 44-gallon drums that took his interest. A giant wall of them divided the floor space. He could cut them in half for pot plants, perhaps. And then there were the tyres. They could be turned into swans, like the ones at the railway station. He pictured them full of geraniums.

'C'mon, mate. I'll give you a leg up.' Tom made a makeshift ladder next to the wall of drums.

Don was ready with a protest, but wasn't able to compete with his friend's enthusiasm. He emptied the 'good things' he'd collected in his cardigan onto the floor and headed over to the wall of tin. Half supporting and half pushing, Tom lifted him up onto the drums.

'Anything on the other side?'

'I dunno. Can't see,' he replied.

'Well, stick your head over.'

Don's foot pushed hard against Tom's open palm. A crack between the drums opened a window into his past. He wiped his glasses as he might the glass pane and peered in.

'What can you see?' The muffled sound of Tom's voice called out impatiently from somewhere below him.

At first he saw nothing, just a crate, a wall of old timbers. But then it slowly dawned on him what it was. He shook his head. How could it be? His hands began to tremble, his breathing became laboured . . . Don closed his eyes and felt the pain of an old wound that would not heal. With each breath, his window fogged over.

'Well?'

'There's nothin'. Nothin' at all. I-I need to get down . . . I need to get down . . .'

The room spun. Above him, the sun pierced holes in the tin roof; pin lights of staring eyes raced past him as his panicked hands searched for Tom's.

Tom held him for as long as he could, before they both crumpled to the floor.

Chapter Three

Perspiration mixed with water from the factory floor made the trip back to Paul's an uncomfortable one for them both. With every movement of the car, Don's second skin leapt off the vinyl seat and clung to his back.

'We'll be home in no time, Don . . . Wind your window down, mate. Bit of fresh air works wonders.'

The wind swept hard onto Don's face, forcing his eyelids shut and accentuating the lines around them. The diesel fumes from a bus eventually forced him back into the cabin.

He glanced down to check the time. A band of pale skin around his wrist momentarily confused him. He pictured the bathroom cabinet, and there sitting next to a bottle of meths, was his watch.

'So what's the story with this Robert what's-his-name, then?' Tom asked at last. 'You and he must've been pretty good mates for him to leave you all that stuff back there. I gather you knew him from the war.'

'The war?'

'Yeah. You do remember the war, don't you, Don?'

'Of course I remember the bloody war. There was a lot of people in that war. I can't remember everybody.'

He put his head towards the open window and wondered if Tom was serious about whether he'd forgotten the war. He felt the wind pushing evenly against his skin; sweeping around the inside of his shirt and awakening his senses. 'I suppose you remember everyone you met in the war, do you?' he asked eventually.

'I'm sure I'd remember somebody like that. I mean, he's got half of it stashed in there.'

'I left my watch on the dresser,' was all Don thought to say in response.

'Don't worry about it. It's gone. It's in the past. We'll just get a new one.'

'Yes,' he replied. 'Yes. Let's forget it. Forget it all.' He wrapped his hands around the seat belt and mouthed the sentiment quietly to himself.

Paul watched the moisture rising from the green leaves of a marijuana plant. A couple of minutes under the griller ought to do it. As soon as he knew his dad would be moving in for a while, Paul had decided to ditch the spindly specimen he'd grown from seed. With an eye on the griller now, his thoughts criss-crossed the room.

Maybe he should move things around a bit, make the place more suitable for the both of them. He could shift the guitar stand and the umbrella tree to somewhere a bit more out of the way; the amplifier he could jam into a bookshelf. And then there was the floor, which had become a moving minefield of textbooks and assignments that came and went with the beginning and end of each school term.

He slipped a David Bowie CD into the player and pressed play. The three-seater lounge was definitely a problem, he realised. He pushed it back against a wall to make a clear path from Don's room to the bathroom.

'Shit, the pot!' He hurried back to the kitchen. It was then that he noticed the front-door key in among the washing-up. It was the same key he'd given Don earlier in the day. Paul cursed himself for not putting it on a ring with specially marked tape. Perhaps he should start marking everything. Perhaps Tom had already dropped him back at the flat and he couldn't get back in and was wandering lost around Bondi . . . Paranoia began to creep into his thoughts. He walked out onto the balcony and looked down to the street below, just as Tom's old Holden pulled up.

Tom put on the handbrake in such an abrupt manner it jolted Don awake. 'We're here, mate,' he told his passenger. 'We've arrived. We're back at Paul's.'

The upset at the warehouse had affected Don to the point where any conversation Tom instigated was met with a solemn silence that eventually led to sleep. Tom held the door open now, and then helped him along the footpath and up the three flights of stairs to the flat.

As they rested against the balustrade of the second-storey landing, it took a full minute before breathing patterns returned to rhythms more familiar to both men. The conversation between them was now starting to repeat itself.

'You can't forget *everything*,' Tom insisted. 'Forget we even went there – what are you talking about?' He lowered his voice before continuing. 'I mean some of that stuff's got to be worth something. It's like what's-her-name said, we just gotta get it all out of there. Come on, Don, it's a gift. Think of the *future*. Maybe we could open a disposal store. Whaddya reckon?'

'A disposal store?' Don asked absentmindedly.

'Yeah. Like the one near Central.'

'Whatever you say, Tom, whatever you say . . . What time is it?'

'Stop worrying about the time, Don. It's not like you've got to be anywhere.'

Don thought about this as he struggled with the last flight of stairs. Tom was right. But it wasn't like he had to be anywhere before either. A routine. An agenda. Things that had to be done before the Channel Ten News. That was what he had before.

The tumblers in the deadlock inside the door ahead of them rolled into alignment. The door swung open.

'Jesus, Pop!' It was Paul, standing there in teacher mode, his arms folded across his chest. 'Where have you been? I nicked off the last period to get back here.'

'What?' was the only response Don could summon.

'The *time*.' Paul pointed to his watch.

'I dunno. Nobody'll tell me . . .' And with that, Don headed straight for the toilet.

The reflection in the bathroom mirror caught him unawares. Another Don, one he didn't recognise, watched him as he let the water run between his fingers. He watched him dry his hands and replace the towel on the rack. And as he turned towards the door, he caught himself staring back at somebody wearing plastic glasses and a new shirt.

Tom's attention turned to Don as he drifted back from the bathroom. 'Anyway, it's all sittin' there . . . Don, I was just telling Paul about your old mate, and about our disposal store idea.'

Don lowered himself onto the lounge as Tom recalled the day's events, some of which sounded familiar, some of which didn't.

'So, Paul, like I was saying,' Tom continued, 'this old mate of Don's has left him all this stuff. *Valuable* stuff. Like this . . .' He produced the compass from his pocket, wiped it over with a handkerchief, and then passed the piece over to Paul. 'I mean this is just a sampler, you should *see* the place. Eh, Don?' The attempt to include his mate met with almost predictable indifference. Undeterred, Tom went on. 'Chockers, mate, absolutely chockers. Location, that's the key. I mean, set this up right and people will come from everywhere.' He paused for a moment as if to take questions from the floor. 'Well, what do you think?'

Paul didn't know what to think. He looked across to his father, but Don was just disappearing into the kitchen with thoughts of switching on the jug. If anything, it seemed to Paul he appeared more distant, weaker than this morning.

'I really don't know if Dad's up to this. Tom, I'm *worried* about him, mate. You said he took a fall at the warehouse. Was he okay?'

'Oh, he was fine, Paul. It was just so dusty in there. Don needed some fresh air, that's all – we both did.'

Paul shook his head. 'Tom, listen to what you're saying. Don is in no position to take on something like this. It's madness.'

Tom sat back on the lounge as a silence descended between them. He didn't see Don as Paul might have done. He and Don had grown old together; it was true, neither of them was in their prime, but that didn't exclude them from pushing on with life.

'Have a think about it, Tom. I mean, really. Have you ever done a BAS statement? It's not like it was fifty years ago.' He gave Tom a reassuring tap on the shoulder and headed towards the kitchen.

'Ground control to Major Tom . . .' In the background David Bowie seemed to echo Paul's thoughts.

The late afternoon sun held its position above the horizon before finally disappearing behind the Swiss Grand Hotel. Tom had left to go home and now Paul sat with his father on the balcony, an empty pizza box between them.

'More stars out here than at home.' Don's eyes tracked across the horizon.

'Yeah, well, the city's pretty polluted,' Paul replied, vaguely. The low cloud mass that had earlier blanketed the coast had now returned. In fact, the only stars Paul could make out were the ones reflected from the lights on Campbell Parade. 'What stars are you talking about, Pop?'

'Up there. Definitely more. Brighter too.'

'Where?' Paul asked.

'There.' Don pointed to the heavens. 'You just have to look.'

'No stars out tonight, Pop. In fact I think I just felt a drop of rain.'

'Other times, distant galaxies.'

'What's that?'

'Stars. That's what stars are.'

'It's getting a bit chilly now. How about I go get your cardigan?'

'Yes, I guess it must be about that time. It's been a long day.'

'You okay, Pop?'

'I'm fine. Tomorrow we'll get rid of all that crap, eh?' Don took one last look at the sky, then headed inside.

Paul watched him leave. The day's events had been too much for Don. The acceleration of change that had taken place over the past week had obviously overwhelmed him.

Before going to bed, Paul quietly looked in on his dad. As he pushed open the door to the bedroom, the light from the hall generated a beam that scanned the human shape under the covers. Don's eyes moved imperceptibly behind closed lids as the strip of light passed over his face. Satisfied, Paul closed the door and made his way towards the couch.

It was just after three when Paul was suddenly awoken. Don stood at the door; his cardigan, buttoned to the neck, covered his pyjamas. He was trying to speak, but his mouth contorted into unnatural shapes. He swung on the door handle, as a boat would a mooring. Clutching at his pyjamas, he tried to make himself understood, but his thoughts translated into nothing but gibberish. Frustration turned to fear as he endeavoured to communicate. Finally his small frame collapsed onto the carpet.

Don came to with the scream of a siren filling the air. It reached deep inside him, breaching his natural defences. Circuits in his brain snapped shut to form a last line of defence. He felt his hand being squeezed, but resisted the urge to open his eyes.

'Pop, can you hear me?' Paul had to shout over the siren. He held his father's hand as the ambulance swung off the expressway and headed for St Vincent's Hospital.

Chapter Four

With his pension card in one hand and a string bag in the other, Tom Barton stepped off the train. He was feeling pretty good about himself this morning. He'd seen a hundred kids safely across the crossing, negotiated a car park within walking distance of the station, and now joined the tail end of peak-hour commuters heading into the city. He'd been thinking about what Paul had said about the shop idea – he was probably right, but it was in Don's best interests to get the best price he could.

At Central Station he approached the ticket turnstiles with caution. Anonymous arms and elbows would have little regard for his centre of balance, so he held back until all but the last of the passengers had made their way through. The Broadway exit had a steep flight of stairs; after that, it was an easy walk along George Street to South City Military Disposal Store.

Campaign medals, from Crimea to Long Tan, were organised into platoons behind the plate-glass window.

Replica bomb casings – *As seen in* Memphis Belle*!* – had been marked down as this week's special. A rocket launcher still in its original packaging appeared to come with ammunition of some sort; while flares, daggers, bayonets, even a landmine, all came under the general category of 'camping equipment'.

A trip wire, in the form of an electronic beam set at ankle height in the doorway, announced his arrival.

'Can I help you?' The male voice came from the high ground, a mezzanine level that overlooked the shop.

Tom tried to get a fix on its position, but by the time he'd swung about, the proprietor had moved to take up another vantage point. 'Just looking,' he replied.

Tom took his time as he carried out an informal stocktake of his own. Racks of East German greatcoats seemed to be the latest addition. A separate display featured the 1991 Gulf War.

'Part of a Patriot missile, if you're interested.' Accompanying the voice, which sounded much closer now, a hand appeared on the display case.

Tom looked up to see a young man wearing an Israeli military jacket. Judging by his appearance, he might have come from that part of the world, but he spoke with a broad Australian accent.

'Dinky-di, that one.' The proprietor reached into the glass-top cabinet and took out a piece of twisted metal.

'How do you know?' Tom asked.

'See that mark? That means it's official – genuine. My uncle had them stamped and sent over. It's a commemorative piece. If you look closely, you'll see that stamp is actually in the shape of George Bush's head, and it's dated March 1991. You don't get more genuine than that.'

He looked down at the scrap of metal the store owner was referring to. The piece looked more like something off an old engine block. If it was part of a Patriot missile, thought Tom, then the rest of it was probably out the back of Robbo's Spares on Parramatta Road. He wandered off as the proprietor rambled on about how his uncle went to Baghdad shortly after the war to pick over the desert.

He noticed an altimeter set apart from the other mechanical devices – definitely a relic from World War II, by the look of it. The long shallow case that displayed it still bore the name of a well-known department store that had recently gone into liquidation. Tom's reading glasses brought the small Bakelite instrument inside into focus. There was no doubt as to its authenticity.

'How much is this?' he enquired.

'That,' said the young man as he lifted the glass top, 'is a very valuable piece.'

'Really?'

'Out of a Lancaster bomber. Lot of history there.' His eyes flicked around the room as he placed it on the counter.

'Right. So how much would it be worth?'

'Sorry, mate, not for sale. There'd only be a few of those left in existence. I'm thinking of sending it off to Sotheby's actually. Should fetch a good price. Had a couple of bombsights a while back, from an old Avro like this – jeez, you wouldn't believe what they went for . . .'

Sotheby's. A small bead of perspiration appeared on Tom's temple as he mentally picked his way through the contents of that factory building out west . . . He remembered a consignment of radio antennas, loosely bound and pointing towards a wooden box. It sat undistinguished among other similar boxes, and contained nothing but old aircraft altimeters. And there was at least one crateful of bombsights, he was sure of it; it might have been next to that box of chronometers.

He started doing the maths in his head, rough calculations. The fact that some of the pieces weren't for sale was an excellent sign, of course. *Sold*, said the auctioneer in Tom's head, *for an undisclosed sum to the telephone bidder from Texas*. The amount of money was getting out of control . . . He was going to have to find a piece of paper and a pen.

Images of the warehouse dissolved into images of the Gold Coast. A meter maid beckoned him and Don onto the beach.

Chump chops, Edgell tinned peas, a few spuds and a bottle of dinner ale. Tom's string bag revealed it all, but the celebratory tin of red salmon lay hidden from the casual observer. The pavement took him away from Botany Road and into the grounds of the Housing Commission flats. Back in the 1960s these apartment blocks were the latest in high-rise, high-density, high-tech living. Preformed pre-stressed concrete windows rose for thirty floors in two separate tower blocks. Each floor had been named after one of the ports of call made by Captain James Cook during his voyage of 1768. Tom lived on the 'Tierra del Fuego' floor, which put him three floors above 'Plymouth' and twenty-five floors below 'Botany Bay'.

Three elevators, one in dry dock, two working, plied their trade from Plymouth to Botany Bay return. Square canvas shopping trolleys on small rubber wheels, pieces of furniture (nothing of worth), form guides in back pockets, lawn bowls in Samsonite school cases – all made the journey from port to port. As the lift doors opened Tom stepped aboard.

'Your phone's been ringin' all mornin',' Bill Maddison said. Bill lived on 'Tahiti'. He wasn't the most boring man in the world – Tom's cousin Geoff was – but he came pretty close.

'Really?' replied Tom. He transferred the string bag from one arm to the other.

'Sure as we're standin' here.' That news imparted, Bill moved on to part two of some yarn from his past. It had started the day before yesterday and involved a now extinct lapidary club.

The numbers in the lift ascended.

'. . . bits of rock from Wee Jasper, felspar from somewhere else, cloudy quartz, diamond saws, volcanic eggs, grinding compounds, and then there were polishing wheels that were driven by belts attached to washing-machine motors . . .'

The lift doors, in an act of charity, parted.

'Oh, and Tom, don't forget. Bingo at the bowlie tonight.'

'No worries.'

Once clear of the lift, Bill's voice was replaced by the muffled ring of Tom's phone. He juggled bags and keys at the front door, but missed the call.

The phone sat beside a long-unused Chrysler record player on a small table, at the side of which leant a pristine boxed set entitled *Springtime Classical Favourites*. The steak knives that came with the records had remained unopened in the kitchen. A portable cassette player that had replaced the Chrysler after its demise sat cockishly above the turntable.

Almost the entire floor plan could be seen from any one point. A once fashionable three-seater clashed with two wing-backs in the lounge-room area. Over in the kitchen, chrome legs with black rubber half-soles supported a green laminex tabletop. The end of a single bed, half dressed, peered in from the bedroom. There, a wardrobe containing an oval mirror reflected windows with metal bars that restricted their opening. A jumper from 'Bay of Islands' had made sure of that last detail.

For a major city hospital, the waiting room at St Vincent's was small. Three rows of chairs were spaced between doors with push-button combinations. On the wall, experienced fingers had embroidered a picture of Christ praying against a rock; he appeared to be watching a television that sat in the corner. The main source of light came from a soft-drink machine.

Paul pulled back a ring top on a can of Coke and thought about last night's events. Don had been neither conscious nor unconscious when the ambulance reversed into one of the two bays at the hospital. A strong gust of wind had accompanied the opening of the doors. It created eddies that swept around him, invisible fingers that lifted the sheet and, like a wave breaking onto a beach, washed over him.

'It's all right, Pop,' Paul had tried to assure him. 'We're at the hospital. Everything's going to be all right.'

Looking up at his son had caused the oxygen mask to be pulled hard across Don's face. It left a thin white line long after its removal. Even if the old man's thoughts had been clear enough to him, it was obvious that his inability to communicate them were causing him to panic. Intense concentration on individual words seemed to come to nothing; and, as he had become more distressed, he began swinging his head violently from side to side.

'Everything's okay, Pop,' Paul had whispered again. But clearly it wasn't. Paul had cupped his hands around his father's face, then watched him disappear into the hospital.

Tom wasn't home. Why wasn't he home? He was always home. Paul hung up yet again before finding his own work number in the mobile's address book. The school secretary answered.

'The old man's had a stroke,' he told her.

Paul didn't particularly like Mrs Barraclough but found himself sharing intimate details, telling her how he felt. A stroke. It was the first time he'd used the word. It had been said to him, but it came from a clinical perspective, devoid of emotion. Machines spoke to machines. Data was displayed on monitors that were fed by wires attached to suction cups. The doctors had received the information, now he was passing it on to others.

'I'm sorry, Paul. If we can help in any way . . .' The school secretary said all the right things. She even sounded reasonable. She rearranged his timetable and wished Don a speedy recovery.

'Yeah, I hope so too,' Paul replied.

But what if he wasn't going to recover? Maybe this was it. Paul wished he was with somebody, somebody who knew Don. He didn't know how it was supposed to be. With Tom still uncontactable, he stopped pacing the floor and returned to his seat.

The waiting room gradually filled as morning wore on. A doctor appeared – one of the ones from the night before – and spoke without making eye contact. Paul wondered if she talked to everybody like this, or was it due to the gravity of the situation perhaps? In lieu of a top pocket, a band-aid had been used to secure a biro. The name *Shauna* had been scratched onto the side of it. Scrubbed hands unconsciously removed the pen.

'. . . embolus, floating matter in the blood,' Paul heard before textbook jargon gave way to a more accessible language: 'Fatty tissue breaking away from the wall of an artery and constricting the flow of blood to the brain.'

The doctor began moving the biro about in her fingers and then brought the diagnosis to an end. 'To what extent he recovers will be revealed over the next few days . . . He's as comfortable as we can make him.'

The two of them stood in silence. In another situation it might have seemed awkward. But in the confines of the waiting room, it didn't seem to matter. Anyway, that was the last he ever saw of Dr Shauna. Paul dropped his half-finished can of soft drink into a nearby bin and headed off down the hallway.

At first a lack of available beds had seen Don left waiting in a corridor. Organised confusion, and the noise that accompanied it, was eventually replaced by a room with a view. In the bed next to Don's, an elderly gentleman introduced himself to Paul.

'If you blow up Bellevue Hill you might be able to see Bondi from here,' the man added with a laugh. Loose dentures gave him a permanent smile.

Paul's attention stayed with his old man. He thought about holding his hand. The bond between them usually manifested itself in far less tangible ways; in fact, apart from during the ambulance trip, and when he was a kid, he couldn't honestly think of any other time he'd considered doing this.

The smiling man gestured again towards the Eastern Suburbs. 'Whaddya reckon?'

Paul looked up from the bed. 'Good idea,' he replied. But his thoughts were with his father.

*

Tom crunched the column shift into reverse and parked the ute. Since finally speaking to a noticeably impatient Paul on the phone – he'd been trying to get through for hours, apparently – it had been a quick trip across town to get to St Vincent's. But then he'd missed the hospital car park, so there was still a bit of a walk. He deposited all his change in the meter and, as a safety precaution, lifted the bonnet and disconnected the coil. With betting slips, form guide and transistor radio, he felt well placed as he finally struck out towards the hospital.

Doric columns ushered him into the main building. As he followed the signs to Ward 15, he began to wonder how long it would be before he too became part of the system. Don was only a year or two older than Tom and he'd seemed fine yesterday – well, as fine as he could be. Perhaps the fall at the warehouse loosened something?

The doorway to the ward was wide, and permanently open. Above each of the four beds, miniature rails extended from the ceiling, supporting curtains that just cleared the floor. Brushed aluminium chairs paired up with single-leg tables that reached out over beds with matching linen. Tom spied Paul sitting close beside one of the beds, on the far side of which an old man with a big grin on his face stood gazing out of the window.

'G'day, Paul. How's he doing?' Tom placed the radio and betting material on a bedside cabinet and his hat on the chair.

'Dunno. We're not sure.'

Tom's attention focused on Don. This was not how

he expected to see his old mate. For the first time he saw Don as being old, fragile. He saw Don as Paul saw him. Any thoughts of listening to the afternoon races or talking about small Bakelite instruments quickly disappeared.

The back of Paul's fingers reached out to caress his old man's face. 'Hey, Pop,' he said softly. 'Tom's here. He's come to see you.'

Tom moved a little closer. 'Hello, Don . . . I brought the radio in for you, mate.'

Don drifted in and out of some place that was a long way from home. The nerve endings surrounding his eyelids pinched his skin, but the message they bore was too weak to be carried out. To those around him therefore, his eyes remained closed; but he felt his lids catching on something, like a window sticking in its frame.

The silver rail of the curtain track reflected brightly against the ceiling. Don found himself travelling along its gentle curves as a passenger. The inside of the carriage felt warm and safe as it circled the bed below. Around him in the carriage were a group of day-trippers, all of whom seemed familiar to him somehow.

From the carriage window, his plight looked grim. His body was clearly visible through the bedsheet, a cotton wall that separated their worlds. He tried to attract his own attention, but he seemed to be too far away.

Turning away from the window now, he looked across to see that the person sitting next to him was his father. How could that be? He'd been dead for almost sixty years.

And Bernadette was there too. She reached across the carriage aisle and held his hand. 'It's all right, darling,' she said. 'Everything's going to be all right.'

Even Miss Peters was there; she smiled from the seat opposite. 'Mr Edwards rang to say thank you for the repair on his watch,' she told him.

The more he looked around, the more he realised that everybody there knew him, and he knew everyone. Seated at the back was a young man in uniform; Don wanted to ask if he was all right, but then he disappeared.

He closed his eyes and, in a single, long circuit around the bed, started replaying fragments of his life, beginning with when his father had left off.

Chapter Five

Father died not long ago, aged fifty-seven. A green dressing gown held him together like a shawl around a newborn. His plaid slippers lay below the bed on the floor, and on his head sat the knitted woollen cap that Mother had bought for him on a trip to Katoomba. On the table next to his bed was a pair of glasses that directed the afternoon sun onto the side of his face; from where I was sitting, it put the colour back into his cheeks. Had he lasted one more day he would've made it to the year 1940. We stared at each other for much of his last evening. He from some other place, me from the side of his bed.

The past month had been spent putting together pieces of paper and legal documents, making sure there were no loose ends to his life. He even struggled down to the shop occasionally and went through a collection of fob watches in the 'Work to be Done' shoebox.

He would sit at his desk holding on to things he knew. Then, for no apparent reason, he would cast himself adrift, wandering around the room in half memories that took him into what used to be the old part of the house.

It was the fags that got him in the end. Most watchmakers smoke – the tins make perfect containers for parts. His are stacked along a bench that runs the length of what was once our lounge room.

The fireplace is still there, and the cat that slept on the linoleum in front of it, but that's about it. The transition from front room to shopfront was brought on a few years back by the Depression; then, because of the house's close proximity to the main street, it stayed that way. Framed family portraits and an excellent oil painting of some roses by Aunty Mary has been replaced by mechanical timepieces that tick fast and slow against the plaster walls.

'Surrounded by time and not enough of it' – that's what he used to say. As a watchmaker, he was first class, and he introduced me to the trade when I was just six. Every Sunday during Father O'Grady's sermon, he would carefully dissect his prized fob watch. The small mechanical piece beat within the pages of his Bible as he explained each movement to me. It was only when he'd pull out his eyepiece in church that my mother began to complain.

She's been gone eight years now. Taken by the Lord when I was ten. I never put much faith in Him after that. So now there's just me and a legacy of shoeboxes that contain watches well past their collection dates.

The shop is divided by a partition, and behind it sit the two spinsters, pearl threaders, in decaying Victorian splendour. They eavesdrop through the masonite walls and dream of faraway places and lives they wish they could lead. Miss Peters is Jewish and keeps the wireless permanently tuned to developments in Europe. Contract work from the Air Ministry has been trickling in for a while now; timepieces at first, then instruments that measure air speed and altitude and changes in pressure. I think that's what made me want to become an airman. I line up the gauges in front of me, and in my imagination, take my desk into the clouds.

'You ever been up in an aeroplane, Miss Peters?' I raise my voice against the masonite wall.

Indistinct chatter filters back. 'Foolhardy' is followed by a request for more tea.

White with one and black with none. I've been making the tea since Mother died. For a time I wondered if I might not have been better off at school. Especially on summer afternoons when my classmates used to push their faces up against the shop window and taunt me with towels, togs and shanghais, and prams turned into billy carts.

But now I have my own workbench. And expandable garters that hold up my shirt sleeves, and long grey trousers and polished shoes. I even have a deposit on my Uncle Neil's car.

A bell above the front door announces a young woman into the shop. She hesitates in the doorway before deciding to enter.

Her eyes drift from watch to clock, then across to meet mine. She is beautiful, like a movie star, but real, and standing right there. Right in front of me. I'm beginning to stare. I pick up a pencil and fiddle with a fictitious set of numbers. She's moving again now. Across to the counter and trailing a scarf that might be used to tie back her hair.

'I was looking for Mr Cameron,' she says, glancing towards the spinsters' door.

'That's me,' I say. 'Don. Don Cameron.'

'Oh. I was expecting . . . an older man.'

'That would be my father. George.'

She pauses, as if I might simply pop out the back and get him. 'He passed away last year,' I explain.

'Oh. I'm sorry . . .' She smiles sympathetically. 'I'm Bernadette Wilson. A friend asked me to bring this watch in for repair. Perhaps you could recommend someone?'

'Well, you could leave it with me if you like,' I reply. 'Probably just needs a clean.'

She hands over the timepiece and stands there for a moment, uncertain as to what to do. I try to look older than my eighteen years by leaning forward over the counter, as my father often used to do. I place my hand to my chin and looked deeply troubled.

'Yes, well, that's the problem with pocket watches,' I tell her. 'Lint. Fouls up the mechanism.' Whatever it is that I say after that, it certainly isn't what I'm thinking. Some sort of a sales pitch the old man taught me perhaps.

'You make it sound quite valuable. Do you think it'd be worth much?'

'Maybe.' I take an eyepiece from my pocket and hold the watch up to the light. 'It's certainly a nice piece. Possibly French. Early eighteenth century – winder through the dial.' I hold the watch in my hand and polish it against my shirt. No doubt about it, it's a beautiful piece. 'Might even be older. You can see where the original gold plating's rubbed off. Years of fingers and fob pockets, probably . . . Still, the face is in pretty good nick. Leave it with me and I'll give it a clean. No charge. Have it ready in a week.'

What I lack in years is made up for in experience. The eyepiece helps. That was another trick of Father's. She seems reassured by my advice and writes an address on a piece of paper while I transfer the watch to the relevant shoebox. Then she turns and heads for the door. A few precious seconds and she'll become part of the streetscape . . .

'Do you think the war'll last more than six months?' I ask, a little too quickly.

'Sorry?' She turns in the doorway.

'The war.'

'I hope not.'

'Oh yeah. Me too,' I agree. 'But, er, if it does – you know, if the Allies go into France – I'm thinking of becoming an airman. It's the way of the future, don't you think?'

She pauses for a moment. She even looks as if she might be interested in what I have to say, but she lets it pass. 'Well, don't fly too close to the sun,' she says.

'The sun?'

'Look what happened to Icarus.'

'Icarus? Oh yes, yes . . . of course.' I smile as if I know him personally.

The smile is returned, the scarf pushed into a pocket, and she disappears into the street.

Even with the propeller turning, the plane looks heavy on the ground. Cumbersome. Part wood, part fabric, with hot oil in long lines staining the cowlings; heat vaporises into the air.

'No smart-arsin' around, all right? Once around the paddock, and back home.' If Henry's nervous about me taking his biplane solo for the first time, he isn't showing it. 'You'll be right. Piece a piss.' He lifts his thumb as a vote of confidence.

I think about yelling something back, but there's little point, as he's partially deaf. Too much time in the air. I release the park brake, aim into the wind and push the throttle through the gate. This is my fifth lesson; and at three quid a go, my last.

The plane waddles at first, wings dipping from side to side, as it gathers speed in long steps across the paddock. Struts pull against wires and canvas against wood. Just this side of the tower, I lift off from the paddock and up into the breeze. I've broken the laws of gravity.

Without Henry on board, the plane seems to soar. The lack of extra weight helps, of course, but maybe it's also as a result of a feeling that comes from within me. Of being alone, soaring with the birds a thousand feet above Kurnell. The beach becomes an ocean and the streets become a city. The world is laid out before me. Tin roofs, tile roofs, chook sheds and fenced back yards pass beneath me. I bank through the clouds and wonder how Uncle Neil would feel about his car payments being strung out a bit. I know this is what I want to do, and it's going to be an expensive hobby. I'll need to raise more money.

The following morning I remove Father's old 'Work to be Done' shoebox from the safe and place it on the bench. Most of the watches are past repair. Not that they aren't any good – it's the availability of parts that is the problem. American watches are the best; they seem to last the longest, and you can swap the workings. Some of the pieces in the shoebox are marked with addresses and phone numbers. Others are in bits, in unmarked envelopes.

Out of a dozen, there are three or four that are redeemable, so I set to work on them. All of them have contact addresses. One of the watches is quite valuable, and I notice it has a fiver owing on it. It was built before mass production, in a time when quality and pride of workmanship counted, when pieces could be traced back to the individuals who worked on them.

Once the repairs are complete, I place them all in my pocket and tell the spinsters I'll be back after lunch. I could take the bicycle, as most of the addresses are local; but because one is over the bridge in North

Sydney, I decide to use the Riley. Besides, there's something about driving. Something about being seen to be driving. First stop a Mr Aitkens, just off Crown Street in Surry Hills.

'A Waltham?' The man who opens the door is short and heavy and breathes in deep breaths that take in all the oxygen around him. 'Could be mine, depends. Depends on how much I owe.'

'Three quid,' I reply. 'Worth heaps more than that.' It's a nice watch. American. Seventeen jewels, ten carats, subsidiary dial for the second hand. The blokes that made them invented a machine for mass production and never looked back.

'Three quid, eh?' The watch all but disappears between his fat fingers. 'Bit short at the minute.' He takes in a particularly deep breath. 'Tell you what, son. You sell it, take out what I owe, and I'll give you ten per cent on top.'

As I walk back to the car I wonder if I should mark it down a bit. Mr Aitkens doesn't appear to be too well, so it might be in both our interests.

The second watch is the one belonging to Bernadette Wilson's friend. It dates back to the 1700s, when looks were considered more important than precision; perhaps that explains the white enamel chapter ring that surrounds an enamelled portrait of the Duchess de somebody. It's a bit of a collector's item, the sort of watch that rarely came out of the safe. The address puts the owner on the other side of the harbour. In Mortimer Street, Milsons Point.

The Riley has good pick-up. Bridge girders flick past. For a few brief moments, I become the harbour master. Below, tugs tow dirty coal barges to listing steamers, and I catch glimpses of men wearing bandanas of sweat as they shovel coal into buckets. Upwind, gentlemen in jackets guide yachts elegantly across the bays.

The house at the end of Mortimer Street was built of stone cut from the site then reassembled to form a two-storey terrace. The second-floor blocks follow a line of stone that runs through the cliff behind. At the top of the cutting, overhanging vines pull the corner of the roof back into the cliff face. Another ten years, it seems, and the house will once again be part of the landscape.

A crack in the front window causes water to trickle over a cardboard sign that leans against the inside of the glass. Through buckled stains I make out the words Piano Tutor, *and sure enough, from the front room comes the sound of a piano.*

'George Cameron, dead?' Mrs Yankovic makes a sign of the cross and whispers something in some other language. 'He was a good man, a Christian man . . .' She stands at the door in silence for a moment, memories of my father drifting backwards and forwards across her eyes. She's elderly, maybe seventy, and despite the heat she's dressed in black. An embroidered stole hangs from her shoulders. 'Come inside,' she tells me. 'Come inside and have some tea.'

The hall is long and lit by electric lamps. The old gas outlets are still in place and now support certificates of music and religious icons. A gentleman's coat hangs in permanent creases next to the front door. It smells of must, of damp rising through the pages of old papers that are stacked along the skirting boards.

She pauses by the door that leads to the front room. 'You didn't tell me about George.'

The sound of the piano is replaced by a younger voice. 'Sorry. Forgot.'

'Forgot?' Mrs Yankovic shakes her head. 'Well, don't stop, my dear. Concentrate.*' She turns to where I'm standing. 'Do you play an instrument, Don?'*

'Not really. No,' I reply.

'You're lucky. It's a gift that can destroy you. Schubert . . .' Her fingers subconsciously play the piece beneath her shawl. 'It's very beautiful, don't you think? Some music just sings to you. And she does play it so well.' She sighs, then continues on towards the kitchen.

I peer around the door. A standard lamp has been pulled up to the piano, and in the half light I see the girl from the shop. Her hair is wrapped into the same scarf that followed her around the room, and the same dark eyes now translate notes into music. She catches my eye as she turns the page. She looks vulnerable, suddenly exposed to others watching her play.

'Sorry,' I say. 'I didn't mean to disturb you.'

'That's all right.' She concentrates on the page of music. 'I've just about got it now. How's the watch coming along?'

'Um, good,' I reply. 'I mean, it's ready . . . Lint.'

She laughs as her fingers trace the notes on the keyboard. 'And then . . . we go back to this bit . . . The music of a madman. What do you think?'

'Not exactly a toe-tapper.'

'It's not supposed to affect your toes. Affects your heart. You have to close your eyes – go on, close your eyes and listen.'

'I've made us a cup of tea,' Mrs Yankovic announces, reappearing in the doorway. 'I hope you like it strong, Don. It's a new pot, you see. I never seem to get it right. Silly really.'

She carries the tray across the room and places it on a low table. 'Such a tragedy', she says, with a quick nod towards Bernadette. 'If it were Russia, she would be playing with Hmelnitsky! But here . . .' She shrugs her shoulders and pours the tea.

I smile in a way that implies I understand the problem.

'The watch belonged to my husband. Well, it didn't really belong to him, the same as it doesn't belong –' She stops mid-sentence, caught between a phrase of music and the watch that sits between us on the table. 'It's worth nothing really,' she continues. 'It's a family heirloom, so it can't be sold. I suppose somebody will sell it, someday, but I'll be dead by then.' The thought seems to comfort her.

I sit back in the chair and close my eyes, drifting with the music. It's as if the pages in front of Bernadette glide around the room like a paper plane, half stalling, spiralling, climbing note over note to the ceiling, where they soar in loose circles that take in every part of the room. Then, with the final flurry of notes, the pages come back down to rest on the keyboard.

'You seem to improve with an audience,' Mrs Yankovic tells her student approvingly.

Bernadette returns her smile as she closes the book of sheet music.

At the front gate, after lingering around in stilted conversation with Bernadette about how well she plays, I ask her out to the flicks. And she agrees. Then she watches me drive off in Uncle Neil's Riley. It's perfect.

It's hot, made hotter by the sun beating into an enclosed cockpit that sits high over the wing. The war in Europe is well under way, and with twenty minutes solo I'd had no problem getting into the Air Corps. I lean forward and watch the shadow of the aircraft racing me across the airfield. It leaps the boundary fence and makes a dash into the bush.

The cockpit allows for an instructor, but this morning it's just me doing 'touch-and-go's along the main strip at Richmond, to the west of Sydney. It's a serious aeroplane, painted canary yellow so as to be easily seen from the ground, and powered by a powerful radial engine. It's a long way from Henry's biplane.

The time is just before eleven. I climb out of the training area and follow the road south towards Penrith. A line of peppercorns point to the Nepean and the old bridge – a place that Bernadette and I know well. We've swum beneath its wooden beams and made secret pacts on its banks. I drop down from the clouds and line up her parents' house.

Through the cockpit glass I can clearly make out Bernadette's younger brother, Frank. He ditches his bike at the sound of the aircraft and races, arms waving, to the front door. I come in low and fast along the river, across the tops of the gums and power poles. Frank's in the back yard now. I pick him up racing to the clothesline, hands gesturing wildly to Bernadette, who's standing with a mouthful of pegs and a basket of washing. She looks up into the sky and waves as the aircraft shadow races across the lawn.

With Schubert in my head, I do a slow wing-over before lifting back into the clouds . . .

Don's hand began to ache, which was a sign at least that his senses were returning. As the fragments of his past life began to slow and fade, the last image he'd caught from his position beside the carriage window was of himself in the bed below: his body, lying beneath the sheet.

A plastic tube came into being. It danced along the side of the track before finally plummeting down to his left arm. He was surprised to find the arm pinned to the side of the hospital bed, and that the tube ran into the back of it. A nurse crossed in front of him. He pushed his head back into the pillow and concentrated on the two figures that watched over him.

'Just relax, Pop. It's us.' Paul tried to sound as laid-back as he could, but the position of his chair, pulled tight against the bed, betrayed his true feelings. He'd been overjoyed when Don had finally opened his eyes. 'You're gonna be just fine, Pop,' he added softly.

'Yeah, you'll be fine, mate,' Tom repeated, perhaps as much for his own benefit.

'Back to bed now, Stan.' A nurse looked at her watch, then took the smiling man by the arm. The light from the window was diffused as the curtain was pulled around him.

The area around the bed now assumed more intimate dimensions. Tom looked across to his old mate. He began thinking about the possibility of him not fully recovering or, indeed, not recovering at all.

As for Don, his bedsheet seemed to be causing him particular distress. For some reason known only to himself, he insisted on it covering his whole body up to his neck, and it had to be positioned exactly straight at the top. Any offer of help now or during the days that followed was met with strong resistance. When it all got too hard he would simply retreat to a position well behind his own lines.

Even in his most rational moments, he was far from okay. He couldn't place where he was or even who he was – words, names, numbers: it all came in a foreign currency and it all came from the past.

Chapter Six

Tom Barton crossed off yet another day on the calendar. Time was running out. Don had been given notice in writing to vacate the factory of its contents, in a letter that suggested some urgency in the matter, and Tom didn't perform well under pressure. There was a lot to organise, but he would have to put the warehouse-clearing issue to one side until he'd got back from seeing Don. He carefully placed a wrapped parcel in his string bag, and headed towards the front door of his apartment on Tierra del Fuego.

An hour later he was stepping through the entrance of the Royal Rehabilitation Centre, a nondescript block set back from the noise of Victoria Road in Ryde. In the reception area, the TV broadcasted a drama to anybody who cared to stop and watch. Oblivious to his presence, the receptionist turned up the volume.

'It's all right, Jade. We'll always have tomorrow.'

'Will we, Camden? Will we? You're full of tomorrows.

Tomorrow you leave your wife; tomorrow we buy the airline tickets.'

'Put the drink down, Jade.'

'Why? Just because you're my drug and alcohol counsellor . . .'

Tom rang the little bell on the reception as the *Home and Away* theme song played over the show's credits. 'I've come to see Mr Cameron,' he said.

The receptionist shook her head at Camden's morals. What a prick, she thought. She leant around the side of a partition. 'Don Cameron. Is he in hydro?'

An anonymous voice confirmed that he was.

'He's relaxing by the pool,' the receptionist said, hardly bothering to look at Tom. 'Left at the end of the corridor. You can't miss it.'

'Good-o.' Tom gathered up his string bag and followed the directions he'd been given. Somehow he wondered if he was in the right building. The sense of urgency that surrounded the scene at St Vincent's had completely disappeared – here, unhurried footsteps were measured in distance rather than time.

Open doors revealed rooms that fell somewhere between dormitories and gymnasiums. Reflected in the convex mirror above the pool entrance, Tom could see machines that resembled wool presses, with sheepskin underlays cushioning arms and legs that rose and fell on levers attached to weights and pulleys.

In the rehab centre's pool area, a travel poster promoting the 1996 Atlanta Paralympics had been placed by the changing room. High-speed film captured athletes in highly modified wheelchairs, lightweight racing machines made of Kevlar that supported their torsos and pushed their knees up high. The wheelchair Don had been sitting in was of a more practical design. It was parked by the side of the pool with the hand brake firmly on. A towel lay across the empty seat.

A woman with a clipboard stood by the pool. 'That's it, Don, you're doing well,' she called to one of the bodies floating peacefully in the pool. 'We'll have you back in the saddle in no time. How are you feeling?'

Saddle . . . Horse riding. Maybe that was part of the program, Don thought. He pulled against the water. It created whirlpools that broke the surface and revealed fingers swimming below. The pool was heated, but it felt cold. A shiver sent ripples of ever-expanding circles across its surface. *Back in the saddle* . . . He thought he'd had a horse once, but he couldn't be sure, so he let the comment pass.

The physio repeated the question, this time a little louder. 'How's it going, Don? Everything okay?'

'Good,' he replied, in a distracted kind of a way. He was thinking about going home; he remembered he'd left a paintbrush by the back shed and thought it really should be in turps.

Don held on to his towel and thoughts of things that needed to be done as Tom steered him down the corridor and into his room. The pool had left him with a smell of chlorine. He'd shaved, or someone had shaved him. Grey slacks gathered themselves over slippers not yet broken in. A walking stick hung from the back of his chair, and, on the table in front of him, sat the aircraft compass Tom had brought in. 'What time is it, do you reckon?' Don asked.

'I reckon it'd be about three thirty.'

'Three thirty.'

'Three thirty,' confirmed Tom.

Don seemed happy with that. He reached up to behind his ear and adjusted his hearing aid.

'Only good for the TV.' He said it as if Tom were privy to some prior conversation on the subject.

Don tried to recall the events of the last two weeks. He remembered much of what had transpired but the first few days in hospital escaped him. Whole chapters seemed to be missing, the pages replaced in some ad hoc fashion. Tom had remained the only constant. Over those past weeks the cafeteria had replaced his back yard, and now an order was beginning to take shape, a routine that gave purpose to the present.

Tom wandered back into an old *Reader's Digest*. Bringing in the compass had been inspired by an article he'd read only the day before entitled 'I am Joe's Brain'. Joe had had a stroke, and this was the story of his survival. Try to keep the mind stimulated – that seemed to be one of Joe's messages.

'What do you reckon about a move up to the Gold Coast?' Tom asked suddenly.

Don pushed his fluoros back onto his nose, as if to improve his hearing. 'You, move up to the Gold Coast?'

'Yeah, Don. You too. You and me – the two of us.'

'Move up to the Gold Coast?'

'Yeah.'

'Why would we do that?'

'To live.'

'But we live in Redfern,' he replied.

Tom picked up the compass and gave it a gentle tap. Perhaps Don wasn't quite ready for the Gold Coast. Not just yet anyway. He weighed up the device in his hand before slowly returning it to the parcel. And with that, in many ways, for him the visit ended there and then. It was just that physically he stayed with Don for another hour or two before heading back towards the car park.

The drive home was far from the easy run he'd enjoyed on the way out to Ryde. He parked the ute and entered the Commission block with the sun already sinking in the early evening sky, as if the day was admitting defeat.

Once inside the flat, Tom's attention returned to the matter of having to vacate the warehouse. This would necessitate a truck of some size and cheaper, short-term storage space. Cash on hand, that was the first requirement. With that in mind, he opened the door to his kitchen cupboard, reached over assorted plates, and removed a vase that contained his bank statements. Tom turned the pages over to the most recent addition and checked his account balance . . . It was not looking good.

Perhaps he'd have to let a few things go, he thought. Too much tied up in capital. There was the ute – but that was a necessity. The beer-can collection, maybe. At the last swap meet, he'd exchanged two bicentennial

Tooheys for a commemorative Pope Paul. All up there might be, what, a couple of hundred dollars worth?

Struggling with this mathematical equation, he headed to the refrigerator and pulled out a beer. Shortly afterwards, a second long-neck thwarted any chance of finding a solution.

He was in the bedroom now, dressed only in pyjama shorts and a singlet. He crossed in front of the wardrobe mirror then reached under the bed. The image he'd had of himself by the plunge pool at Paradise-sur-Mer didn't quite match the image reflected in the mirror now. On all fours he looked frail, thin arms and legs protruded from his torso. His shorts hung loosely around his body. A drawstring of aging skin pulled a web of scars that ran down one of his arms.

Under the bed, beside the spare ticking, was a suitcase stuffed with papers, photographs, old tax returns and various documents that summed up who he was and what he did. It wasn't much really, a life in a port, bound by a leather strap more suitable to harness racing. He always felt depressed looking in this suitcase; it was like a geological dig into his past. Near the surface he hoped to find something for Don. Something to help him piece together his life.

He sifted through the contents of the case as one might wander down a familiar street, stopping occasionally for a beer at once familiar landmarks. Photographs of Don and Bernadette were put to one side. There was a shot of the Sydney Opera House with skeletons of scaffolding; and if you knew what you were looking for, you could pick out Don clowning about, pretending to be part of the army of workers. There he was, holding the plans to the chook shed in one hand and pointing to the rising sails with the other.

Deep into the dig, Tom unearthed his parents, and the farm he grew up on, and the old Dodge, and seaside holidays. Black-and-white postcards of ships – cargo carriers such as *Adelaide Steam*, *Burns Philp*, BHP's *Iron Chieftain* and various other *Iron*-named ships; war service medals, and the stories that came with them; the two-up pennies that came out every Anzac Day; a sketch of his younger brother Harry that had been done at the local show.

Harry looked about twelve. Tom didn't know why he had the sketch, but there was one of himself somewhere too, he was sure. He remembered Harry telling the artist he wanted the town included in the picture, so the sleepy hamlet of Ariah Park ended up in the background. Funny what you remember and what you don't, he thought.

Then he came across a photograph of Emily Taylor. He stopped for a moment and held it at arm's length. Emily Taylor . . . She and Tom stood together on Terrigal Beach, holding a fish, before a backdrop of sea and sky. They were probably fifteen or sixteen at the time, but she could have been in a magazine. She truly was beautiful. He knew it at the time, but back then he was just this kid from the country. Back then, almost sixty years ago.

Tom was about to pack it all away, when he saw a picture of a house. His mind sped forward the best part of two decades from his memories of Emily Taylor, and somewhere in the corridors of his mind he heard a dog barking. It belonged to the people who lived at number 30, the house next door to the one in this photo. He had an image of himself cutting up vegetables at the kitchen sink, a half-full bottle of beer beside him, and the dog going off on the other side of the fence. He still couldn't say if he had the kitchen knife in his hand or not as he approached the dog . . . According to the neighbour, he did. He could remember having the beer in his other hand, though, and that this was one of the times he took 'the pledge'. His wife Catherine was there. She was yelling something unattractive from the picket fence.

And then there were the wedding photos. Very flash, with all the trimmings. But the marriage never worked out. Ten years later it might've worked – it might even have worked now. It was the timing that was all wrong. He felt sad about that, but at the time he didn't. At the time, he couldn't have given a shit.

And on Tom continued, each picture or memento dragging up another long-gone moment. There were the years spent damming the Snowy. He pictured the scene as the river's backwaters silently tiptoed under the door of the boarding house he'd once stayed in, and, inch by inch, climbed up the stone stairs that led to the church where he'd worshipped. Building by building, the whole town was flooded, a generation lost as the waters filled the valley. And when the job ended on the Snowy Scheme, there was a railway being built up north, then a housing estate, then another river to dam. That was how his whole life had been: itinerant. Right up to the school crossing.

And with that realisation, the dig was complete. Tom tightened the strap around his past, placed the photographs of Don on the dresser, then passed out on his bed.

Morning brought with it his last day on the school crossing. Tom didn't feel old. It was just the way others perceived him. He took a little extra care shaving, found a shirt without a fray, socks to match; then he took his orange safety vest from the cupboard and closed the front door behind him.

It was a perfect day. No wind swirling lunchtime wrappers from gutter to gutter. No late entries rushing him from behind. Good visibility. A perfect finale. As a professional, he should've been thinking about the blind spot and the position of the sun in relation to a motorist's eye, but he was distracted. The sight of the army of backpacks and school ports took him back to his flat, back to the suitcase under the bed, back to the memories.

The red Bronco caught him off-guard. It was in the approaching zone, well over the speed limit, and wasn't going to stop. And little Tuscany Scanlon was still on the yellow stripes. Without a thought for his own safety, he stepped into the gutter, gently reached for her hand, and helped her onto the pavement.

'Watch it, driver!' he hollered. 'I've got your number, pal!' He smiled, satisfied with his reflexes. Tom Barton still had what it took. He watched Tuscany skip off into the school yard, his mind drifting off to other places.

He remembered the deliberately straight guard of pencil pines that ran up to Jock and Emily's farmhouse. Marsden was her surname now. She and Jock had met in Wagga during the war, and got married almost the day after hostilities ended. It was summer; a country town summer – Grenfell, that was the town. It might have been 1950 or thereabouts when he'd last seen her, on the way home from visiting his parents at Ariah Park. In country miles, the towns weren't all that far apart. A Christmas harvest – yes, that was it. He remembered pigeons chasing wheat trucks, like gulls following trawlers, and feasting on grain that never made it to the silos. Jock was there, looking the part, and their girls; the names of which he couldn't remember. They might've been about three and five at the time, too young for school at any rate. It all seemed pretty perfect. He pictured the handsome farmhouse, and beside it . . . Yes, he could still see it now, clear as day: there, to the left of the house, was a large machinery shed. The front doors were swept back to reveal a floor space only marginally smaller than that of the warehouse.

With the sound of the bell, he put the stop sign under his arm and headed across the school yard to the auditorium. Inside, the junior school began to settle down. Excited voices were hushed by class teachers as the school's deputy principal began his speech in Tom's honour.

A sense of occasion lay before him. He straightened his socks and walked towards the stage. Some of the children gave him discreet waves from chairs they couldn't really see over; others sat like grown-ups. The real littlies sat cross-legged down the front.

With Tom now beside him on the stage, Deputy Principal Carmichael continued with his address. 'And so it is with sadness in our hearts that we see you leaving, Tom. On behalf of all the children at Dawson Street Primary School, we'd like to present you with this small gift in appreciation of all the safe crossings that you have presided over.'

Spontaneous clapping erupted as the school captains helped him unwrap a photograph of the student body. With it came a card, and in a child's hand was written: *To Tom. Goodbye and good luck. Come back and visit us. We will miss you.*

The finality of it all had hit home. Quick reflexes or not, Tom Barton was old, past it. *Goodbye and good luck . . . Come back and visit us* – the words stayed with him for the rest of the day. They were still resonating in his mind when he went to visit Don late that afternoon. In half steps, their arms linked, the two of them made their way around a bed of marigolds that seasonally spelt out the name of the rehabilitation centre.

Occasionally Don would lift his eyes from the bitumen as they walked and quicken his pace. 'What time is it?' he asked again.

'For Chrissake, Don, why do you keep wanting to know the time?'

'It must be late.' Anxiety underscored his voice.

'It's early,' Tom told him, tapping his watch. 'Not yet five.'

Don stopped and repeated those last words.

'Don't worry about it, mate.' Tom stepped forward but Don held his ground.

'But aren't we going somewhere?'

'No, mate, we're not going anywhere.' He spoke slowly, using his hands to get the point across. 'You've had a stroke. You're recovering. It's five to five and it's Wednesday.'

'But we're in the car park,' Don replied.

'I know, mate. It's the repat car park. We're just going for a walk.'

Don took a small spiral notepad from his cardigan pocket and very carefully wrote *Wednesday*.

'What else you got written in there?' Tom asked him.

'I dunno. I can't remember.'

Tom glanced over his shoulder and saw his own name. He took a deep breath and put his arm around his friend.

From his Tierra del Fuego apartment, Tom looked out over the city. A week had passed. Pension day had come and gone. Another trip to the disposal store. A couple of visits with Don at the rehab centre. Don did seem to be improving; perhaps the jigsaw pieces he brought in were helping, Tom wondered, or perhaps it was just his company. He'd thought more about that shed out at Grenfell, at Jock and Emily's farm. It would be perfect for their needs now. But what could he do, just turn up and say hello after five decades?

It felt odd not having a job, not having anywhere specific to go to. No responsibilities. No uniform to put on. Tom had suddenly become misplaced. On the Thursday, he'd even gone back to the crossing. Just to see how the new bloke was working out.

Tom's replacement was wearing a new vest and a new orange cap; he looked even older than Tom perceived himself to be. Slower too. Out of the corner of his eye, Tom had spotted young Imogen Welding – never one to obey the sign – dashing towards the middle of the crossing. He watched the new man waving the lollypop and yelling something inaudible, but she'd continued on regardless.

Amateur, Tom had thought aloud. An accident waiting to happen. He pulled the ute into gear. It was time to move on.

CHAPTER SEVEN

The train no longer went through Grenfell, in central New South Wales. The line stopped at Cowra, thirty miles to the east. In fact, just about everything stopped at Cowra, and that was the kind of town Grenfell had become. Once the town had boasted a department store, specialty shops, a sit-down restaurant, six hotels with rooms booked ahead, a presbytery with two priests and a housekeeper, and grand houses containing drawing rooms and maids' quarters. But it all got left behind, like a bend in a river that slowly closed its banks.

From the summit of 'Hospital Hill', as the locals referred to the incline on top of which Grenfell Hospital still perched, the town might have seemed like an illustration from a children's storybook. A 'pop-up' town – with a main street, with gums along its asphalt banks, and a garage, a fire station and a church spire. An island cenotaph comprised a stone-carved soldier, head bowed, in a roundabout of small shrubs. If one looked hard enough at the scene below, shopkeepers, farmers in elastic-sided boots and other townsfolk could all be seen going about their business. Somewhere on the page there might even have been a miniature statue of Henry Lawson.

Emily Marsden's red Laser would have registered to the hilltop observer as it pulled out of the Grenfell Bowling Club car park. Inside the little Ford, a mixed-pairs trophy lay on the seat beside her. It had been a great victory, a day to remember. Emily replayed the last bowl in her head now as she turned into Main Street. At first she'd thought it had too much speed – 'Slow, slow,' she mouthed the words to herself again. She could see George Tooney watching from the scoreboard, no doubt hoping for it to go wide. And then, like in a story out of the scriptures, rain began to sprinkle. Just enough to wet the green; just enough to slow the ball's trajectory and ensure it started to curve in gently towards the jack. In that moment, the sounds from the clubhouse nearby fell away to nothing. George Tooney's jaw dropped and Beryl Davidson put her hands up to her mouth. It was the perfect bowl.

'Lovely, Emily. Lovely bowl.' Lynton McCabe gave Emily a kiss on the cheek and dreamed of going that one step further. The luck of the draw had put the two of them together as mixed-pair partners this year, and since the passing of his wife, the club president had shown more than a passing interest in her.

'Thank you, Lynton. Teamwork. That's what it's all about.'

'Exactly,' he replied. 'Now, what about a celebratory tea at the Chinese?' Lynton removed his glasses and smiled his McCabe's Second-Hand Machinery smile.

'Why, that's a lovely thought, Lynton. But we've got the Festival Committee meeting tonight, remember, and . . . and it's important we're all there.' Safety in numbers, she thought.

'Absolutely,' he agreed. 'I know, I'll make a booking for after.'

Emily's sigh brought her back to reality just as she reached the town limits. In the rear-vision mirror now, she caught the reverse image of the Grenfell sign and another promoting the upcoming Henry Lawson Festival of Arts. The festival was held in June of each year, over the Queen's Birthday long weekend, and allowed the whole town to come together to celebrate its claim to fame as the birthplace of the great Australian poet. And Emily had been in charge of appointing the festival's guest of honour for as long as she could remember. It was a fairly thankless task and had become increasingly difficult as the years went by. These days she dealt with minor celebrities usually, most of whom had never heard of Grenfell; and even when they had, they'd want a fee or a return airfare or major press coverage or something else the town simply couldn't offer.

After a long day at the club, Emily was keen to get home and change out of her bowling whites. As she drove the last ten minutes to her property, she realised she was peering through the steering wheel, rather than over it. Aged seventy-something, it was as if she'd somehow shrunk a little – or maybe it was the springs in the seat, she thought. She remembered the day she and Jock went over to Cowra to buy it. You never think of a car outlasting you, but this one had outlasted her husband and would probably outlast her as well. As she pulled off the Mid Western Highway, she thought of having to have dinner with Lynton this evening after the committee meeting. It was not something she looked forward to.

Emily's mailbox had been made from the petrol tank of an old tractor, a present from a grandchild who demonstrated a flair for making such things. It came complete with a glass float bowl and sat bolted to the top of the front fence post, above the property name, Duraminar. She slowed down sufficiently to check its contents. The sampler pack of teas should've arrived by now. And then there was the 'lucky key' to that BMW . . . Still, it was only Tuesday – give it another couple of days before giving up on that one, she thought. She continued on down the dirt drive, past the overgrown tennis court, which long ago her girls had always pretended was Wimbledon, and pulled the Laser to a stop in the garage to the right of the house.

The kitchen was filled with the sound of voices. For years now Emily had made it a habit to leave the radio on. She told people it was to fool burglars, but in an empty house, it was like a welcoming, familiar voice to her. Old Bert, the gardening presenter, was just taking calls about garden bugs. With a cup of tea and a sympathetic ear, Emily sat down to share each caller's anxieties, as usual.

'Exactly,' she said in reference to an aphid problem that Arthur from Dubbo was experiencing. 'Don't delay – *spray*.' Other callers came and went, each one seemingly comforted by Bert's suggestions.

Her teacup empty, and the program now over, Emily headed off to the bedroom for a lie-down. A couple of hours' rest to prepare herself for tonight.

Evening fell quickly on the pop-up town. Street lights illuminated circles on the black bitumen. Only the pubs showed any signs of life. In the ladies' lounge of one, the Shearers Hotel, the Festival Committee meeting had been in progress for the past hour.

George Tooney leant back in his chair and shoved his hand in the air. He was a wide man, and this balancing act made those around him nervous. A broad smile seemed to add to his width.

'We need something *new*,' he began. 'No one does art and craft shows anymore, 'specially ones pushin' dead poets.' He'd had a couple of drinks beforehand, and from where he stood, he thought he was sounding pretty solid. 'Let's get something happening, something that's going to attract a lot of people. Twenty years ago the town could've had the Cherry Blossom thing . . . Well, we know who got that. Cowra, of course. Long before that, a POW camp was up for grabs. And who got that one? Cowra again. I mean, they're even selling barbed wire from the camp breakout – for *eighteen* dollars and fifty cents!' With all in attendance now turned towards him, George felt he was on a roll.

In truth, his message was falling on deaf ears. To his fellow committee members, George Tooney was something of a troublemaker, and worse still, an out-of-towner. He was a public servant who'd only been living in Grenfell for nine years, and he could move on at any stage. Everyone else was there for the run.

'Aw, shut up, George,' Rose McIntyre said, not quite as light-heartedly as she could have. 'Mrs Mac' worked at the local council, so she dealt with him on a daily basis. She looked over her glasses. 'And what about the Iris Festival? Who got that? Anyway, what are we gonna do with a whole lotta tourists? We can't accommodate 'em here. Perhaps we could send 'em over to Cowra as well?' Mrs Mac ignored the sniggers this last comment produced around the room, and went on. 'No, George, it's for *us*. Us and the kids. The kids love this festival.'

'All I'm suggesting,' George countered, 'is something a bit more *with it*. I mean, how many times have we seen old Teddie doing the bushranger thing? Nothing personal, Teddie – but, you know, it's the same every year. You fire off the old rifle, there's a big noise and a lotta smoke, and you run down the street.'

It wasn't clear whether Ted Foster had taken it personally or not, but Mrs Mac was ready with a rebuttal anyway. 'People expect it, George. It wouldn't be the same without Teddie.'

'Well, maybe we ought to try something new. Like an outdoor film festival, which could be combined with, say . . . I don't know, a blessing of the tractors, or something.'

'A blessing of the *tractors*?'

'Yeah, like on the coast when a town has a blessing of its fishing fleet. It could be big on the religious calendar.'

'Could work,' said Lynton McCabe of McCabe's Second-Hand Machinery Centre. 'Could be something in it, you know.' He pictured his sales tent decorated with a suitably religious theme, useful exposure in the local paper – it could all be good. 'Lot more accidents on tractors than there are in boats,' he added.

Emily's thoughts were drifting between tractors and free tea samplers when an elderly gentleman on the footpath outside caught her attention. Through the window, she watched him stretch his arms against the door of a light-coloured ute. Meanwhile, back inside the pub, yet another poetry competition was being added to the agenda.

'Eight forty-five – meeting adjourned,' committee chairman Trevor Styles called at last. With that, Race 4 from Wentworth Park took over the bar.

Tom Barton put his car keys in his pocket and took in the surroundings. He thought there might have been trees dividing the street when he was last here. Peppercorns maybe. Mind you, that was almost fifty years ago. The banks and the pubs had remained constant. Like giant bookends, they kept the shops in two ordered lines that began at the cenotaph and continued down to the grain silo.

He sported old man's trousers, an open-neck flannel shirt and a felt hat that covered a five-dollar haircut. He'd been behind the wheel for five hours and he was feeling it. He wiped his hand across his forehead, picked up his plastic bag full of toiletries, and headed through the entrance of the Shearers Hotel and into a small central hallway. At the same time, a group of about twenty locals came barrelling through the door from a lounge bar on the right.

'Woops-a-daisy – sorry, mate,' said one of the older members of the group as his elbow collided with Tom's. The man, heavily scented with aftershave and immaculately dressed in moleskins and a Pure Wool tie, picked up the plastic bag that now lay on the floor between them. 'Looks like you've got your life in there, son.' He held Tom's gaze with a used-car salesman's smile, before slipping off to follow the crowd as if in search of someone in particular.

'Closing down this section,' a voice called out from the same doorway that had deposited the group. Tom turned to see a middle-aged man approaching with a trayful of empties.

'Just wondering what the chances are for a room,' he said in reply.

'No problem. Twenty-five bucks including breakfast,' replied the publican. 'And the missus cooks it good old

English style, by the way, not one of them *con-tin-ental* ones.'

The missus's breakfast was indeed a pearler. It had started without him, but the smell of steak, eggs, chops, black sauce and pineapple rings, the squeals of young children and the thump of a football bouncing down a corridor had all found their way to his room on the first floor. It was gone ten o'clock by the time he'd decided to rise from his bed and make his way down to the hotel's dining room.

His morning meal now finished, Tom laid the local newspaper out on the table before him and flicked through the pages. Squeezed in among the plethora of small businesses advertising their wares, there was plenty of talk of an upcoming festival, he noted, while a weather report predicted rain. He used to know this world, he reflected – long ago, long before his life in the Housing Commission flat at Redfern.

Tom moved on to the tourist brochure he'd grabbed on his way into the dining area. The 'Open Town' program sounded interesting – you had to register for a weekend stay, he read, and the town would turn it on for you, culminating in a real estate tour.

Grenfell appeared to have a lot to offer. Its rural history, the Lawson weekend, historic buildings, the Weddin Rangers – and, of course, there was also the golfie and the bowlie. In the leaflet's centre was a map of the town and its environs. He tapped the spot where he remembered Emily's farm to be. He'd ask at a garage for more specific directions.

He drained his cup of tea, placed the serviette-wrapped leftovers – a sausage and a hard-boiled egg – inside his pocket, and headed back upstairs.

The publican had given him a time of 'midday, or thereabouts' to vacate the room. It was a far cry from the urgency Tom had left behind in Sydney. Whether it was the real estate agent's underlined bold type on another 'final reminder' letter, or Don's increasing obsession with knowing what hour of the day it was, he was relieved to find that out here, at least, clock watching didn't appear to be contagious. He took advantage of his country timetable by resting up for a bit. Just for a moment, to catch his breath. The long drive the day before was catching up with him. Maybe he wasn't quite as young as he thought he was.

It was well into the afternoon when he was woken by a knock at the door and the missus's voice. 'Will you be stayin' on, Mr Barton?'

His budget had not extended to a second night at the 'flash pub', he had in fact intended to drive back to Sydney after visiting Emily. 'Just packing up now,' he replied. He pulled a comb through his hair, gathered up his plastic bag of possessions and headed down to the ute.

His tie was all wrong. It was a last-minute thing, but now he'd found it made his neck seem thin; something wasn't quite right. Added to that, from the moment he set off he began to have serious misgivings about what he was doing. Maybe he was being rather presumptuous in thinking she'd remember him after all this time. And even if she did, why would she want to help him with his venture? And who was to say that the large shed was still there anyway, or that Emily and Jock hadn't sold the property and moved on? The adage 'There's no fool like an old fool' rang through his mind for the duration of the short drive east.

He had no trouble spotting the turn-off. The bloke at the BP garage had alluded to a bright red metallic mail-box that heralded the start of the dirt track winding off to the north of the highway. Once he'd slowed the ute down and negotiated the turning, Tom noticed a dog racing behind him, close to the back tyres. Ahead were the pencil pines – still there, just as he'd remembered them. The wheat trucks hadn't travelled down this road for many years. But the Marsdens' house was there all right, and the machinery shed too.

The dog took a short cut through the bush then re-emerged closer to the house, crossing straight in front of the ute at the last moment, like a warning shot across the bows of an enemy. Clouds of dust swirled on either side of the Holden as Tom stood heavily on the brakes.

Inside the cabin, discarded betting slips flew into the air, while a sticky-taped Gold Coast meter maid slid from the dash to the floor. For a moment, everything outside turned to dust. The dog ran in frenzied circles around the car, barking all the while. Tom wound down the window and reached for the door handle, and instantly recalled the brief weather report he'd read that morning.

Raindrops began to explode into the dirt. Not a gentle rain that would leave a sweet smell in the air; more like a downpour that had been threatening for weeks. Tom could hear it hammering down on the corrugated-iron roof of the machinery shed and waterfalling over the doorway. Dirt and dust erupted from the ground as rivulets of water cut deep channels into the yard.

The sound of the dog barking brought Emily out onto the verandah. Through the rain she made out an old ute, but she didn't recognise it, and there, in the doorway of the large shed, its driver appeared to be trying to shelter from the downpour. For a second or two, she thought about how her daughters were always pushing her to move into town. She turned to go back inside but the wind beat her to it, slamming the door before she got to it. She called the dog as her fingers traced along the window ledge for the spare key.

Water chased down pipes and gushed into the yard. Gutters were rendered useless. Through the waterfall that filled the doorway around him, Tom could see the figure standing on the verandah. He cupped his hands around his mouth and yelled across the open ground, but his voice was drowned before it left the shed.

Emily held the dog by her side as the stranger began jumping the puddles that separated the machinery shed from the steps up to the verandah.

'Emily Taylor?' A smile lifted the lines around the stranger's eyes. He waited for her acknowledgment, then removed his hat. 'Hello Em. Long time no see.'

Emily feigned a smile as she finally got the key into the lock.

Emily Marsden stood at the kitchen sink and studied Tom Barton through the flyscreen door that opened out onto the verandah. The rain had abated; still falling, but not enough to make conditions unpleasant on the covered deck.

She thought about hearing her maiden name again. It sounded odd, as if it belonged to another person, the person that Tom knew. As for him, he looked old, like someone's grandfather, and used words that evoked images of another time. A turn of phrase, an inflection, a hand movement, all brought with them a familiarity that had initially unnerved her. But there was no mistaking him. He spoke of their shared past as though it were just the other side of the Grenfell turn-off.

'. . . and Mr Insill, and Mr Coopes, the general store man – how could you forget him? Terrigal days.' He shook his head as he reached across the verandah deck to stroke the dog. 'And what's your name?'

The dog looked back towards Emily.

'Turps,' she answered on the blue heeler's behalf. 'He fell off the back of a painter's truck.'

Tom laughed. 'Landed on his feet by the look of him.' He settled back into the chair.

'More tea?'

'Ta. I don't think I've had this one before.'

'It's new,' she explained. 'I received it in the post only

last week. I often test new brands – market research, you know. Mind you, it can be a bit of a bother sometimes.' She poured the tea with chosen responsibility, then got down to business. 'So what did you want with my shed exactly?'

Whatever Tom had expected, Emily's direct approach unnerved him somewhat. He had found himself mentioning the machinery shed within seconds of arriving out of the rain, but it wasn't what he'd planned. Certainly, back at the pub this morning, back when he was driving out this way the day before, even back in Redfern when he'd first considered coming to Grenfell, he'd always envisaged an easy, more natural reunion between the two of them. He searched for the words to explain his reappearance after all these years.

'The shed. Yes, the shed . . .' he began, unconvincingly. 'You see, Em, an old mate of mine has inherited all this stuff. War surplus, camping gear, that sort of thing . . .' As he told the story, he kept thinking how unbelievable it all sounded; more than that, how unbelievable it must be to Emily that he'd have come all this way for something as commonplace as storage space. He found himself referring to Don as his 'business associate', which only made his speech patterns sound more nervy. In the middle of it all, he launched into stories from the past that involved both him and Emily.

A look from Emily finally brought him back from Terrigal. 'Let me make sure I've understood you correctly, Tom. The two of you are thinking of setting up a shop together, but until then you need somewhere to store this "stuff" – is that about it?'

'Um . . . well, yes. That's about it, I guess, Em,' Tom stammered.

'And how long do you envisage you'll need to store it here?'

'Coupla weeks, Em. Tops. Just need to sort everything out.'

Emily had no problem with Tom using the shed. The problem she had was having to deal with what was currently in the shed. 'All right then, Tom,' she told him. 'A couple of weeks.'

Several pots of tea and an early evening meal later, and still the rain fell, but heavier again now. Emily spoke of her late husband Jock and their four girls – two 'glasshouse flowers' and two 'wildflowers'. The first pair had gone to boarding school in Sydney; the 'wild' ones had attended the local school here in Grenfell. And she spoke about their children, their lives, their achievements.

Outside, the wind hurried past the shed to the clothesline, where it lifted pegged sheets into the light of the kitchen window. This weather wouldn't be letting up. Emily suggested he might prefer to use the spare room for the night rather than drive back to town, and Tom was quick to accept the offer.

Accompanied by thoughts of her girls, Emily escorted him down the hall. They were a constant source of worry, but she felt blessed that they'd all turned out so well. Megan was the eldest of the four and the only one still living in the area. She'd married into the Morrises, of Morris's Furniture and Electrical in Bathurst. By virtue of her being the firstborn, Megan had had an organisational role thrust upon her. For Megan, keeping an eye on her younger siblings had carried over into adult life, which inevitably led to confrontations over the dinner table. There was always a problem with somebody's life that needed sorting out, and if there wasn't a problem, well, that was a problem in itself. Rosie fell into that category. Rosie carried the burden of being the youngest – her life always seemed perfect and she could do no wrong. Her presence always brought out the worst in the other three. Kate, the second eldest, had married well by bringing a barrister into the family. Unfortunately he was a complete twit, but as long as Kate was happy. And then there was Jane. She'd gone to art school and was always an exhibition away from greatness.

With all of them having left home long ago, there were at least four rooms that could have been described as 'spare', but only one that Emily used regularly as a guest bedroom. Faded horse ribbons covered its single bed, while gymkhanas and district shows were depicted on strips of brightly coloured cloth that had been sown together to form a quilt.

'This was Megan's room,' she said. 'You'll be comfortable here.' She placed a clean towel on the end of the bed and bade Tom goodnight. 'Night, Em,' was all she heard him say before she'd closed the door and headed down the hallway to her bedroom.

Emily turned on her bedside lamp and reached over for a glass of water. She wasn't feeling too good today, in fact she hadn't for a while now. She knew she'd meant to call Megan tonight to discuss something important, but Tom's arrival had been the perfect excuse to put it off again.

Tom Barton . . . Terrigal. The two of them had been children back then. How extraordinary life was, she thought, that things had turned full circle. An afternoon and evening of conversations that hung on people and events she could barely remember, of childhood reminiscing prompted by his memories of their shared past. If he wished to use the shed, she would have to face going through Jock's things, though, and she'd always intended to leave that up to the kids.

Emily closed her bedroom door and turned the key in the lock. It felt odd with the door closed, let alone locked, as if she'd somehow lost the rest of her house. She returned to the bed and lay there thinking how there had to be some other reason for Tom to have come. Surely he and his 'business associate' could've found a storage unit closer to Sydney, particularly if it was only for a couple of weeks. Tom seemed like a nice enough man, but for all she knew, in the intervening years he may well have turned into a mass murderer . . . Emily dismissed this last thought as over the top, foolish, but realised that it was exactly what Megan and the girls would be saying to her if she were to tell them. She warmed instead to the idea of having somebody around for a while. Someone who didn't live around Grenfell. Someone she didn't really know.

Down the hallway, Tom's eyes traversed fifty-odd years of Emily's life in the room around him. Overlapping photographs of children and grandchildren had been placed under the glass top of a dresser. Their lives could not have been more different, he thought. Emily's was a work in progress; a photograph of Emily and one of the grandchildren could've been taken last week. As his fingers ran over the glass top, he figured that Jock Marsden must've passed away around the time one of the grandchildren had graduated from university. Tom thought of his own collection of photos, all strapped up in a box back at Tierra del Fuego. There were no generations of families there, just events.

He undid his lace-up boots and fell back onto the bed. This was how it had turned out. At the end of the bed, a framed wedding photograph of Jock and Em looked down on him. That smile she had given him during the evening, it was the same smile as in this black-and-white photograph. And when she'd spoken of Terrigal, the sea and the sun were reflected in her eyes. Whatever the differences were, it didn't matter; it was the same beautiful Emily.

The rain gave way to a silence Tom had not experienced for a long time. He fell asleep with images of Emily filling his thoughts, of Terrigal at a time when their lives had overlapped.

Chapter Eight

Long lines of breakers erupted in front of him. Tom Barton was in another world, of sand dunes, and bluebottles. And mothers with dresses tucked into knickers, playing with children in rock pools. This was the world of the coast people. They lived in an environment so vastly different from his that he was amazed to find they spoke the same language.

'Back with us again, eh, Tom?' Terrigal was where the Barton family had their annual holidays. The owner of the cottages was a man who faced danger every day of the week. 'The sea wall collapsed in that last storm, so make sure you don't go near it. And the rip at the end of the beach'll drag youse straight out to one of them Pacific Islands, where there's cannibals that'll eat ya . . .'

It was Tom's younger brother's health that took the family there. Back home in rural Ariah Park, every time the wooden paddle wheels beat their way across the heads of the wheat, Harry would start coughing and wheezing. 'Add a tablespoon of this to boiling water and get him to breathe deep,' Dr Gilmour had advised while handing their mother a brown bottle with Chinese writing on it. The doctor came with the reputation of being a good horse man, indeed he'd brought Dominic Murphy's horse back from the dead. 'And if that don't work, try a bit of salt air.' And so began the coastal holidays.

The journey really started at the base of Mount Victoria, with the annual discussion as to whether the car would make it to the top this time. Every bit of car space was packed with something in case the existing 'something' broke down. 'Of course the old girl'll make it,' his father would insist. 'She's still got another trip in 'er.' With each gear change she'd develop a second wind. The old man never doubted her, and Tom never doubted him. The optimism was rarely shared by his mum, who by journey's end was always shattered. She'd spend the first day of the holiday trying to recover – or 'putting her bones back together', as she used to say.

The road across the mountain was part dirt, part sealed, and followed the route the first Europeans took. At the top of the range they had marked their trail with an axe that cut deep into an ironbark. Here they'd rested and taken their bearings. And so did the Bartons.

'Hey, you kids, get right back, will you. Stand back!' Hissing steam added to the old man's theatrics as he loosened the radiator cap. When the thermos appeared, the two boys would nick into the bush, in search of mountain devils, ancient rocks and long splinters from the ironbark. Tom presented Emily Taylor with a piece once, and she was greatly impressed. 'You can even see where the explorer's axe went,' he told her. In truth, he'd done a little work on it with his penknife.

Tom first met Emily when he was nine. It was during the family's second visit to Terrigal. He and his brother Harry wandered up from the beach one afternoon to find a car parked in front of the neighbouring cottage. The cottage's windows on the front verandah had been opened to the breeze. Up until this point, the house was just another outbuilding, like one of the sheds that surrounded the house back home. But now there was someone living in it. Three suitcases sat on the front verandah.

'I've invited them in for tea,' Mum said as she opened the oven door and pushed a skewer into the roast. 'I'm sure they won't feel like cookin''. Now, boys, what about helpin' your father clean up the outside table?'

It felt odd to Tom, having people they didn't know over for tea. Back home at Ariah Park, they knew everyone. He tucked his bare feet under the table as Emily arranged herself on the seat next to him. She was the same age, slender rather than thin, and gave the impression of someone uncomfortable in her body. Her legs were too long and continually needed adjustment, or her arms were too short, or her elbows stuck out – some part of her was always at odds with another. She wore a pair of shorts and a top that might have doubled as swimmers. Her hair was still wet from the sea and flowed straight down her back. A peeling nose blistered between blue eyes, and had an excessive amount of cream rubbed into it.

Tom was going to ask her something about the beach, but before he could say anything she slapped her hand hard against his leg, causing his knee to bash the underside of the table.

'Got him!' She lifted what was left of a mosquito up by its legs and smiled at Harry, who always enjoyed it when any sort of pain was inflicted on his elder brother.

'Yep. Got him a bewdy,' Tom replied, rubbing the sting out of his leg. He always thought Emily Taylor had something going for her. Right from the start.

There were four kids and two sets of parents, but the folks didn't count. Em's youngest sister, Coralie, didn't count either. She was four and when entrusted in the kids' care only slowed them down. 'How come we have to take her?' Em would plead with her parents, but it was to little avail. 'Because she's your sister,' would come the reply. Which meant that was that.

And so for four weeks of every year, Tom and Em grew up together. A part-time friendship that was held over from one year to the next. Emily's family lived in Sydney, near The Spit (which seemed an odd name for a suburb, he always thought), while the Bartons came from somewhere so small it had to be linked with the bigger town of Temora to be given any credibility. Ariah Park was the sort of place where you skidded over bull ants' nests on your bike and detoured around rabbit traps on the way to school.

Terrigal was a halfway house in a way, and Emily an introduction to the city. But, for the moment, it was the coast people that the two of them shared. Like Mr Insill, whose land they had to cross to get to the beach, and his dog Max, who had little back wheels instead of hind legs. Taken by a shark, or so Mr Insill said. Even the coast people's dogs led dangerous lives.

Each day brought with it something new, and it was always to do with the sea. The high tide washed around the rocks and over the sand dunes and into the lagoon. It washed away the day before and left a clean slate for the morning.

'Quick! Quick!' Emily called out one day, running towards the Bartons' cottage. 'On the beach . . . there's, there's a man taking a picture of a . . .' She could hardly contain herself, she was so excited. 'A *whale*. A whale!' Her arms bolted outright as an indication of its size.

The whole town surrounded it. It stood higher than the front verandah and longer than the back fence, with flukes that stretched a full ten feet to the side. It was hard to imagine such a creature even existed, and with it came other creatures – denizens of the deep that clung to the sides of its mouth, and barnacles and other crustaceans that seemed to form part of its skin.

Tom squeezed in between the legs of the postmaster, Mr Willis, while Em did the same between Captain Bell's. The latter was a retired sea captain who now occupied a permanent berth in the town's main hotel. And there they all stood, waiting for something to happen. Waiting for the whale's mighty tail to flick the pushers and prodders high into the air. Waiting for a mighty geyser of water to shoot from its forehead, or Captain Ahab's *Pequod* to appear on the horizon. But there was nothing, no movement, only the sound of waves washing sheets of foam over its back and tucking it tighter into the sand, and voices carried on the wind.

Mr Coopes, who ran the general store, suggested dragging it to the end of the beach, where the rocks might hide a temporary slaughterhouse. 'I got a cousin down at Eden,' he explained. 'And what they do down there is cut big holes in 'em, then, with a rope tied firm around your chest, they lower youse inside. It's the oil – fixes gout, rheumatism, arthritis. They got people queuin' up for a dose. Payin' good money too.'

Captain Bell, whose jurisdiction the whale seemed to fall under, dismissed the idea. 'No, we're gonna try to get it off on the high tide,' he said. 'And if that don't work, Eric's gonna organise a tug.'

The group stood together for more than an hour, the surf rolling against their bodies, and willed the sea to take the whale back. Through distant breakers, ropes strained against anchors holding the big fish against the incoming tide. Then it happened. The eye moved. The lid rolled back to witness the alien world that surrounded it. Emily saw it first. It stared straight at them, an unfathomable blue as deep as the currents that took it on its long migratory trails beneath the oceans. It seemed to understand its plight and that these humans were its only hope. Tom had seen that look before, in farm animals, as drought brought them to their knees. A film of sand washed out of its eye.

'It's *crying*,' said Emily.

Maybe it was. Emily certainly thought so, and Tom couldn't deny it.

By late afternoon the shadows that reached down from the cliffs had ventured into the surf. And as the night fell, the townsfolk drifted back to their cottages and their houses, and their teas on the table. Emily and Tom stayed until the darkness and the black currents that tugged at their ankles eventually took hold of their imaginations and forced them back to the beach.

By morning the whale had gone. And no evidence had been left to say it had ever been there. They spent the remainder of the day in Tom's homemade canoe, paddling the lagoon and venturing into the bay, but the creature had simply disappeared. Only the hump-backed rocks of the shelf remained, and in the imaginary pilot vessel Tom and Emily guided them safely out to sea.

'Ya gunna need a more seaworthy craft than that if ya wanna be pilotin' whales,' Em's Uncle George told them. 'What ya need is a motor!'

With each stay, strange relatives from both sides made brief appearances. Tom's mother's sister stayed once; she was a woman who, according to Mum, was always 'on the verge' and lived on nerve tonic. And then there was George, Em's uncle, who spent his whole stay pulling his car apart. That was probably how she developed her interest in mechanics, because a year or two later she'd definitely got the bug.

'Get out of the light, Harry! I can't see what I'm doin'.' She dug deeper into the engine.

'Well, ya shouldn't be doin' what you're doin' anyway,' he replied, hanging over the fender. 'Anyway, what are ya doin'?'

'Cleaning out the carby,' Emily replied without once breaking her concentration.

'I can see that – I'm not totally stupid. Best left to the blokes, I think, Em.'

'Piss off, Harry,' Tom told him. 'The old man wants you inside.' He took his younger brother's place as Emily wiped clean the inside of the float bowl.

Her hair had been cut to a bob and revealed a line of sunburn across the back of her neck and the tops of her shoulders. She seemed taller than last year, her slender body hidden by overalls that continually needed adjustment. A birthday watch had been pushed up her arm as a means of protecting the timepiece. Tom wanted to say something about her appearance, something about her, something about how beautiful she looked, but he was defeated by adolescence.

'Hey Em, what do you reckon about doin' a little fishin' this arvo?' he asked as casually as he could. They knew each other too well, and that was the problem. If it had been anybody else, it would've been different.

The sound of a front door banging shut took their attention to Harry and the old man heading for the gate.

'Give up, Em. It'll never go!' Harry's laugh carried across the lawn.

Tom always thought he might end up living in Terrigal someday. Become a fisherman and get a trawler, or rent out some cottages. Or maybe open a garage with Emily Taylor.

Emily's Uncle George turned up again at the end of what was to be the penultimate holiday together for the two families, in October 1939. 'It's on,' he declared. 'The war's on.' For those old enough to know the consequences, it was a sombre moment. 'Thank Christ I'm too old,' George said. 'And I've got that old knife wound.' He helped himself to his brother-in-law's scotch.

Like so many young Australians looking for adventure, Emily was excited by the prospect. A year later, having followed the recruitment adverts with interest for some time, she was considering a posting to Wagga Wagga Air Station as a mechanic. She was a few months shy of her eighteenth birthday.

'You got a gift for it, Em,' said just about everybody, 'but nobody's gonna give you a job.'

'We'll see,' she'd reply. There was going to be a shortage of blokes, and mechanics were always blokes.

Tom was the only person who really supported her in her dream. But maybe he hoped there'd be something in it for him too. 'A good spot to live, Em, that's what you look for if you're lookin' for a job,' he'd tell her. It was a place more than a job that he wanted; a place on the coast. And a war couldn't offer that. To live someplace where you felt a sense of belonging, where there were things to do, places you could go – that's what mattered to him. The job was almost irrelevant. The trawler idea seemed to be the thing that people did on the coast, and for that Tom knew he needed 'sea time'. So maybe he could get the war to work for him, he figured.

'Navy could be the go,' he told her. 'The merchant navy – see a bit of the world as well, eh?' Not that seeing the world really held much interest. From what he'd seen in magazines and books, it didn't look half as good as Terrigal. A place on the coast, that would do him. For sure.

Chapter Nine

Tom Barton was eighteen and a bit, and it was the bits that now counted the most. A bit more of 1941. A week. A day. He was a long way from his corro canoe and the carefree days of Terrigal. A long way from the wheat belts that straddled the dirt road leading to his parents' farm. The adventure was over – it had been over for some time. What had started as an entry into the ways of the sea had turned into a daily battle for survival.

He listened for the sound of the ships' engines. For the past forty-eight hours they'd been as constant as the fuel stove at home that burnt day and night through farm winters. But there was nothing, just the sound of the wind channelling deep furrows in the Pacific Ocean, shifting walls of water that hid the funnels of his travelling companions.

From the ship's bridge he'd counted five other ships, but there could have been more, and a corvette that worked the convoy as a dog might a mob of sheep, sometimes ahead, then back in a tight circle nipping at the heels of stragglers.

The seas that broke against the ship's hull now came without warning. The boat was momentarily suspended, then crashed deep into the next wave. The MV *Trident* of the Maclay Line was four and a half thousand tons and three hundred and forty feet long, single stack, with cargo gantries forward and aft. She was registered in Sydney and carried an Australian crew. The captain had arrived from Scotland on a sailing ship in 1910 and spent his career in the Asia Pacific. 'Called to the sea I was, a true seadog, he used to say – indeed, one almost expected to see a parrot on his shoulder. But his accumulated wealth of local knowledge had been invaluable in navigating relatively uncharted reefs and restricted access ports. The *Trident* had been a welcome sight to the locals of the many small islands that were becoming increasingly isolated by the Japanese advance.

Tom took a deep breath of salt air and looked at the walls of green water pounding the foredeck. It was obvious the weather was the ultimate ship's master. Nobody would choose to put to sea in these conditions.

In the coffin-quiet depths, a Japanese submarine waited. Inside, the foul stench of diesel and oil and battery acid hung still in the air. For the past eleven hours it had been travelling just below the surface, stalking a scent of smoke and oil. Just before dawn, a periscope broke through the Pacific swell. Now the convoy was in sight. Its moment had come. Enveloped in darkness, the submarine's diesels pushed it towards the line of shipping. The patient days of waiting and watching were over.

'Ay Tom, you still 'ere?' The bloke in the bottom bunk kicked the metal frame with his boot. 'I reckon they missed a few rivets when they built 'er, mate. There's water pissin' in 'ere.'

Tom groaned. 'Mallet and plugs are in the aft lockers, if you can be bothered. You want the bucket?'

'After you, mate.' He paused, concentrating. 'How's the time?'

'Dunno. Six, maybe.' The last time he'd felt this ill was in the beer garden of the Criterion with Harry. On the way home he'd spewed against the Chev window. Harry had complained about the smell before passing out on the back seat.

Somewhere between bucket and pillow he began piecing together a mental scrapbook of his brother. It would have been two years since he last saw him. It was back on the farm, in midwinter, when hooves cracked the frost on the ground and cheeks were permanently red from the icy wind. Bridle to bridle they raced the cockatoos to the dry creek gums. Harry's asthma had all but gone. The horse doctor's advice had put him back into the saddle, and the pollens that constricted his breath were no longer a problem. Tom wished he'd written things down, things they did together. Emily always kept a diary, a journal that by year's end was filled with undeclared secrets. It would have been a way of remembering him.

In the first week of his war Harry was shot through the head by a sniper, and two days later he was buried on the beach where he fell. There would be no funeral, no body to mourn – just his name added to the town cenotaph they played on as kids.

It was all so wrong. Being the eldest, the responsibility of taking over the property had laid with Tom, but he'd always figured on handing it over to Harry. He was the one who loved it, every dry acre of it. It was the isolation that got to Tom; weeks would pass without seeing another soul. If someone was coming, you could see the dust a mile away. Ossie Henstridge was one such person, their only regular. Every three months he would swing past the property with a boot full of leather suitcases. The family would all gather around the side of the car as he pieced together a portable clothes rack, then filled it with a season of ladies and gents clothing. Tom recalled his mother had bought a Mass dress from him once, and a hat for Harry that had to be stuffed with newspaper to make it fit. 'She's a bewdy, mate,' said their dad. 'You'll grow into it.' And he did.

The town was always the same. Nothing ever happened, nothing ever changed, and nothing was ever replaced. When the picture theatre burnt down, it became a vacant block, and when Mrs. D., who operated the telephone exchange retired, her daughter Kim would be entrusted with the town's secrets. It was a town that existed out of necessity, its inhabitants rarely venturing past the wheat silo at the end of Main Street, and to which news of the outside world was carried by the wireless.

Generations of Bartons had lived on that vast flat and unforgiving piece of land. Three generations of them had fought against it, as if it were an enemy that had to be subdued, clear felling, controlling, then repopulating with wheat and hard hooves. And now it was going to be up to him to continue the tradition. But he knew that 'Elderslee' would never be defeated.

The light in the companionway began to flicker as water found its way into the ship's wiring. Tom lay back in his bunk and watched the trickle roll with the ship. At least with coast people there was a certain unpredictability, and change came with every visit, new houses and asphalt roads, sea walls that had been demolished and new ones built. There was even a sit-down restaurant in Terrigal.

He closed his eyes to the sound of bodies rolling against canvas straps and thought about the calm that would come with being swallowed by the ocean, the tranquillity of floating below the confusion and the noise. And he thought about the whales that passed off Terrigal. And his perfect life, a house by the sea, his trawler, a voice – Emily's – beckoning him into the wheelhouse. 'Come inside, Tom . . . It's too hot. There's ice water in the esky.' She looked beautiful, inviting. But then came the dry heat and the dust that blew across stripped paddocks of wheat. He forced his head back against the canvas and drew in the salt air.

He would catch up with Emily as soon as he got back. Maybe he'd ask her to marry him, and live on the farm. But he knew she couldn't stand it. How could he do that to her? She was a coast girl, for sure. He rolled over and turned out the light, his life suddenly insignificant in the vastness of the seas that surrounded him.

At 0630 hours the submarine's bow rocked back as compressed air fired a series of four torpedoes into the convoy. Propelled by a mixture of pure oxygen and kerosene they left no trail, no wake that might be detected and avoided. At five thousand yards, their running time would be about three minutes.

Tom's early morning journey back to Sydney was punctuated with images of Emily. His thoughts bypassed the highway he was travelling on and took him along a slower route, a side track that allowed details to linger. At one point during the evening, he had felt self-conscious about his appearance, and placed a hand over the frayed cuffs of his shirt. He glanced at himself in the rear-vision mirror now: he thought he looked old, and wondered if Emily thought the same. He wondered if he should buy a new shirt.

Emily still looked beautiful, just like she had in the photograph he had back home. He thought about their youth and the times they had shared, and found himself yearning to be that young man holding the fish once more. A second chance. This time the shutter could catch them running along the beach, laughing. Chasing each other's footprints. He would tell her how beautiful she looked, and then they would fall together onto the sand.

Tom caught the thought, surprised at where his daydreaming had taken him. He'd learnt yesterday that Jock Marsden had passed away, and for the first time since Harry's memorial service, he saw her as Emily Taylor from Terrigal.

At Lithgow, Tom broke the distance with a cup of tea from a thermos and a chat with a semi-trailer driver. He was hoping to sort out the transportation issue, from the warehouse to Emily's shed, but the conversation soon headed off in an entirely unexpected direction.

'Elvis just started speakin' to me, out of the truck radio,' the driver said, pointing back to the cab. 'To me, personally. Like we're talkin' now, only outta the speaker.' Dave Blainey whistled up his dog and lifted it into the cab. He might have once been a taller man, but years of sitting behind the wheel had compacted him down. Layers of sediment in the form of burgers and fries had settled over the straining elasticised waistband of a pair of faded Stubbies. Skinny legs stuck out of socks and work boots. 'Grenfell, you say?' Dave clearly had his problems, but he was willing to get a couple of his mates together and do the removal job at pensioner rates.

'Yeah. It's a property just this side of the town.' Tom made it sound like it was just down the road. 'Direct access. No problem. The place belongs to an old friend of mine named Emily Marsden. Must be fate,' he added. 'I've been putting a lot of thought into how I'm going to transport all this stuff, and then, out of nowhere, you turn up. More to do with luck I guess.'

'Luck?' Dave said, an edge of interest entering his voice. 'I mean, nothing's a coincidence, you know. These things are . . . ah, what's the word? *Preordained*, that's it. Preordained, beyond our control.'

Tom screwed the lid back on the thermos and began writing out the address of the warehouse on a beer coaster. 'In God's hands, eh? Isn't that what they say?'

'Maybe some people think it's God. All I know is that it's a small world, and even more so out there. I do a lot of driving in this job. So I see everyone, everywhere. Over the course of a year I'm bound to cross paths with the same people – I mean, it could be I pass them coming in the opposite direction down the highway; maybe I drive by their house beside the road; maybe I'm in the room next to theirs at a motel; or maybe . . . maybe I pull over one morning and get chatting to them over a cup of tea.' His eyes fixed on Tom at this point, almost as if to rope him in to the logic of his argument. 'The point is, that over time the chances of meeting that person you passed at the gas station, or wherever, will become more likely.'

Tom leant against the ute door. Long distance driving obviously gave Dave a lot of thinking time. 'The old numbers game, eh?'

'Connecting Forces, that's what I call it.'

'Connecting forces?'

'Exactly. Something that ties us all together. Who knows, maybe we were meant to meet. I mean, if you don't believe in something greater, something outside of us, what have you got? The here and now. Not much really.'

Tom had a second or two to consider his well-worn shirt cuffs and plastic bag filled with toiletries, his ute with the faulty doors, the flat on Tierra del Fuego and the suitcase that accounted for nearly seventy-five years of Tom Barton. 'Well, no. I guess I'd feel a little disappointed if I thought that was all that life amounted to.'

'Exactly. There must be a greater force that contributes to all our lives. Perhaps swaying the law of averages and dictating who exactly passes who on which highway at what time.'

'Riiight . . .' Tom said the word slowly, measuring it out. 'And how does that relate to, say, me deciding to visit an old friend in Grenfell?'

The truckie tilted his head to one side. 'Maybe someone was trying to connect the two of you – either an inner part of yourself or,' he looked at the address Tom had handed him, 'this Emily person, maybe. Connecting Forces, Tom, nothing to do with luck.'

Tom shook his head.

'Believe what you want, Tom. If it's not coming from you or Emily, perhaps it's a relative or a friend trying to guide you to Grenfell. Or maybe someone's influencing the present from the afterlife. Who knows?'

Tom's scepticism was put to one side as he mentally ran through a list of friends and rellies.

Dave gave a short laugh and suddenly remembered

where the conversation had started. 'Don't mind me, Tom. It's not like I start rabbitin' on like this to every bloke I meet. It's just *we* have a connection here, if you follow my drift.' He paused to check the second address that Tom had given him. 'Okay, so this is a the warehouse address for the pick-up?'

'That's the one,' said Tom. 'It's a disused iron foundry.'

'No worries. And we're talking World War II bits and pieces, some stuff that needs to be crated.'

'Yep.'

Dave nodded in agreement. He was about to expand on his theories when the appearance of his dog in the driver's seat of the cab diverted his attention. 'Ayy, Colonel . . . Waay back,' he shouted. 'In the back – waaay back!' He then handed Tom a business card.

'No worries, Tom. Any change of plan, just give me a call.' He held up a mobile phone.

Tom eyed the words 'TCB Trucking' and an embossed thunderbolt that made up the front of the card.

'Takin' Care of Business,' Dave explained, suddenly adopting a convincing Deep South accent.

Tom gave a wave as the truck's air horns sounded a final farewell. Maybe Dave had a point. Maybe there were some sort of forces at work here. Either way, it all seemed to be falling into place. In less than twenty-four hours he'd managed to secure both temporary, rent-free storage space and haulage between the two locations at a reduced rate. 'We're getting there,' he said to himself. 'We're getting there.'

*

During the long climb up into the Blue Mountains, the rain returned and he thought about the passing of time. He didn't feel any older than he did twenty years ago. Maybe that was how Emily felt. He saw time as an abstract period, punctuated by moments of lucidity that seemed just as real now as they did then. These moments could've happened in the last month or the last year. Fifty years. It didn't seem that long ago.

Somewhere along the M4 motorway he thought about the canoe he'd built as a kid. It was a simple affair, a flattened piece of corrugated iron folded in half and nailed at each end to a bit of four-by-two. A short plank forced it apart at the centre and also doubled as a seat. The corro came off the back shed, and he'd used road tar to fill in the nail holes.

On school days the canoe was berthed alongside the wood heap, where it collected leaves and long pieces of stringy bark that drifted down from the trees and acted as mooring lines. At night, he used to imagine that it carried Aborigines with hunting spears silently across the back lawn. They'd drift past his bedroom window, dipping paddles into the long grass that grew like rushes down the side of the house. By morning, the canoe would be back on its stringy-bark mooring, with no evidence of its nocturnal journey.

For a time it was kept at Terrigal, Harry's too, alongside the cradles holding a generation of wooden clinkers that ventured past the sea markers. He and Em had taken it out on the bay in search of the whale, of course. He remembered these things well.

A diesel electric train passed over a railway bridge and followed alongside the road. Tom kept pace with it for a bit, watching the faces in the carriage windows and the rainwater flying down from the gutters, listening to the wheels clicking over expansion joints. And he wondered if, at some future point, this would be one of those moments he remembered.

It was early afternoon when Dave Blainey's Mack pulled into the truck stop just before Gosford. He reached into the glove box, retrieved the beer coaster that Tom had given him and carefully transferred the details into an old school exercise book. Years of contact numbers and business cards filled the pages, all fellow travellers, all carefully documented. Dave was someone who knew everyone but knew no one. There were plenty of lost and lonely souls out there, all searching for someone, and Dave was in the perfect position to bring them all together. Even if they didn't know they were searching for each other.

He flipped back to the previous month's entries. Todd Davitt. That was him. That was the man he needed to call. 'War Memorabilia' – that was his bag. He'd met him at the Caltrex outside Goulburn. He and his wife were on a caravanning holiday, visiting museums, historical sites, that sort of thing. He remembered him as being the same vintage as Tom – might even have been in the war himself.

He turned down the volume on Elvis's 'Always on

My Mind' and reached for his mobile phone. Sometimes the Connecting Forces needed to be pointed in the right direction. Yes, he thought, there were a lot of lonely people in the world. And if he'd held that thought long enough, he might well have put himself in that category.

With that, he dialled Todd's number, then slipped the exercise book back into the glove box.

CHAPTER TEN

Emily Marsden sat at her kitchen table as the familiar sound of the *Neighbours* theme song drifted through from the lounge room. She was researching potential candidates for the 'special guest' slot at the festival, and the actor playing Dr Brixton looked perfect. She dashed in to catch the show's end credits and made a note of his name, before attending to a whistling kettle in the kitchen and returning to the table. Beside her was a coupon from a soap box and a ticket that she hoped would win her a new washing machine. She placed them both in an envelope and opened the local newspaper.

The *Grenfell Record* usually sat on the kitchen table for a couple of days, so it always got a few reads. Mass times over the festival weekend would remain unchanged, she read, while entries were being called for the Henry Lawson Festival Art Competition. She thought about a painting she'd entered one year. Jock reckoned it should have won. In his eyes, it was a Rembrandt passed over by judges who wouldn't know a good painting if it jumped up and bit them.

The next item that caught her eye concerned Alec Wilson, who'd died recently. Well, she already knew that, of course. He was eighty-nine, according to the paper. Half the houses in town were probably built by Alec from timber milled at his long-gone timber yard. His obituary, including a photo, took up a whole page. That was the good thing about dying in Grenfell – the town made something of it. She took some comfort in that. The town wasn't big enough to warrant a full-time funeral director, so Stan Pemberton did a little wool classing on the side. As word of her husband's death had gotten around, he'd discreetly opened the parlour doors and put the hose over his hearse. Everybody showed for that funeral. Shopkeepers closed their doors as the black LTD slowly lapped Main Street. He was a good man, Jock. He always made an effort.

For some reason, Emily was suddenly overwhelmed with thoughts of him now. She was quite used to living alone, but perhaps seeing Tom Barton had brought back old memories. With a deep sigh and a soft shake of the head, she rose from the table and took her cup of tea out to the verandah.

She'd never really noticed how old Jock was, she realised. She just woke up one day and he was old. And that was when he gave up. Her children had pressed her into agreeing to a nursing home for him – respite for her, more than professional care for Jock, the girls insisted. He went in on the Wednesday and died in the early hours of Thursday, and in her heart she always felt that was what did him in in the end. She'd been with Jock Marsden for fifty years, but she wasn't with him at the end. 'You weren't to know,' everyone said. But she should've known, and she never forgave herself for that.

Emily took a seat on the verandah and a sip of her now lukewarm cup of tea. She lifted her eyes from the decking and followed the stop–start trail the blowflies took, a trail that would eventually lead to the creek. She rested her thoughts in the shade of the peppercorns and wished she could turn back the clock, just enough to be able to say goodbye to her life-long partner. She thought about when they'd met and the journey that had led her to Grenfell.

Two girls from Rockhampton had arrived at Wagga Wagga Air Station during the week, so that made eight in total. Plus there was Mrs Smallwood. She wore a WAAAF uniform, but appeared to have no other role than that of chaperone, and made great use of a bosun's whistle that hung from a lanyard around her neck. The night before, at the sight of some poor bugger at the window, she'd blown a long ear-piercing note and followed it up by hollering out, 'Piss off, ya little pervert!' It was a job to which she seemed well suited. But Mrs Smallwood had surrendered her security detail this evening, allowing Emily Taylor and some of the other girls to make their way unchaperoned into town for the Saturday night dance.

Along Goodsall Street, kitchen windows blinked squares of light onto lines of washing that ran down to the river's edge. The sun's slow twilight journey continued through the back yards of the town, past Ed Malronie's hire boats with bilges that stank of mullet, past the showground and the picnic tables, past the peeling weatherboards of the Wagga Wagga CWA, and into the town centre.

At the Bayliss Street bridge, Emily was graduating towards the front of the queue of people waiting to enter the community centre. It was a hot evening, and the women at the ticket windows stayed close to the small holes in the glass in front of them. On the footpath over the road, groups of men in military uniforms drank bottles of beer, smoked cigarettes and laughed uproariously at the punch line of a joke that had taken some time to get to. The sound of a swing band came and went with the opening and closing of the community centre's front doors.

It was the photographer from the *Wagga Gazette* that was holding up progress ahead of Emily. 'Won't be a minute,' he said, juggling a hot bulb. 'Just one more shot.' His subjects, three RAAF-uniformed young men, stood patiently, holding their positions at the front of the queue. She noticed one in particular – a big, tall man of post and beam construction, his strong arms hanging gantry-like from his shoulders. He ditched the cigarette from his huge hands onto the footpath.

A new flashbulb now installed, the photographer's face returned to the eyepiece of his camera, but soon he pulled away again, raising his hand in apology as he did so. 'Sorry, fellas, think we need to balance things a bit.'

He moved down the line to where Emily and another WAAAF girl stood. 'Ladies, would you mind?'

The photographer guided the young women past the other queuers and gently nudged them in among the group of soldiers. Emily's eyes met those of the bloke next to her, the tower of a man she'd been watching earlier, as the photographer surveyed the group through his lens.

'What about puttin' your arm around her, like you're sweethearts?' he called out to the big man. 'You don't mind, do ya mate? It's just for the social pages.'

The young man didn't seem to mind at all. In fact, he looked like he couldn't believe his luck. Emily linked her arm through his and the photograph was taken.

'What names should I put in the caption?' The photographer licked the tip of a pencil and held it over the page of a scruffy-looking notepad.

'Jock Marsden.'

'Emily Taylor.' She turned to look at this Jock Marsden and held out her hand. 'Pleased to meet you, Mr Marsden.'

Once they were inside the hall, it was all swing. Jock's voice competed with the band.

'Yeah, me mates enlisted with the AIF but I figured I'd be better off here,' he told her. A streamer happened between his fingers. 'Someone's got to look after the fort, eh?' He smiled for a bit then looked down to the ribbon of coloured paper. He was always picking things up, Emily would later learn. Things that could be passed between fingers and pockets. As a kid, Jock would tell her, it was usually a stick or a piece of bark, or a good flat skimming stone, too good to throw.

The band drowned out all conversation as couples regrouped for the next bracket. He seemed to be about to ask her for a dance, Emily thought, but then dropped the matter at the very moment the band hit a particularly upbeat swing number. She looked out to the dance floor to see a handsome young American, judging by his uniform, heading her way.

'Excuse me, ma'am,' the GI said with a smile. 'This song's about my home state and I was wonderin' if you might care for a dance?'

Emily accepted the invitation, checking with Jock as she did so. His country-boy smile was still there, no doubt about it, but as he nodded his approval the smile wasn't quite as genuine as before. Like so many young Australian men on the home front during the war, Jock felt he had a distinct disadvantage: the lack of an American accent.

The US serviceman was a snappy dancer, oozing confidence as he moved, and the smooth grin never once left his face.

Jock went off to get a drink and was waiting with it when she came off the dance floor. 'Thought you could do with a drink, Em,' he said, handing it to her. 'Looks like you've been workin' up a bit of a sweat out there.'

Emily dipped into the glass and removed an ice cube. 'Ta. Do you dance, Jock?'

'Pride of Erin specialist, actually, but there's not much call for it here.' It was the only dance he knew, he added, something he'd learnt from his sister. 'This your home town, Em?'

Emily laughed. 'Nah. I'm from Sydney,' she replied.

'The big smoke, eh?'

'Hardly. The Spit. It's on the way to Manly. How about you?'

'Grenfell.' He waved the streamer in the direction of the band. 'About a hundred and fifty miles that-a-way.'

'That'd be the sticks, then?'

'Weeell . . .' He drew the word out before continuing. 'You have to see it at night to see how big it is.' He lifted his glass towards the ceiling. 'Lights from one horizon to the other. By day it's a little less imposing – five pubs and five banks. My folks have got a property out there.' He jingled some loose change in his pocket for a bit, then shuffled into a conversation about a trip he'd made to Queensland once, but it wasn't really going anywhere. A breeze from the front door saved him. 'Startin' to cook in here, Em,' he said. 'Might have to nip out for a bit of fresh air. Whaddya reckon?'

Night rushed past as Emily's arms gripped tightly around his waist. Jock opened the throttle on his Indian motorcycle and watched the needle climb on the speedo.

At the bottom of the street, where the river met the road, he slowed and yelled across his shoulder. Words were lost to the wind – something about the night air perhaps. He reached back from the handlebars and placed her hands into the pockets of his jacket.

*

It was another hot Saturday in Wagga and the heat that rose from the tarmac put a twist into a line of aircraft that waited outside the hangar. Dressed in overalls that were rolled up to the knees, Emily leant over the leading edge of the Avro's wing and dangled her legs in the sun as if she were at the local pool.

'Give up, Jock,' she called out. 'It's not going to happen.'

'All right, Em. If you're so smart, *you* fix it.'

The problem was in the ignition, Emily realised. Same principle as her dad's Morris, and she'd fixed that heaps of times. She slipped down from the wing, picked up a screwdriver and set to work.

When it came to mechanics, she always thought about her Uncle George. He was the engine man, a stoker, who worked the 36s out of Forbes and Parkes. As the day warmed up, you could smell the oil and soot rising up through the pores of his skin. He'd park his Austin on the front lawn of the house and then spend an afternoon drinking beers while he pulled the car to bits. According to Emily's mother, it lowered the tone of the whole street. 'A good soak in petrol, then the wire-brush,' he'd say. 'That's the way, Em.' By late afternoon, he would be fairly pissed and end up staying for tea. Dad and he would then go down to the pub and get more beers, which fuelled George with stories about what he did 'before the railway', stories he swore were true. About living on the lam, pub brawls and a scar that ran down the side of his leg – stories with language that brought Mum in from other parts of the house.

Once he got so carried away, he stabbed the kitchen table with her best knife.

'Okay, Jock,' Emily said at last, as she climbed down the ladder that led up to the engine cowling. 'Pull her over.'

Jock lifted the propeller blade to the point of compression, and snapped it hard through the arc. The engine gasped for air, then leapt to life. Spinning blades dematerialised into a background of aircraft hangars and the smell of high-octane fuel.

'Ta-daaa!' Emily gave a theatrical bow as the whine of the engine increased with each turn of the screw. Backwash from the spinning blades caught her shirt and buffeted it wildly against her skin. She closed her eyes and leant forward a little into the slipstream. 'Timing, Jock,' she shouted. 'It's all in the timing.'

'You reckon?' He captured a strand of hair that whipped across her face. 'All in the wrist, I reckon.'

Emily laughed. His voice competed with the sound of the engine, but she wasn't listening. Her senses were lost in turbulence as he wound his fingers through her hair.

Emily couldn't help thinking she'd made a big mistake mentioning him to her mother. Jock had just received word he was to be posted to Brisbane that week and Emily had found herself needing to share that item of news in a letter home. She could just picture her mother on the verandah at the side of the house at The Spit. Everybody would be there, all throwing in their two bobs' worth.

How long did she say she'd known him? Aunty Faith would ask, a woman who tended towards theatrics. *A month? Did you say a* month? Yes, Aunty Faith, Emily thought now, one month. And I've managed to get a three-day pass so I can catch the train to Sydney to see him off.

Sometimes Jock's hand would search out hers on the seat beside him, and she would rest against his shoulder and they'd listen to the rails clicking them further and further from the town they'd both got to know. And sometimes she'd fall into the rhythm of the locomotive and wonder if Uncle George was up the front on the footplate.

At Goulburn a young man in an ill-fitting suit steadied himself against the sliding door to the compartment. He dumped a rifle and a kit bag on the floor and fell back into the seat. This was somebody from the real war. Last month it had come to Wagga in the form of a shot-up Hudson. What looked like blackened clothes pegs in the cockpit turned out to be severed fingers gripping a control line that ran through to the tail of the aircraft. A government man arrived shortly afterwards and placed the charred remains in a tin, the sort used for storing coloured pencils. No one said much, but everybody knew about it.

From Goulburn through to Sydney, she dozed in half thoughts of Tom and coastal holidays. He'd joined the merchant navy, just like he said he would, and his last postcard came from a seaside village in New Guinea. It reminded her of Terrigal, and the crying whale. She prayed that he was all right.

At Sydney's Central Station, drifting eddies of fine ash coated the line ahead in grey dust and forced passengers back from the edge of the platform. Jock and Emily would only be staying the one night – he'd be heading north the following morning – so they didn't bother looking too far for accommodation.

'No doubles, I'm afraid,' the hotel receptionist said in reply to Jock's question. 'Can do you a room with two singles, Mr . . .?'

'Mr and Mrs Smith,' Jock answered quickly.

The receptionist looked over her spectacles to view Emily waiting by the front door. She sighed, then turned the register for Jock to sign. 'Third floor, bathroom's down the corridor. Leave the key at reception if you're going out.' Somehow she doubted Mr and Mrs Smith would be venturing out tonight.

A shower rose dripped slow drops onto the stained porcelain around the taps. Her mother's 'little chat', before she'd left for Wagga, had failed to mention the ecstasy that had shivered through her body, or the rush that came with skin on skin. She peered into the water now, half expecting her body to have somehow changed. From where she lay, she appeared disjointed. She broke the reflection with an underwater wave that washed around the rim of the bath, exposing knees and breasts, then travelled behind her in a high arc. She drifted into her bath, her eyes travelling the room like a tourist's . . . past peeling paint and brass fittings, to the window and the handbasin, and around to the bathroom door.

Somewhere a pipe began to shudder. Her eyes followed the sound up the wall and into the ceiling as a water heater ignited above her head. But below the surface, her thoughts were immersed in Jock. She intertwined his imaginary hand in hers and, with slow fingers, retraced the journey of his hand from the night before.

The outside world had been deliberately shut out by closing the curtains on the bedroom windows. Faded light fell through seams and veiled the cheap furniture and frayed linoleum. A radio in the room next door played softly through the wall. Jock's arms felt smooth, his body all consuming, inviting. The backs of his fingers had trailed down the buttons on her dress, and in a slow dance of anticipation, they had explored each other's bodies. The sensual feelings that came with skin on skin, of soft necks and hard shoulders, brought them together. As lovers they fell onto the bed, arms and legs entwined. It felt dangerous, uninhibited. She caught her breath as ecstasy shivered through her body.

'Hey! You haven't drowned in there, have ya?' The sound of an older woman's voice came from the other side of the door. 'You're not the only one on this floor, ya know.'

Emily sank into the bath and let thoughts of Jock wash over her.

*

As they stepped out together into the morning light, Emily held on to Jock's arm and watched the passers-by, wondering if anybody noticed the knowing smile that passed between the two of them. And so they walked, back to Central, across the station concourse and through the ticket barrier towards a waiting train.

The Brisbane Mail broke their long embrace with a sigh of steam that softened its industrial edges and hid the edge of the platform. It was Jock who spoke first.

'I know it's not in the right order of things, Em, but I bought you a present. I didn't get it engraved or anything, in case, you know, you didn't like it . . .'

In the time it took her to unwrap the small package, Jock had boarded the train. Emily looked up to find him leaning out of the carriage window. He pointed to her hand. 'It goes on the fourth finger of the left hand.'

She walked beside the moving window. 'Was that a marriage proposal?'

Jock smiled. His outstretched arm reached for hers. 'What else? Of course.'

Emily looked into his eyes, then leaned up and kissed him on the lips. 'In that case, I accept,' she said.

The carriage shuddered as it slowly gained momentum. They held hands for as long as the platform would allow, until eventually Jock was replaced by other faces in other windows.

Chapter Eleven

Torpedoes had ripped open the MV *Trident*, exposing the hull and spewing fuel oil from ruptured tanks. Muffled explosions fuelled rivulets of fire that flowed black and red across the Pacific Ocean. Below decks, Able Seaman Tom Barton began a desperate race through twisted hatches and broken frames. Concussed, stumbling, half falling, he was being driven by men pushing their way along dark tunnels, like miners in some terrible underground fire that sucked the oxygen from their lungs and blackened their bodies. United in a bid for survival, the merchant seamen fought their way to the surface. Behind them, steel deck plates began buckling from the heat, as below the seas spewed flames of fuel and oil into the troughs of waves. At the stern of the ship the men waited, but there would be no rescue party, no miners with lamps to show the way clear.

Tom fell through the fiery membrane, into the darkness below, where it was cold, calm and inviting. It was where he wanted to be – drifting down to the ocean floor. Then someone grabbed hold of his hand. He fought to let go, but it was replaced with another, and then a different pair of hands pulled him violently back into the hell from which he'd come.

Men were frantically rowing, desperately pulling the lifeboat away from what they were looking at. He turned to see his ship, its propellers still turning, as it rose into the air. As its boilers flooded, it exhaled a massive cloud of steam that hung over it like a flag over a coffin; and then the vessel slid into the deep like a body buried at sea.

He'd been in the lifeboat for two days when the nightmare began again. In the late evening, the silhouette of a submarine broke the surface. It sat not twenty yards away. With empty ballasts, it wallowed on the sea. Gun crews appeared, scrambling, closing up on weapons. A man yelled something from the conning tower, then scanned the skies with a pair of binoculars. The sound waves from the exploding torpedoes had ruptured Tom's eardrums and the nightmare ran like a silent movie over and over in his head as a life-boat was pulled alongside.

He felt oil being poured on his face. His burns were cooled. In the submarine's world of artificial light, he could just make out an American pin-up girl taped to the underside of a bunk. Only then did he realise he was safe. This would be the end of his war. He was going home.

The farm at Ariah Park was where Tom had needed to hide, to recuperate from his wounds. The skin on his arm had baked, then twisted into pitted knots of tissue as it cooled. Back home, he'd been spared the mortification of strangers staring, or consciously looking away. For once the isolation had worked for him, but only in the last few months had the scars healed over.

When he'd first got back, Tom could feel Harry's presence everywhere – down by the timbers, racing high in the saddle to the front gate. The woodshed, the side verandah. But now it was getting better. Sometimes a whole morning, even a day, might pass without him.

In the spring of 1945, Tom and his father had built a basalt memorial for Harry.

They had placed the basalt rocks in a corner of the top paddock and asked Father Brougham to come over and bless the memorial. A lot of people turned up – people that Tom and Harry had gone to school with, people who knew their parents. And there were a number of other families from the district who also had lost their sons.

As Tom stood silently remembering, he caught sight of Emily and Jock. They were late, but that didn't surprise him. Emily's timing had always been pretty crook.

'Shockin' road, lucky to make it at all.' Jock stretched out his hand. 'And I'm sorry about Harry, Tom. Emily tells me he had a lot goin' for him.'

'Yeah, well . . . that's how it is,' Tom said quietly. 'Harry'd appreciate you both coming over, that's for sure. He was a good bloke. Eh, Em?'

Tom had only met Jock in a description given by Emily. She wasn't far off target: her husband did indeed have the mark of a country kid. Not far removed from himself really.

'Yeah,' she said with a nod. 'He was a good man. Smart too.'

'I'll take those if you like, Em.' Tom took her cake tin of scones and the three of them started walking towards the house. 'How was your trip then?'

'Dry, mate. Bloody dry out there.' Jock nodded in the direction of the paddock. 'Looks like you haven't had too much rain here either. Been dry over Grenfell way, mate. Real dry.'

'Same here,' said Tom. That was another thing about the country: life revolved around seasonal rain. It was always 'too' something. He caught Emily's eye as he unlatched a gate. 'How're you settling into life in the country then, Em?'

'Good. Different.' Her reply could have gone either way.

'It'll get better.' Jock stuffed a tobacco tin in his pocket and felt around for some matches. 'We're livin' with my parents till we build something of our own. Got the stumps in, savin' for the tin. Eh, Em?'

It was easy to see Jock Marsden's appeal. He spoke about the farm, his experiences in Brisbane and his plans for the future. Tom held his conversation with his eyes, but he wasn't really listening. He'd found another conversation, one that revolved around Emily. One that spoke of how beautiful she looked, of how he'd felt, of how he'd always felt. Of all the things he'd wished he'd said.

'I mean, you'd have to agree, eh, Tom?' Jock shifted his weight from one foot to the other as if to punctuate his point.

'For sure.' His imaginary conversation dissolved into farming and everyday events.

'Brought over a few beers,' Jock said brightly. 'Can I get you one?'

'My word.'

Emily watched Jock return to the boot of their Chev and then turned back to face her old friend as the two of them kept walking. 'I'm pregnant, Tom,' she told him. 'We're having a baby in the autumn.'

Tom stopped at the foot of the stairs. For some reason he was thinking that this marriage wasn't going to work – a Sydneysider like Emily would never survive on the land. And somehow she was still a part of his life. But not now, not with a baby. 'I guess that's what usually happens, Em. You get married; you have kids. Are you happy?'

'Yeah,' she replied. 'I'm happy.'

'Then I'm happy for you. I'm happy for the both of you.'

Emily gave a squint that could only have been a legacy of the Terrigal sun. 'So how is it with you?'

'Dunno, Em.' It was the truth: he didn't know how it was with him. So much had happened in such a short period of time, and his thoughts changed every day. He looked across to his parents. They were the only thing keeping him here. After the harvest he would think seriously about leaving.

'I'm really sorry about Harry,' she said. 'It's just so unfair. Life can be so unfair.'

'Yeah, it can,' Tom agreed, and he wasn't just thinking about Harry.

With that, they entered the house and joined the other guests. Different versions of Harry's short life circulated around the room. Knowing smiles would inevitably fall away to sadness, only to be resurrected by someone else's memory of an incident that could only be shared with those who'd known him. The service had served its purpose: Tom and his parents had said a farewell of sorts.

The months passed, and soon Christmas with them. The harvest had come and gone; now it was time for Tom to be gone too. He flicked his fingers along the reins of his horse and made his way down to the dam, where he'd first seen the fox. Hungry and lean, it could smell the water and the horse and the human sweat that filtered into the air. Spotting the animal now, Tom reached for his rifle, but a squeak of leather betrayed his intentions. Harry would have pursued it, racing his horse through the long grasses that followed the fence line. This was Harry's place. This was where he was meant to be.

Tom turned his horse for home and settled into a slow gait. He looked back to the dam and watched the fox go back to drinking by the water's edge. He knew he wouldn't have shot it. He'd never pulled the trigger on anything.

The sea was where he now needed to be. A source of life that stretched to eternity.

The teredo worm does most of its damage in a warm tropical environment. It grows up to a foot and a half long and loves cowie and bluegum. It'll even have a crack at teak. The worms enter the timbers in the larval stage through holes too small to be detected by the human eye, then they eat away at the timber from the inside. In July of 1949, Tom Barton bought a boat that had a history of them.

He'd known it at the time, but she'd been 'cured' and was going for the right price. Besides, she'd recently been recorked and sealed and sat high in the water. The little money he had left he spent on replacing planks as necessary – which seemed to be an ongoing expense. Still, the *Dolce Bella* had a beautiful line. She was thirty-six feet long and nine feet wide, with a big Detroit diesel that pushed her through the water.

An offshore breeze brought the smell of land and small insects that clung to the decks. Tom stood in the wheelhouse. He wore a captain's hat and a loose coat that billowed in the breeze like an unfurled jib. For the first time in a long time he felt truly happy.

They were a long way off the coast, and the mountains that shadowed the afternoons in town appeared only as a reference point. He slowed the boat until it rolled uncomfortably with the swell.

'What's goin' on?' Ted Bailey stuck his head out of

the companionway. He was old, weathered by salt and wind. Once sharp features had been rounded off like the rocks at the end of the point. As a deckie he was a bit slow, but he knew everything about the sea, its fishing grounds and the deep trenches that dictated the line of their nets. He held onto the gunnel and peered over the side. 'Not yet,' he said. 'Not yet, son. Keep 'er goin' . . .'

Ted was a fish diviner. His old man was a diviner too, so in a way there were two generations of fish finders looking for fish. This gave Tom hope. He'd missed the last boat payment, and there was another one due on Thursday.

'Over there,' the old man instructed, pointing further out to sea. 'Drop a gang line over the side. Not deep, mind – just over the side.'

He knew Ted from before, from his holidays on Terrigal Beach, along with Captain Bell, Mr Insill and Mr Willis, the last of whom had recently retired from the post office. They all seemed smaller in stature than he remembered.

'There!' shouted Ted. A baited line whipped across the deck. It was travelling fast, racing along gunnels before disappearing over the edge.

It might have been the shadow of cloud that brought the school of kingfish to the surface, or Ted's sighting of the solitary seabird that glided above in ever-diminishing circles. Or perhaps it was, as Ted would have everyone believe, 'the electro-kinetic energy that steers me towards 'em'. Whatever it was, the fish were there.

'Can't go near Ollie's fish shop no more,' he bragged now. 'Not unless I wanna get electrocuted.' He slewed the line with his boot. 'Nooosir.'

Electric flashes of silver passed beneath the boat. Fast and slow, stem to stern, leaping, diving, running deep on tethered lines. On the surface a rolling sea of fish were being picked over by seabirds that dropped from nowhere.

For twenty minutes the two men retrieved fish and baited hooks. No sooner would the lines hit the water than they were pulled with four or five fish jagged on the line. The deck was alive, with many spilling back into the sea.

Tom felt the sting of wind peppered with salt. He gripped the wheel and held his ground as the overladen boat speared down the swells. This was as good as it got. He stuck around for as long as was necessary before swinging the 36-footer about and heading home.

Back at Terrigal, the Angling Club was situated at the edge of the car park that led to the main wharf. An odd assortment of chairs surrounded a 44-gallon drum with the top removed and a series of holes punched in the bottom to allow for the flow of air. A fire had been lit and loose timber chucked inside. The club members gathered around it.

'I've passed more lighthouses than youse lot have shithouses . . .' Merv Trumper stirred the ashes as he spoke to the fishermen. 'And I'm tellin' ya, we got more barg'nin' power if we stick together.' It was a good turnout. Talk of setting up a co-op always brought them out from their bunks and their fishermen's cottages, away from their nets and their needles, their wives and their teas.

The co-op had come too late for Tom. The day's catch was good, but it wasn't good enough. He would need to fill the hold every day for a week to turn a profit. Even if the weather was perfect, there was no guarantee on the fish, and it was just a matter of time before the *Dolce Bella* would be repossessed. He'd survived everything the sea could throw at him, and now it was the bank that was going to finally sink him.

'They're movin' the Snowy.' The lobster man sidled in beside him. His pots and buoys marked the channel, and, in even the foulest weather, he would be seen out in his clinker, putt-putt pulling his cane baskets from the sea floor.

'What are you talking about, George?'

'Movin' it inland.'

'The Snowy?' Tom picked up a handful of chips then wiped the neck of a bottle of beer that was being passed around.

'Yeah.'

'Why?'

'I dunno.' George brushed away the remaining chips and passed over the wrappings.

Sure enough, it was true. They were moving the Snowy River. A whole river, diverting its flow back to the inland. It was right there on page one. He folded up the article and shoved it in his pocket.

Chapter Twelve

The social worker had suggested a nursing home for Don Cameron. At age seventy-seven, his needs were becoming more specialised. Staying with Paul would not be fair on him or Don. Apart from any other reason, a third-floor walk-up would amount to a prison gate.

'You're lucky, Don,' she'd said, speaking with an even voice and looking directly into his eyes. 'We've managed to find you a spot at Wentworthville.'

'Wentworthville?' Paul had been thinking of someplace between home and his work, but Wentworthville was way out in Sydney's west. 'You haven't got anything closer, have you?' he'd asked.

'I'm sorry, that's the best we can do.' The social worker had smiled at Don before turning the evenly spoken voice on Paul. 'We have an ageing population problem. I had to split up a couple just last week, been together all their lives. She stayed in Sydney, he went to Canberra. It's a terrible situation. It should never have been allowed to get like this.' She had then handed over some legal-looking documents and a pen. 'Everybody thinks only for today and only for themselves. I strongly suggest you take up the offer.'

Paul closed the door of his father's blue Beetle and compared the photograph on the front of the brochure with the building opposite them now. There were some similarities. Maybe it was the light. With an accountant's eye for design, a wing of dormitory bedrooms had been added to the rear of the nursing home. 'Just looks like someone's house, from the front anyway,' Paul said, trying to sound enthusiastic. 'What do you reckon, Pop?'

On entering the building, they discovered there was a reception but no receptionist. Paul rang a small bell that was attached to a chain. Cooking smells mixed with antiseptic and age filtered into the foyer. From somewhere nearby came the sound of a suburban train. Paul wondered if you were allowed to build so close to the tracks; then again, the residents probably wouldn't hear it anyway.

Don pushed his fluoro glasses onto his nose and looked up at a pinboard of photographs. He read the childlike script: *Edith's 93. Hooray for thee!* A smiling, if somewhat bewildered Edith looked back at him. He took in the cake and remembered his own birth date – 18 April 1921. He felt pleased about that. He turned to mention it to Paul, but it suddenly slipped from his mind.

Other photographs pictured residents shuffling by rose gardens, on shoes unevenly worn. A community bus waited in the wings.

'Mr Cameron?' The voice preceded a woman who appeared from the dining room. Through the swinging door Paul and Don glimpsed snapshots of elderly people sitting down to the evening meal. 'Just in time for dinner,' the nurse said. She might have been forty, and wore her auburn hair in a tight bob that met the corners of a generous smile. She reached over and took Don's bag. 'Is this all you've got?'

Don looked down at his bag.

Paul answered for him. 'Er, was there something we were supposed to bring?'

'Not at all. Really, it's a welcome change. Most people bring in everything, their whole life sometimes. Not that we mind, but some of the rooms are awfully cluttered.' She turned her attention back to Don. 'It's nice to have you with us, Don,' she said softly. 'Come and meet some of our other residents. You're going to have a lovely time with us.'

The nurse made it sound like first day at school with an anxious parent. After settling Don into his room, she pressed on with a 'Best leave now, it'll be all right' tone in her voice.

'I'll give you a call tomorrow, Pop, to see how you're settling in,' Paul said as he gave his father a hug. He felt frail somehow. Frailer than before they arrived.

Don nodded his head and then, in an old-fashioned fatherly kind of way, shook Paul's hand.

On the way home, Paul took advantage of the abundance of streetlighting along the M4 to snatch phrases from a typewritten poem that had, over the years, made its way from the glovebox to the floor of Don's car. *Each time I drive, Lord, may I feel / Your hands on mine upon the wheel.*

He wound down the car window and welcomed the night air. There was a permanency to a nursing home, he felt. People lived there, they weren't staying for a few days or a few weeks. This was it. The bloke sharing his dad's room had a sideboard with rounded glass doors – a time capsule that held photographs in silver frames and small pieces of china aged in hairline cracks. Paul thought about a few things he could take over for Don, but his bag had contained it all.

He gave a weary sigh. Leaving his father sitting on the bed was foremost in his mind. He looked across to the poem and tried to remember how Don had acquired it. Paul had always seen it as being part of the car.

'Your hands on mine upon the wheel . . .' He gave the line a bluesy country interpretation, which made it sound sadder than it might have been.

It was night, but it never really got dark in Don's room, and there was always the noise. Somewhere a cleaner pushed revolving discs around the lino floors of the nursing home. An extension cord meant no peace. Don looked across to the man lying in the bed next him – he thought his name was Harold, but he couldn't be sure. Maybe Paul was still here, he'd know. Maybe he himself had written it in his notebook. He felt his pyjama pocket, but found it to be empty. The bedside table left no clues. In a rush of anxiety, he pulled the covers up to his neck. Everything was different here. Everything had to be learnt again. He lay back into the pillow and closed his eyes.

Morning came with the sound of trains urgently clattering their way to the city and a cheery greeting from the man who may've been called Harold. It was a weekday, but by lunchtime the dining area of the nursing home had been transformed into a Saturday afternoon hair salon.

It was a different woman who addressed the residents now from the nurse who'd shown Don to his room the night before. Or maybe it wasn't, he couldn't be sure.

'Ladies, your attention please,' she said. 'This handsome young man is Mr Cameron, who's now sharing a room with Mr Murphy.'

Heads of tightly packed rollers emerged from plastic domes on chrome stands. A line of vacuum-cleaner hoses linked wheelchairs, stockinged feet, knitted tops, cameo brooches and tissues tucked into sleeves. A fine mist of hairspray held the whole scene in place. Walking frames had been parked around the perimeter.

The nurse continued with the introductions. 'Mary, this is Don. Mary painted those beautiful paintings in the reception area, Don.' Mary's smile lit up the inside of her plastic bubble.

The woman, whose name still remained elusive, steered Don further into the salon. 'And this is Peg.

Peg used to be a journalist. She's travelled all over the world, haven't you, Peg?'

'All over the world,' Peg replied. She beckoned Don down to a more conspiratorial level. 'Haven't got a smoke on you, have you, pet?' Swollen fingers with rings well past removal reached out for his hand.

'You don't smoke, do you, Don?' The woman with no name answered for him.

'That's a shame.' Peg withdrew her hand and retreated into her own thoughts.

In the background, a resident held the swinging door open just long enough for Don to see a man standing at the reception with a hat in his hand. The man was a stranger to Don, but he'd announced his name as Tom Barton to the girl at the desk.

In the foyer, Tom's eyes wandered past the photographs of Edith's ninety-third birthday and onto a framed poem that sat on the reception desk.

In your eyes you're frail and old,
In your eyes your beauty is past,
But in your heart, you laugh and sing,
And in your mind your feet have wings.

Don Cameron could not have looked more earth-bound, Tom thought. His old mate was standing in the doorway now, concentrating hard on him.

'G'day, mate. You didn't think your old mate Tom'd be far behind you, did you?' His eyes searched Don's face for some sign of recognition.

Don's weight shifted onto his back foot as the stranger moved towards him.

'Come on, Don. I'll walk you down to your room.' Tom smiled at the receptionist, then, his hat in one hand, he took Don's arm and led him down the corridor.

The room he shared with Mr Murphy was divided in half by a curtain. Don's bag had been placed on a bedside cabinet and its contents placed in the drawers. The previous occupant had left a travelling clock, which now faced the bed. On the other side of the curtain, small pieces of furniture and household effects waited for the auction rooms.

Don took a seat on the edge of the bed and stared out of the window. 'I can't remember things anymore,' he said at last. He wiped his eye with the sleeve of his cardigan. 'Everything's different.'

'It's all right. You don't have to remember things.'

'I'm still Don.'

'That's right, mate. You're still Don.' Tom placed an arm around him. 'That's all you have to remember.'

Tom had intended to tell him that he was going away for a few days to sort things out, to set things up for them, and that he'd be back at the end of the week. But he thought better of it, and decided it might be wise not to mention it at all. Likewise the recent trip out to Grenfell. Instead, he helped Don up from the bed and guided him out through the glass door and onto the verandah. There, they found a seat and watched the trees slowly shadowing the garden.

Some hours later, a worker appeared and announced that dinner was being served. Don passed on an evening meal – he'd had lunch, and he and Tom had shared an afternoon tea. Don had dozed through the afternoon, and was now asleep, so Tom pulled a blanket up over his friend's shoulders before making his way down the corridor and back to the reception area.

Somewhere in his wallet was a piece of paper with Dave Blainey's phone number and the address of the warehouse on it. Tom had earlier transferred the details from the truck driver's business card and the warehouse address onto the sheet of notepaper; he liked having all the important information in the one place. He dug about in its folds and picked up the payphone receiver.

'Hi Dave, it's Tom Barton,' he said, as exhaust brakes machine-gunned down the phone at him. He hated these new mobile phone things. 'Just making sure you're right for Thursday to move the stuff.' He placed his hand around the mouthpiece and raised his voice. 'I was hoping my mate Don would be joining us, but it doesn't look like he can make it. So it'll just be me there with the agent. She's got the key.'

'Sweet, Tom,' came the reply. 'No probs. Thursday it is. See ya, then.'

Tom put the phone down, feeling useful again. He put his wallet in his back pocket and headed for the exit. Maybe this was the only way he could help Don. Get this deal together, and then the two of them could clear off to a better life. The same evening breeze that swept gently through the doors fluttered the piece of notepaper he'd mistakenly left behind on the shelf beside the payphone.

Don woke up the next morning to find it was party-hat day. But there was no party as such. The hair salon had been transformed into an arts and crafts centre.

'. . . and this little bit goes underneath this little bit.' The woman holding the demonstration folded a piece of card back onto itself. In front of her, the 'advanced group' were working on miniature animals, but arthritic fingers gave them little hope. Angles of cardboard lay scattered around the footplates of wheelchairs.

Don's hat was not progressing well. He looked around to see how the others were faring. At ninety-three, Edith was not really a contender; while down at the far end of the table, the gentleman who shared his room was being assisted by the woman with no name. She caught his eye and smiled. 'That's excellent, Don,' she said. 'You can wear it in the hat parade.'

Parade? He had to be in a parade? He suddenly remembered his dark suit – it was hanging in the wardrobe at home. Next to his cream bowling pants. He could picture it quite clearly, but what concerned him was that it probably needed to be drycleaned before he could take part in any parade.

The woman was coming towards him now, a piece of paper in her hand. 'Oh Don, your mate Tom must have left this at reception. How about you give it to him when he next comes to visit?' She folded it into a tight square and placed it in his shirt pocket, and then pointed to the hat. 'Definitely for the parade.' She stroked his hand before moving over to join the lady who smoked.

By early afternoon all evidence of the morning's activities had disappeared. Instead of hats in various stages of completion, it was cups of tea and side plates containing pieces of cake that covered the craft table.

'Has anyone seen Don?' The woman with no name made a general announcement from the swinging door. Mary the painter thought she'd seen him in the garden, but she couldn't be sure. Don's room-mate, Mr Murphy, wasn't able to help either.

After a thorough search of the nursing home grounds, the hunt was extended to include neighbouring front yards. The woman with no name took a shortcut to the staff car park. In the time it took her to reach the main entrance onto Wentworth Avenue, she'd convinced herself that Don had more than likely wandered off towards the shopping mall. It was only a short walk. She took comfort in the fact that residents rarely made it past the traffic lights at the end of the street, and even if they did, they were usually returned by a local shopkeeper.

She rang in on her mobile phone. 'Nothing here, Val,' she told her colleague. She wasn't worried, but there were procedures to be followed in such circumstances. 'Better give the police a call.' She hung up and hurried off towards the mall.

But Don Cameron was nowhere near the shopping mall at Wentworthville. He sat watching electricity stanchions flicking past billboards and back-yard pools, and felt the railway carriage clicking its way across a set of points. He was thinking about his suit, and his old mate Gordon, who ran a drycleaning business just around the corner from his house on Knox Street.

Chapter Thirteen

Tunnel walls rushed past the train windows. Fluorescent lighting threw the inside of the railway carriage into a world devoid of shadows. Images from the present retrieved days from Don's past. An advertisement for watches led him to the front of a jewellery store. It must have been 1940-something, because his neighbour's new Morris motor car was parked outside. A signwriter was painting *Cameron's* on a plate-glass window. Don went to step inside the store, but instead found himself alighting from the train. The outgoing tide of people swept him along the raised platform and down some stairs to the ticket barriers.

'Got your ticket there, mate?' the guard asked him.

'I'm going home. Home to Redfern.'

'Redfern? No, this is Central, mate. Redfern's one stop back. You must've missed it.'

Don tried to confine his thoughts to the present. He followed the line of the man's arm across the concourse as the guard directed him to the correct platform. He climbed the stairs again, realising as he did so that he was wearing not his good black shoes, but bedroom slippers. And without socks too.

Once on the southbound train, Don remembered more about the jewellery store. He saw himself quite clearly behind the counter. Bernadette was showing a ring to a customer. Under the counter he could see baby Paul peacefully asleep in a makeshift bassinet, while there before him a watch lay disassembled. As Don tried to fit the pieces together, he became more and more agitated – there seemed to be bits missing, and of the pieces he had, none seemed to match.

The train travelled the short distance from Central, during which Don made a point of standing right by the doors of the carriage, so as not to miss the stop a second time. A large man of Aboriginal descent was most adamant that this was indeed Redfern. He wore a City Rail uniform and sat on a stool at the station exit. 'Got your ticket?' he asked.

Don looked anxious. How could he not have had a ticket? The more he searched, the more agitated he became.

'No worries, bro,' the man leant over and whispered in his ear. 'Pensioners free today, okay?'

The guard helped him through the turnstile and pointed him towards Redfern Street. The 'don't walk' sign stopped flashing as Don stepped up onto the pavement. He didn't recognise this part of town at all.

'Hello, Don. How've you been?' A young woman in an Australia Post uniform fell in alongside him. A mailbag hung between them.

'Oh good, good. Yeah, everything's good.' The woman was familiar to him, but only because she knew his name. She spoke in small-town talk that included gossip sourced over letterboxes. As they turned the corner, he realised something was terribly wrong.

'Where are you living now, by the way?' she asked.

Don stopped to think. The Mobil garage had gone. Not only that, but there appeared to be no evidence of it ever having been there.

'Well, that's it for me,' the postie said with a smile, as she switched the mailbag over to the other shoulder. 'See you later, Don. Take care of yourself.'

It was all different. The fruit shop had gone, the Portuguese butcher had gone, even the drycleaner had gone. He turned back to ask the woman who seemed to know him, but she'd gone too. Only the milkbar offered refuge, except it wasn't a milkbar anymore. It was a seconds clothing store. In fact the whole street was made up of clothing shops. He stopped for a minute and had a think.

The tobacconist was just around the corner, he remembered. He turned onto the side street and put his hands up against the shop's plate-glass window. On the floor inside, a battlefield had been set up. A model army of French foot soldiers marched across the meadows of Waterloo.

'See something you like?' The man from the hobby shop stuck his head around the shop window.

'I was looking for the tobacco shop. I was looking for . . . Martin.' The name came to him at the last second.

'Sorry, mate, don't know any Martin. But there's a smoke shop at the station.'

But Don had just come from the station, and he would have recognised Martin for sure. He was English, and sometimes played the piano with Bernadette. Don smiled at the man, who then directed him back to the main street.

Paul Cameron thought carefully about the possible consequences of his actions. A direct hit to Nick Thoulous's eye would probably result in a law suit against him. He faced the blackboard and secretly loaded a piece of chalk between his index finger and thumb. Not worth the risk, he thought. Besides, the second-floor windows of the school classroom opened directly onto Cleveland Street, so the diesel fumes would get young Nick in the end.

Only ten more minutes, then he could have a cigarette. Half the class were probably thinking the same thing. He threw the piece of chalk into the bin.

'Hey, sir! Somebody's at the door, sir.' A rowdy discussion ensued as to whether there was anybody at the door or not.

The head that finally appeared was that of the school secretary, Mrs Barraclough. 'May I see you a moment, Mr Cameron?' she asked.

'Sir's in trouble! Are you in trouble, sir?' The room filled with laughter as Paul headed for the door.

'The nursing home just rang,' she told him

sympathetically. 'I think you should give them a call.' A telephone number passed between them.

The staffroom was small and offered little privacy. Paul wound the telephone cord between his fingers. 'Wandered off?' he repeated. He could hardly believe what he was hearing.

'It's not uncommon,' the matron from Wentworthville replied. 'We've notified the authorities and I'm sure he's fine. Your father's probably at the local mall. Is there anything special he might've wanted to buy?'

Electrical tape and biros was all that Paul could think of. 'No, nothing really.'

The matron seemed to have no doubts that Don would turn up. 'We'll give you a call the moment he does. Please don't worry.'

Paul hung up the phone. Don't worry? How could this have happened? He was dumbfounded. They'd seemed like responsible people, *professionals*. Getting out to the nursing home was now foremost in his mind.

Don pushed his glasses back onto his nose and, as an aid to thinking, put a finger to his lips. The town hall was just there . . . Wilson's Lebanese was on the other side . . . and he lived just the other side of that. In measured footsteps he made his way down Pitt Street and turned into Knox. House keys? He must've left them under the pot plant, he supposed.

Everything was familiar again. He saw himself pottering in the back yard, and from the kitchen he could hear the kettle whistling him inside, and the sound of Schubert being played on the piano. He'd forgotten why he'd gone out in the first place, but it didn't matter – he'd most likely remember once he got home, like he always did. He lifted his eyes away from the pavement and up to his front gate.

Blistered paint on wrought-iron pickets had turned into scabs of rust. A garden of weeds flourished in charcoal-enriched soil. Previously blackened walls, now washed down, supported an enclosed verandah of broken louvres. The front door appeared to be open. But Don noticed none of these details.

The missing pot plant was uppermost in his mind. From the doorway, an angle of light caught him as he fossicked among the weeds. The flash of white bit into his eyes, forcing a retreat to the fence. From there he saw a clean sheet of corrugated iron nailed to the architraves of what was once the front door.

He stood for a moment, silent and still. This was his house, he knew that. It was exactly one hundred and twenty-seven steps from the town hall to his front gate, and he'd just counted them out. Something must have happened to the door. There seemed to be no other explanation.

He retraced his footsteps to the laneway that led to the rear of the house, only to find the back door was locked. And not just that, but someone had nailed some of his good bits of wood across it. Wood he'd been saving. The kitchen window was boarded up also. He used some house bricks to lift himself up to a gap in the timbers, and, with his glasses against the grain, he peered inside. Everything was black. The natural light had been boarded out; all that remained were the shadows of what might have been. Stagnant air caught him by the throat and forced him back against the side fence.

Something had happened here, something catastrophic. He looked around the back yard, unsure of what to do, and began wringing his hands in an attempt to make sense of it all. If he could just get into the house, maybe he could phone Paul. Paul would know what to do.

Twilight passed unnoticed. Anxiety turned to fear, and the outside toilet became his refuge. Don looked across to his house, then back to the dunny's cement floor.

Tom Barton was trying on a new shirt when the phone rang. As he spoke to Paul, he placed the pins and packaging in the bin. 'Why would he be with me, mate?' he asked.

Paul was becoming more agitated. 'Because someone saw him get onto a train that was heading into the city. That's why, Tom.' He paced the reception area at the nursing home, his mobile glued to his ear. On the other end of the phone, he heard the rustling in the background stop – he had Tom's full attention now, he realised. 'Look, maybe you should pop over to the house and see if he's turned up,' he suggested.

'Sure thing, Paul. No worries,' Tom replied.

Paul hung up and shook his head. It was serious now; even the staff had lost their cheery confidence. Paul looked out of the window and saw that night was beginning to fill the car park. He was going to have to head back to the flat at Bondi, to make sure his father wasn't sitting on the doorstep.

As he drove towards the city he found himself reciting the motorist's prayer. It wasn't really appropriate, but it was Don's and it was on the seat beside him. At Cleveland Street he took a detour via the old house, just to be sure. But there was no sign that his father had been there recently.

At the prospect of spending the night alone, Don had left his back-yard refuge in search of anybody who might befriend him. In the local park he'd found it in a couple who helped him into a small minibus. On the sliding door was written *Matthew Talbot Hostel*. As it closed behind him, the door brought together the cradled hands of Jesus Christ holding a vessel of water.

Don now found himself sitting in the gutter outside the front of the hostel building; the man beside him had the luxury of a milk crate to sit on. He tried to place the last few hours, but nothing seemed to fit anymore. Don locked his arms around his knees and pulled them up to his chest. As he did so, he wondered what had happened to one of his slippers.

'I fell out of a car and onto the road,' the man on the milk crate was saying. The stranger was obviously feeling the heat. He peeled his singlet off a gut that rolled like unsecured ballast from one side of the crate to the other, and wiped his face with the garment. 'Course I was pissed at the time.' He laughed and pointed to a scar on his windpipe. 'That's where they put the air into me. It affected me brain, so I just kept drinkin'.'

'G'day, Anick,' said another voice. 'Had a bit of a top-up, have we?'

Don looked up to see a young man standing over them. Rosary beads hung from a black bum bag around his waist.

'Aw jeez, give me a break. I'm still savin' up for a cask. I was just tellin' me mate, er . . . What's ya name again?'

Don felt the sweat from the bare arm that his new friend suddenly wrapped around his shoulder. He tried to think of his name, or any name, but Anick cut him short by shifting his weight and farting.

'Oops! Let the duck outta the bag.' He laughed and settled back onto the crate before picking up where he'd left off. 'Now, about me accident.'

'You mean your finger?' The black bum bag was replaced by the face of the young man sitting on his haunches.

'Nah, that was when I was a slaughterman.' Anick proudly held a hand up in front of Don. 'You gotta get right inside 'em, that's the trick. Then it's lungs down one shoot, livers down another . . .' The four-fingered hand gestured left, then right.

'Why don't you invite your friend inside?' The man with the bum bag introduced himself to Don. 'Hello, I'm Father Michael. I gather you've met Anick.'

'I've lost a slipper,' was all Don thought to say in response. He put his head on his knees again. He was trapped in the present. He closed his eyes and felt the security of the slaughterman's arm.

An hour or so later, they'd moved back indoors for the night. All around him, bodies in beds appeared as small mounds of earth over freshly dug graves. The light gave no clues as to the hour of the day. Don opened his eyes from a brief sleep and remembered his name.

From the inside of a perspex dome, a holy statue watched him slowly change from the pyjamas he'd been lent by the hostel volunteers into familiar clothes. But everything else was alien to him. He crossed the dormitory floor in shoes that weren't his and peered down a hallway.

'Not on me floors, mate!' a voice hollered. The man and the mop were not dissimilar in their appearances. Don waited until they'd both disappeared before venturing any further. He pulled back the glass doors and stepped into the laneway.

Out on the street, a radio tuned between stations played static from the inside of a plastic bag that hung from a No Standing sign. Below the sign, Don recognised the slaughterman's milk crate. A pre-dawn shift of young men had gathered around it. Along the footpath, empty bottles in brown paper bags betrayed figures crumpled in doorways. Don detoured around knuckles inked with the words *Love* and *Hate*, and disappeared behind a man who whispered lines from the Bible he was reading.

The form that the police officer had given Paul to fill in didn't allow for much in the way of detail, relying instead on the accompanying photograph. Don Cameron's cheekbones accentuated his tired eyes. His skin looked fragile. He had little hair, but needed a haircut. Even in the photograph he looked lost. Paul placed the negative in an envelope and walked out of Redfern Police Station.

As dawn began defining the streets, he felt a little less uneasy. The light would peer into unseen corners, lifting covers for all to see. But regardless of this ray of hope, he still felt it was all his fault. Don was his responsibility. Paul thought of all the sacrifices his father had made for him, and in return he'd dropped him off with strangers in the middle of nowhere. He wiped the tiredness from his eyes and regretted that he hadn't spent more time with his dad. This was one hell of a wake-up call.

He was overtaken by an ambulance on the drive home to Bondi. His stomach knotted as he pulled over to let it past. For the rest of the trip, Paul suddenly found himself aware of every old bloke on the street.

From his position over the road, the soft-drinks machine shone like a lighthouse beacon. Don followed the light down the railway concourse and into the relative sanctuary of the station building. An unintelligible platform announcement ushered in a train, after which he looked up to see a small crowd of people milling around a man collecting tickets. Had it not been for the blue uniform, the man could've been mistaken for a feral. The stale air that preceded the train's arrival lifted matted hair that he'd tied with string more suited to wrapping parcels. Eventually the City Rail worker gave up on the last few passengers and took shelter from a strong gust of wind.

Old tickets were whipped up in swirling eddies and dumped around the human shape that was slumped against the Coke machine. Don's memory waded in and out of the shadows of his mind. Only concentrated breathing kept him afloat.

'You right there, mate?' The feral ejected a can of Fanta from above Don's head, then worked a dustpan around him.

Don looked up to see a man standing over him. He pushed his fingers into a wire grille that protected his lighthouse and attempted to pull himself to his feet. Below his right knee a tattoo of dried blood had stained trousers past repair. His orange fluoros had been missing since he fell, but only now did it seem important to find them. His fingers probed the empty pockets of his trousers.

'Lost something?'

Don's thoughts remained on his glasses. He removed a tightly folded piece of paper as he extended his search to a shirt pocket.

'This where you're going?' the stranger asked him. The paper was taken from Don's hand and an address was read from it. 'C'mon, Pop. Looks like you've got a bit of a way to go. Suburbia. You want to be careful out there, it can be a dangerous place.' The feral took him by the elbow and led him into a labyrinth of tunnels and out onto another station platform.

An hour later, Don watched images of suburbia flicking past the carriage windows. Big blocks with triple car garages, trees, bush, tiled roofs, tin fences, shingled cabanas with swimming pools that backed onto railway lines – they all blended as one.

'All change.' A man in uniform tapped the outside of the carriage window.

Don stepped onto a deserted railway platform and watched the tail end of the train disappearing into a landscape of red-brick houses, television aerials and industrial estates. An aching knee made him look for a place away from the morning sun, and soon he found his way out onto a busy street in front of the station building.

It wasn't until he saw a leaking bubbler that Don realised how thirsty he was, so he limped over to it and leant over the spout. Water guttered across his shirt and down his trousers. He felt around for a handkerchief, but only came up with the piece of paper that had led him here. He was about to wipe down his shirt with it when a large dog appeared. Its eyes squinted out of a square head scarred from fighting. They watched each other for a time, Don from the shade of a tree, the dog lapping water from the base of the bubbler. A sharp whistle diverted their attention to a semi-trailer parked over the road.

A steel-capped work boot kicked into the wall of a tyre. Dave Blainey had started the week a thousand kilometres away. In that time, he'd driven by countless roadside houses, passed even more vehicles on the highways, stopped off at gas-station forecourts in two states . . . all the while adding new entries to his exercise book.

The two kids who'd just finished helping him load the loose bits and pieces of war surplus were themselves entries from a year and a half back. Dave had helped them move house and once transported their band's equipment down south from a rained-out festival in Queensland. In return, Dave occasionally called on them for assistance when a bit of muscle was needed.

They'd been a big help today. The final container was so big they needed the assistance of the hydraulic crane that was situated at the back of the cab.

From under the coupling, Dave looked up to see an elderly man limping towards him. He looked like a straggler, from an army in retreat. In his hand he held a piece of paper that could have doubled as a small white flag. He handed it to Dave.

'Yessir. That's me,' Dave said, 'and this is the address, all right.' The piece of paper was returned and the old foundry building pointed out. 'Looks like you've been through the wars,' he added, but the comment seemed to draw a blank from the old man. Dave pulled hard against a rope.

'You'd have to be a mate of Tom's, eh?' he asked. 'Don, is it? Tom said he didn't think you'd be coming along.'

At this, the stranger finally appeared to acknowledge the truck driver's banter. 'Don, yes . . . yes, I'm Don,' he replied with a smile.

'Pleased to meet you, Don. I'm Dave. You haven't seen Tom today, have you? He was supposed to be here.'

Tom. The name didn't sound familiar to Don. His eyebrows folded in concentration.

Dave sighed and looked down at his watch. 'Are you supposed to be meeting him here, or what?'

Don didn't answer, but looked over at the semi instead. It reminded him of a tourist bus, which reminded him of the *Women's Weekly* cruise he thought he'd been on once.

'Well, we ain't gettin' any younger, Don. Tom's got my mobile number – he'll work it out.' Dave loitered around a pin-up girl stencilled to the side of the cab and whistled up the dog. 'Get in there – way back. Waay back! Front seat, 'umans; back seat, dogs!'

Dave held the door open and looked across to Don. 'I take it you are comin' with us?'

A minute later, the *Lisa Marie* pulled away from the warehouse with Don Cameron perched high in the cabin.

Part Two

Chapter Fourteen

Emily Marsden had stopped reading some time ago. She sat on the verandah with the sun on her shoulder and a book in her lap. She'd been thinking about moving Jock's things out of the machinery shed all morning, and now it was time. She pulled herself out of her chair and crossed the lawn to the shed.

Since his death five years back, things had just piled up. Boxes and suitcases and tools that had once lived on shadow boards now lay scattered around the perimeter. Along the back wall, leather reins lay stiff and cracked, and glass jars with screw-top lids hung from the undersides of shelves that buckled their way along the studs. As a way of putting off the inevitable, Emily opened a window to let in more light. A blowfly beat itself repeatedly against the glass. Exhausted and senseless, it now rested on a wooden cross-frame. She slipped the latch and let it drone into the slow afternoon.

Emily turned away from her late husband's possessions now and leant against the huge doorframe of the shed, but the feelings they inspired stayed with her. Feelings about the temporariness of life, about mortality. The same applied to her property, she realised, as she gazed out across the paddock. In the far distance, she could just make out the heavily wooded western boundary of Duraminar, where the bushrangers Ben Hall and Johnny Gilbert once kept stolen racehorses.

The property had originally extended to some six thousand acres, but the kids didn't want it, and she wasn't leaving. Megan had thought about taking it on – she had a love of horses, but it had never really carried much past her teenage years. The reality was that country life was a struggle for the most part, and you had to love it. When David Morris had come along, with a solid job and an interest in a local stable, it was perfect for Megan. Over the years, Duraminar had been divided between the neighbours, so now its boundary fences enclosed only the house, the bottom paddock and the shed. The heavy machinery had been sold to Lynton McCabe, and for nearly a year their Massey Ferguson had sat in the dealership yard. It finally went to a bloke out at Cobar and was the start of the process of 'letting go'.

With that in mind she picked up the closest suitcase of Jock's clothes and made a mental note to drop it off at the church when she drove into town later that afternoon.

*

Don watched the countryside floating by. He was a long way from the city but he felt safe because he was with somebody who seemed to know him, and he was on his way to somewhere.

'Ever been pig shootin', Don?' Dave gave himself a little more height by racking up the driver's seat another notch. 'The right tool for the right job, Ruger rifle, bolt action, .308 calibre.' Dave had no real interest in pig shooting. His knowledge on the subject had been acquired only the week before from a bloke he'd delivered a machinery part to in Walgett. 'And get yourself a decent sight'. He passed over a reassuring look. 'Leopold's the go.'

Don nodded. In fact, Don had agreed with everything Dave had said. Although Don wasn't a great conversationalist, Dave had found his travelling companion a good listener, and had taken the opportunity to expound his views on Connecting Forces. Well satisfied with the grasp Don seemed to have on the matter he moved on. 'Don, maybe you oughta get someone to look at that leg.'

Don looked down to his knee and picked at the dried blood that surfaced through his pants. He thought back to the night before and remembered the fat man without his shirt and being lifted from the pavement by a man who may or may not have been God.

'Ever been to Graceland, Don?'

'I don't think so.'

'You'd remember, mate. Beautiful, it is. What he did to that place . . . and the *colours*. He knew what to do with colours. And he always knew what was goin' on around him, because he had a room full of tellies, you see. Can't be too careful these days – someone's always watchin' you. And the gun room . . . Weeell, you name it, he had it.' He pushed back in the seat and stalked his way through the lower gears of the semi. 'What you gonna do with all this stuff here, anyway, Don?' he asked after a brief pause.

'My son's borrowing a ute and taking it away.' It was an automatic response from his past.

'A ute? Need more than a ute, mate!' Dave applied the truck's brakes as they approached Emily's property. 'Something, something, *vision splendid* . . . Something, something, *sunlit plains extended*.' He looked across to Don. 'Henry Lawson,' he said rather smugly. 'We're here, mate. We have arrived.'

At the far end of the dirt track, the sound of the truck's air horns brought Turps to life. At full pace he burst, dirt brown, from under the house. Emily heard the commotion and emerged from the shed, and caught sight of her dog short-cutting across the bottom paddock. He surfaced briefly in a sea of Paterson's curse before embarking on a submariner's course that led into a travelling storm of dust and chrome.

A *semi*? A few crates, that was what Tom had said. Emily stood in disbelief as the truck hissed to a stop.

Inside the Mack's cab, the sudden silence of the engine jolted Don Cameron from some distant place. And now all around him, it was different, again. In the background, Elvis sang softly to Priscilla. Don consciously rolled back his eyes and glanced around the inside of the cabin. Through the windscreen he could see an elderly woman standing in front of a shed. She blew strands of grey hair away from her mouth, then strode purposefully towards the truck.

'G'day. You must be Emily,' Dave called as he swung down from the driver's side door. 'I was wondering if Tom was about? Just need his signature.'

Emily looked back at the truckie through the settling dust. She was under the impression that Tom would be following in his ute. 'You haven't seen him?' she asked.

'Nope. But here's his mate Don. Where do you want it?' He pointed to the back of the semi with his thumb until his attention suddenly turned to the dog inside the cab. 'Get back in the back, Colonel! Get back . . . *way* back!'

The passenger door swung open now, and Emily watched as an elderly man lowered himself to the ground and stabilised himself against the side of the truck. He stood there for a while before acknowledging her with a smile.

'The shed maybe? It won't all fit in there.' Dave began answering his own questions. 'Whatever doesn't fit in the shed, I'll dump on the lawn, eh?'

'That's fine. You go ahead,' Emily replied, distracted, more concerned about the state of this frail old man. She left the truck driver to it and crossed over to where Don was standing. 'Hello, Don,' she said. 'I'm Emily. Emily Marsden.' She reached out a hand. 'You're Tom's friend, are you?'

Don saw the hand as a means of support. A lifeline thrown the moment he began sinking to the ground. He clung to her wrist as she led him across the gravel to the house.

Once inside, she steered him into the kitchen and onto a chair by the table. The two of them shared a pot of tea there in near silence before Emily stood up and took the cups to the sink. He seemed less confused now than he had been ten minutes before. He sat at the kitchen table and accepted whatever it was she had to say.

'Dave gave me a lift,' Don said suddenly, and stood up from his chair as if he'd remembered something important. Something that would explain everything. He reached into his pocket and pulled out the piece of paper. He carefully unfolded it and passed it over as a schoolboy might a late note.

The warehouse address and Dave Blainey's name and phone number meant nothing to Emily, though it gave her a name to put to the face of the man out in her driveway. She'd been so shocked by the size of the rig, she couldn't even remember whether he'd introduced himself. 'Is this where you've come from?' she asked Don. 'Does Tom know you're here?'

Certain words caused a spark to light up his eyes, Emily noticed. But then the spark would be smothered by his eyelids and he'd slump back into his other world.

'Well, don't worry, Don. You're safe here. I've got Tom's number, so I'll give him a call.'

Out the front, Dave Blainey had finished unloading the various crates and boxes. It was an easy job at this end compared with the pick-up operation at the warehouse. With the Colonel now returned to his position in the rear of the cab, Dave coiled the last of his ropes, packed them into the dog box and made towards the house. It might have been a homestead once, he figured, with grand verandahs that stretched out like a well-worn Stetson, but neglect had turned to decay, and the once expansive gardens had turned to weeds. A recently mown lawn now defined only the perimeter of the house, at the front and down the right-hand side. Just out of reach was an orchard of rotting fruit, while back towards the highway, the roots from a windbreak of pines surfaced in a tennis court. He tapped the flyscreen door. 'Ya there, Emily?'

A reply came from a distant part of the house. Dave entered a kitchen that smelt like his grandmother's. A tea cosy covered a recently made pot of tea. Proper cups sat on proper saucers.

'Won't be a minute.' The distant voice took its cue from the closing of the screen door.

Dave waited by a bookcase full of old paperbacks. Catherine Gaskin seemed to be a favourite, and there were a few titles on farm management, he noticed. Tall skinny books on art mixed with videos and car manuals. *How to Cut Your Family's Hair* even came with a set of clippers.

'Come on through,' the voice called, from what Dave supposed was one of the bedrooms.

Inside the room, Don Cameron's eyes were closed. The gymkhana quilt covered his body and at the foot of the bed was a pair of shoes. A face washer and a bowl of water sat on the floor.

'Jeez,' Dave whispered from the doorway. 'He hasn't carked it, has he?'

'He'll be all right.' Emily spoke softly. 'Right now, I'd say he just needs to sleep.' She stroked Don's forehead in a way that implied she knew what she was talking about.

'D'you think we should call the ambos maybe?'

'He's fine.' She placed the bowl of water on the dresser and looked back at Don. 'He's just tired. Very tired.'

'Well, he's not much of a talker, that's for sure.' He pointed a finger and clicked a thumb towards the window. 'Bit more stuff there than Tom thought, but I've managed to get a tarp over the gear on the lawn.' He thought to bring up the subject of Tom's cash payment, but the moment didn't seem appropriate. 'Tell Tom I'll be passing back through in a couple of days and he can fix me up then.'

'I'll pass it on, Dave.'

'Well . . . nice meeting you. I'll see myself out.' He shook her hand and then leant forward to tap the end of the bed. 'See ya, Don. Take care of yourself, mate.'

The sound of the screen door closing was soon replaced by the sound of Elvis being cranked up on the truck's stereo, and then the Mack's engine burst into life.

Tom wound the window up tight into the ute's door-frame. He'd been driving now for a good few hours and was beginning to feel a sharp drop in the temperature. An invisible stream of cold air blew into the cracks and crevices of doorways and inside the double-buttoned coats of pedestrians who walked in quick time down the main street of Cowra.

He was tired and his foot was starting to cramp. He'd spent the previous night scouring the inner city, a journey that took him to places where he would not normally venture. A grey in-between world lit by neon, where hunched-over figures in heavy coats pushed shopping trolleys filled with toaster parts, pram wheels and other small treasures from block to block. He'd passed around photos of Don but received little response. It would've been a miracle if Tom had found him, he knew that, but then maybe somebody might have at least seen him. He'd had to do something. He couldn't just sit at home.

His search had taken him to Wynyard Station, where an unreliable source reckoned he'd shared a bottle of Royal Reserve with a bloke that might have been Don. But it had all come to nothing. To add to Tom's frustrations, he'd lost the piece of paper with Dave's details and the warehouse address – he was forgetting things himself now, doubting his confidence. It was midday before he'd arrived back at his flat, and it was only then that Emily had phoned him and put his mind at rest. He in turn had then put a call through to Paul.

'He's out at Grenfell, mate,' Tom had told him. The relief in Paul's voice was palpable, although it had taken some time on Tom's part to explain how and why Don had ended up in Grenfell. In the end it was agreed that Don was fine, Tom was on his way to see him, and Paul would join them the following day.

Tom arched his foot again to relieve the cramp, then reached across to the passenger side of his ute and pulled a cardigan from an assortment of clothes he'd gathered for Don. In a string bag on the floor of the ute were potatoes, chump chops, his celebratory tin of red salmon and a bottle of sparkling wine that he'd been saving for a special occasion.

Cowra seemed like a pretty nice town. For starters, it had a river, and that always helped. It might even have had a set of traffic lights. He followed the sign to Grenfell and wished he'd fixed the heater. It didn't matter so much in the city – he rarely travelled far enough for the engine to heat up – but this afternoon he felt the seasonal chill that blew down from the Snowies and swept across the plains. He placed the cardigan across his knees and thought about the cold that was part and parcel of the job he once had up there, almost fifty years before.

Most of his time had been spent in the front seat of a Land Rover, ferrying men and equipment through the mud and the rain. That's where he'd met the clairvoyant. Funny the things you remembered, or chose to remember. Frederick Koman was his name, originated from 'the Continent' – well, nearly everyone on the Snowy Mountains Hydro-Electric Scheme did. Frederick came from one of those places that ended in 'stein', one in a long line of gypsies that had roamed around Europe since forever. Or so he said. *I see riches*. Those were his exact words. *Lots of riches, but it's distant. You won't have to worry.* He went on about a whole pile of other stuff, but it was the riches bit that stuck. Tom thought about his age now. Seventy-five years old . . . there wasn't that much time left. The riches, however 'distant', must be getting pretty close, he reckoned.

The previous night was beginning to catch up on him. Despite the cold, he opened the window to allow an icy blast of air to wash over his face. As he approached the turn-off to Emily's house he looked in the rear-vision mirror and pulled a comb through his hair. The dirt track he was driving on seemed wider than before. Small shrubs had been crushed and overhanging branches lay broken by the side of the driveway.

The tarpaulin was the first thing he saw. In the fading light, broken shapes reached up to wooden pegs that weathered on the clothesline. An exposed corner revealed webbing and water bottles, uniforms, desk lamps, shell casings. As Tom crossed to the house, he wondered if he shouldn't have been more specific with Dave. After all, nobody wanted old tyres. Emily wasn't going to be too impressed. His thoughts were interrupted by Turps, who raced around the car before disappearing into the folds of mouldy smells.

Inside the house, Emily looked up at the broken kitchen clock. It had stopped at a quarter to twelve, but its ornate casing meant it was there to stay, although it certainly wasn't worth fixing. She viewed it out of habit, then returned to study Don out in the yard beside the house. His physical stance reminded her of Jock – when he was older, towards the end. Maybe it was the dressing gown.

In the back of her mind was Tony Jenkins, who'd just been talking to her on the phone about this year's festival production of *South Pacific*. He was the only gay man in Grenfell and ran the local drama society with the flair of a West End producer. 'Numbers, Emily. We need numbers,' he'd stressed. She liked Tony but declined his offer all the same. She'd been involved in other productions, but this year she felt it was all too much. Being on the committee was stressful enough. Emily wiped her hands on her apron as Tom stepped onto the verandah.

'Hi, Em.' Tom stood in the doorway with the bag of groceries in one hand and Don's clothes in the other. 'How is he? How's Don?'

'Good, Tom. He's fine,' she replied. Tom looked different somehow. Neater than before – his hair had changed and he was wearing a new shirt.

Tom peered down the hallway.

'He's down the side, feeding the chooks,' Emily said, as if reading his mind.

'Feeding the chooks?'

Tom followed her gaze and walked over to the window. The chook yard was partially overgrown with the kind of blackberries that, once preserved, lasted from one street stall to the next. The gate, if it could still be called a gate, had been pulled to the side and half a dozen of Emily's chooks fought over bits of bread that fell from Don's hand. Dressed in Jock's robe and slippers, he looked almost biblical, like a picture from a Sunday school book. Tom could almost imagine a small bird floating down from the sky and perching on his finger.

'It's a *miracle* . . .'

'More to do with sleep and country air, I suspect. Anyway, he doesn't seem half as bad as he was this morning.' Emily motioned for him to follow her and together they went out through the flyscreen door to the verandah. She leant over the side rail and gave Don a wave, before turning to look again at Tom. 'He's mentioned someone called Paul a few times.'

'Paul's his son,' Tom explained. 'He'll be down tomorrow, if that's okay.'

'Someone here to see you, Don.' Emily waved again from the verandah.

Don looked up from the garden to see a man striding towards him.

'G'day, mate!' Tom pulled the robe tight around Don's shoulders. 'It's me. Tom. You okay?'

'Yeah. No, I'm good.' He shifted from one foot to the other, then leant back as if to bring the new arrival into focus. Tom . . . Tom had arrived. Tom could explain everything. 'I'm staying the night,' he said.

'I know, mate. Here, at Emily's house.'

Emily's house . . . 'That's right. Emily's house.'

Tom slipped an arm through his. 'Everything's going to be all right, mate. Everything's going to be all right.'

Emily joined them among the chooks, and the three

of them then shuffled round to the back of the house. Behind them, a dozen of Don's disciples followed him to the door. 'Worried sick, I was,' Tom said as he helped Don up the four stairs that led past the laundry. 'I was lookin' for you everywhere . . .'

Emily went on ahead to the kitchen and laid out three cups and matching saucers. From the window that looked out from the front of the house, it was hard to miss the pile of crap that Dave Blainey had deposited. There were things that looked salvageable, as curiosities from another time, but on closer inspection, most of it looked fit for the tip.

'Now, I know what you're thinking, Em,' Tom called out behind her after settling Don in a chair. 'But don't worry. I've got it under control. I'll have it all sorted over the next couple of days, and then it's just a matter of loading up the ute and doing the rounds of a few Sydney dealers. Simple.'

The only thing Emily was worried about was the state of her lawn, but she knew she could always get Joe Baker over from the neighbouring farm. He had a front-end loader and a tipper that could deal with it all very efficiently. 'A couple of days, you say?' she said, turning around from the window. 'What do you think, Don?'

Don gave a vacant stare, then looked to Tom for advice on the matter.

'A week, at most,' Tom continued. 'No worries. Lotta good stuff here, Em. Valuable stuff. Aeronautical memorabilia, that sort of thing. Come on, I'll show you.'

The three of them went out to the verandah and descended the stairs. 'It's all good, Em. I've got a bit of an eye for this sort of thing.' He latched onto a corner of the tarpaulin and began dragging it across the lawn.

'And the stuff in the shed?'

'The shed?' Tom looked across to the machinery shed, where a large crate filled the spot that might once have been taken by a harvester. Dave must've got it wrong. There had to be some mistake . . . Tom looked to Don for an answer, but the chooks had gathered again and taken him back towards the verandah. Tom couldn't remember there being a crate this size. He circumnavigated it, but came back with nothing.

'Stand clear!' he shouted. 'Stand clear, everyone!' He shooed away the last of the chooks with a spade, then slipped it between the timbers of the crate. A crack turned into a crevice. A brief moment of instability was followed by a heavy groan as the timbers split apart. And then there was silence.

Laid out before them was the fuselage of an old aeroplane, like a mummy from some ancient tomb. Its wings, like shields, were attached to the remaining side of the crate; and, as if to help it into the afterlife, preserved mechanical pieces lay soaking in inhibitors.

Tom's mind began to race . . . to the warehouse and the wall of forty-fours. He stared in disbelief, then turned back to where Don had been standing, but only the chooks remained.

'A plane? You didn't say anything about a plane, Tom.' Emily was looking at him for an answer.

Tom was lost in arithmetic. The altimeters had already turned out to be a valuable asset, and now they had the aircraft they were housed in. He continued to borrow tens and carry ones – the number was going to be big. He knew that now. Very big.

Chapter Fifteen

Emily woke to the sound of Lynton McCabe's voice. She pushed her head into the pillow to wake herself from what could only be a dream, but the voice persisted. *If it's a tractor you want, it's the tractor we got.* She opened her eyes and in the dim light inspected the shadows that crept in with the dawn. *Fully guaranteed with a McCabe warranty. No bull. Just tractors, and just for this week!*

Another voice slipped under the bedroom door. *What have you got for us this week, Lynton?*

Kubota, Johnno – heapsa tread, fully optioned.

A tap at the door forced her to pull the blankets up around her neck.

'Morning, Em. Breakfast's up!' Tom's voice sang out from the hallway. 'Would you like it on a tray?'

On a tray? She had to think for a moment where she was. She couldn't remember the last time she'd had breakfast on a tray – with Jock and the kids in a motel somewhere, maybe? 'No thanks, Tom. I'll be right out,' she replied.

Emily opened the door almost expecting to see Lynton sitting at the kitchen table, but the voice came from the top of the fridge. The radio had been tuned to a commercial network. Never in the radio's history had the frequency been changed from the ABC. And now 'Johnno', the second voice she'd heard, was droning on about the virtues of McCabe's Second-Hand Machinery Centre. And the screen door was open. And Turpentine lay sprawled across the floor.

'Hello, Em.' Tom greeted her cheerfully as ever. 'Fog in town today, according to the wireless. A pearler of a day out here, though. Brekkie's all organised. Paper's there as well.'

Emily picked up on the headline: *Japan Capitulates*. A photograph of General MacArthur, complete with corncob pipe, shared the front page with an advertisement for du Maurier cigarettes.

'It's a bit out of date, but makes excellent reading. Found a whole pile of old books as well. They'd have to be worth something to somebody, I reckon.' Tom ejected a piece of toast. 'Don seems a lot better this morning, by the way.'

'I'm sure he just needed a rest,' she said blearily. She gave Tom an encouraging smile, but she still had grave concerns about Don's condition.

'Exactly. Just taking a cuppa in for him now.' With that, he headed down the hallway, cup of tea in hand.

Emily sat down at the table, unsure of what to do next. Should she help herself or wait for Tom? Yes, it was her house, but . . . She avoided the situation by thumbing through an old aircraft maintenance manual as she waited. Detailed pictures of engine components filled the pages. Technical information rekindled a once familiar language that dealt in suppressors and superchargers, longerons and ailerons. Emily tucked a lock of grey hair behind her ear and peered out of the window. There had been a point during the night when she'd thought it was all a dream. But no, there sitting in the shed was the aeroplane. A 1943 Spitfire Mark Vc.

Two rooms down the hallway, Tom pushed back the door to Don's room. 'How's it goin', mate?' he asked, placing the teacup on the dresser.

Don stood at the window and stared into the front yard. 'Good. Good,' he replied, but he appeared agitated. He wrung his fingers backwards and forwards in the manner of a childhood game. He moved away and sat back on the bed, the sleeves of his pyjamas falling over his hands as he did so.

'Cup of tea for you there, mate.'

Don acknowledged the cup, then began an inaudible discussion with himself.

'There's a lot of money sitting in that yard, Don,' Tom began. 'Enough to set us up somewhere. What do you think?'

Don reached for his tea, and then moved back to his position by the bedroom window. He was in the same room as the one he remembered from last night. And Tom was here.

'We could get a little flat together up at Surfers,' Tom continued patiently. 'Do a bit of fishin'. What do you reckon, Don?'

'Did you remember to put some cold water in my tea?'

Tom sighed. 'Yes, mate, I put some cold water in your tea . . . You know, Don, you can't ignore that stuff out there. It's not gonna just go away.'

The more he pressed his friend on the point, the more elusive Don became. Maybe it was nothing, maybe he genuinely couldn't remember. But it was obviously upsetting for Don, so Tom changed the subject. 'Hey, I spoke to Paul last night. He's coming down this morning, to see how you are.'

'Paul?' That seemed like a good idea. One thing he did remember was that the car needed servicing.

'Now, Don, he's going to want to take you back. Back to the flat in Bondi. But . . . well, it's nice here, don't you think? And I was thinking maybe you'd want to stay on a bit and catch your breath.' Tom looked out the window now and saw that Emily had taken her cup of tea out into the front garden. 'I mean, you don't want to be in too much of a hurry to get back to that nursing home, eh?'

Emily stood in front of the stack of crates and assorted debris and wondered what she'd let herself in for. Having Tom to stay was one thing, but Don was another story. She'd seen Jock through his final weeks and now recognised the signs. She turned the leaves in the bottom of her teacup as a fortune teller might, then walked to the machinery shed and rolled back the doors.

The plane was definitely the real McCoy. There was no mistaking it. Some parts of it looked new, others like something you'd find at the wrecker's. She ran her fingers along the outside of the cowling and thought back to another time. A time in which she'd been able to tell the compression ratios of the engine she was now looking at.

'A mechanic? You've gotta be jokin'.' Dave Rowley watched pinwheels turning petrol into pennies. 'Don't you read the papers? It's 1946. War's over, sweetheart. I got half a dozen blokes out there lookin' at this job. Why would I give it to you?'

'Because I'm qualified, and I'm more than capable.'

'Is that right?' He placed the nozzle back into the bowser then pulled his hands across the bum of his overalls. 'Well, how about throwin' that tyre onto the back of the tray then?'

Emily took in the truck, the heavy metal rim, and the tyre that encased it. She would not give him the satisfaction of trying.

'Why don't you try your local area? Somebody you know might give you a go.' He gave a smile that said 'I'm sorry,' and cranked over the truck motor.

Everybody had told her she was wasting her time. She would have given up weeks ago but she'd persisted out of stubbornness.

'Sounds like the timing chain, Mr Rowley.' She shook her head and walked out onto Parramatta Road.

So now it was back to Wilson's drapery. Wilson's drapery, next to the park which was next to the school which was a five-minute walk from home. Wilson's drapery. Wilson's Drapery and Manchester on Smith Street, where she'd gone with her mother on so many occasions to buy fabric for curtains and ribbons for dresses. It had come to this.

Mr Wilson looked old, but he probably wasn't. Maybe it was the inside of the store that made him look old. It seemed to have a funereal feel, with a smell of camphor and oiled timber cabinets – perhaps even formaldehyde.

'Well, if it isn't little Emily Taylor.' Mr Wilson came to life. 'Well, not so little anymore. Looking for anything in particular?'

'A job.' She smiled a shopkeeper's smile and wondered what it would be like to live with Jock in the country.

Turps ran alongside the driver's side door, choking as he gasped for air through the dust. For Paul it had been one hell of a trip, and now he had some crazy dog to deal with. The car was badly in need of a service, and the radio so old it was tuned into Europe. As the Volkswagen came to a halt, the dog broke through the cloud of dust and made towards the verandah, where it fell, tongue flagging, into the cool earth that lay beneath the decking. Paul extinguished a joint and wound down the window.

A haze of smoke hung heavy across the yard, and through it the remnants of a fleeing army began to emerge. Pieces lay where they fell. The dope might've had something to do with it, but the scene reminded him of a diorama he saw during a school excursion to the

War Museum in Canberra. A battlefield of waste and carnage with a painted sky.

And there, emerging from the trenches now, was Tom, wearing an officer's cap. He coughed as he advanced through the smoke pushing a wheelbarrow full of gas masks.

'G'day, Paul,' he called. 'Barbie's a bit out of control, mate. Must be the wrong kinda wood.' He pointed to the source of the smoke. 'City wood seems to burn better than country wood. Perfect timing on your part, though. Lunch is all but served.'

Paul stepped out of the car and looked around for his old man. 'Bit out of the way for a disposal store, Tom. Maybe you ought to put a sign out on the road.'

'You reckon?' Tom pictured the sign, but dismissed the idea as being too small-time.

'Well, you weren't kidding about there being a lot of stuff,' Paul said, indicating the collection on the lawn. He peered into the shed. 'But I don't recall you mentioning anything about a plane.'

'Didn't I? Must've slipped my mind. Yep. It's the retirement package, all right.' Tom tipped the gas masks out onto a space on the lawn and put the wheelbarrow down. 'Your dad's been waiting for you,' he said, pointing towards the verandah outside the kitchen. 'And I want you to meet an old friend of mine.'

Over on the verandah, Emily waved at the new arrival and watched the two men as they headed across the front yard. Maybe the aeroplane was Tom's big chance, she thought. Something to gamble everything on. She'd had her big chance, and her grandchildren were the proof of it.

She looked over to Don now, who was dozing in the midday sun in one of her winged chairs, a travel rug wrapped around him. 'Well, look who's here,' Emily said gently, before opening the flyscreen door and returning to the kitchen. He lifted his head at the sound of her voice.

'G'day, Pop . . .' Paul's handshake developed into a hug. 'God, I've been worried about you. You all right?'

'Yeah, yeah, I'm good. I'm good. Best I've been for ages actually.'

'Where's Emily, Don?' Tom removed his cap and joined them on the verandah. Don looked across to her empty chair. 'Never mind, mate. I'll see if she's inside.'

Paul settled into the seat next to Don and briefly eyed the table in front of them. It was tempting to revert to his school teacher role, but at the same time he couldn't stop thinking about how ludicrous the situation was. 'Now, Tom tells me you hitched a ride out here. Is that right?'

'It's all a big mix-up. Such a mess . . .' Don tried to explain about God and Elvis the rifleman, but it all came out wrong.

'That's okay, Pop,' Paul said, seeing his father's distress. 'Don't worry about it now. We'll piece it all together later.' He leant well forward and placed his hand on his father's knee. 'I even had the cops out looking for you, you know?'

'The cops?'

The creaking of the screen door grabbed their attention. They looked up to see Tom stepping through from the kitchen, followed by Emily. Balanced between the two were various condiments, a salad and a plate of sausages.

'I thought you men might be hungry by now,' Emily said. The silver teapot also made an appearance. 'Tom was responsible for the sausages,' she added by way of an apology.

'They'll be fine. Proves they're barbecued,' Tom replied, before stopping to introduce their host. 'Paul, this is Emily.'

Paul stood up and shook her by the hand. 'Emily, I just want to say how grateful –'

'Oh, don't you worry about that, Paul,' she said quickly. 'Now, Don's told me all about you. Haven't you, Don?'

Don couldn't remember any such conversation, but seemed to accept the situation all the same. He beckoned her across the table. 'Paul reckons the police are lookin' for me.'

'Doesn't surprise me,' Tom chimed in as he helped himself to a sausage. 'Doesn't surprise me one bit!' He winked at his old friend but wasn't surprised to find that the joke simply drew a blank.

Don settled back into his chair and began thinking about his past . . .

'Tom's only joking. Just ignore him, Don.' With the unfolding of a napkin, Emily adopted a more formal tone. 'I'm glad you could make it down today, Paul. I've been a bit short on testers, so I've had to make up a few of the results.'

'Testers?'

'Exactly.' She placed a card on the table. 'So, Paul, what do you think of this tea? Would you say it was: *A, full-flavoured*; *B, mellow*; or *C, bland*? And would you buy it again?'

Paul returned the fine-bone china cup to its saucer and took a deep breath. 'Jeez . . . I don't know really. I mean, it just tastes like tea to me.'

'Okay, we'll go for *B, mellow* . . . and let's say you *would* buy it again. A little encouragement can go a long way,' she said with a smile. She then ticked the appropriate boxes and placed the card in an envelope. 'The sooner I send it, the sooner they send out the next lot of samples, which will be . . .' Her eyes scanned the letter that had come with the tea. '*Breakfast cereals*. Mmm, that sounds good. Will you be here for breakfast, Paul?'

'Um . . . I don't think so, Emily. Thanks, but I have to be back for work.'

'That's a shame, because I understand you're a bit of a singer. The drama society's looking for a male lead at the moment. Could be a good break.'

'Is that right?' Paul Cameron looked down at his sausages and wondered what he'd walked into.

Don woke in the bedroom. The afternoon sun lit up the edges of a drawn curtain. Paul was talking to him.

'I'm sorry, Pop. You're going to have to go back.'

Paul moved around to the side of the bed and sat on his haunches. 'You could stay at my place. In fact, I'd really like that. I'll get some help in – you know, with the cooking, that sort of thing.'

Don shook his head from side to side. 'It's all a mix-up. Tom knows what's happening . . . I can't leave Tom. He knows all about it.'

'Knows what?' Paul asked, confused.

'You know, about me staying on here for a bit.'

'All right, Pop. I'll have a chat to Tom.' He reassured his father with a smile, then closed the door behind him and walked back out to the verandah.

Emily had cleared away the remains of the lunch and replaced it with her embroidery. With the sound of the screen door opening came the final patch of blue that made up her patterned sky. 'How's he going?' she asked as Paul returned to his seat.

'Oh, fine. He'll be right for the trip back.'

'The trip back?' Emily looked up and over to Tom, whose attention was likewise diverted from the pages of the *Grenfell Record*.

'Well, obviously he can't stay here,' Paul began.

Emily returned to her needlework. 'Tom tells me he's going to have all this stuff packed away by the end of the week . . . Isn't that right, Tom?' She stitched the coloured thread through the material. 'And as long as he's here, then Don may as well stay too.' She was thinking about Jock as she spoke, about her decision to put him into a home. She'd carried that for a long time. It was obvious Don wasn't well, but it was just old age, another stage of life. Something to be celebrated.

'I think it would be easier for everyone if he comes back with me,' Paul said firmly.

'For everyone?' She caught his eye. 'Paul, I respect that you're all he's got left in the way of family – believe me, I do. But have you asked Don what he wants to do?'

Paul already knew the answer to that. The last thing he wanted to do was place him somewhere against his will, especially after the disaster at the nursing home. 'Well, you're not really all that well set up here for . . . well, you know.'

'No, who? The elderly?' Emily looked at him over her glasses. 'What could possibly happen that hasn't happened already?'

'Ummm . . .'

'Exactly.' She went back to her needlework. 'If he needs specialist care, the hospital is just down the road.'

Paul could see the sense in it. Perhaps it would be best if his Dad did stay, at least till he got things sorted back home. And Tom and Emily would take good care of him. He leant on the railing and looked across to Tom. 'How long's it going to take to sort all this?'

'I dunno. Not long. Coupla weeks, kinda thing. Coupla loads to the tip, maybe.'

'The tip?' Emily interrupted. 'If you're going to the tip you can take the rubbish behind the tank.'

'No problem, Em.' He continued with the plan. 'Then I get the auction people down here to sort out the plane and whatever's left, and that's it. Don can come back with me in the ute. All solved.' For Tom, life was simple. As far as he was concerned, Don was on the road to recovery; if he needed specialist care, then Tom and Em probably weren't far behind him – and that certainly wasn't the case.

'Goodo.' Emily held up her needlework. 'What do you think, Paul?'

Paul didn't know what to think.

'It's a stag with a waterfall in the background. Anyone can see that. You just have to step back a bit.'

Paul drove away from the property with a plate of Gladwrapped sandwiches and a thermos of tea. There was no point arguing with Tom and Emily, not that that had been his intention. The plan had obviously been put in place before he'd arrived. It was the best outcome, really, and it did take the pressure off him for a bit. He'd come back the following week and see how Pop was travelling. When he was back in the city he'd pull into the nursing home and tell them Don was staying with relatives for the rest of the week.

As he dug a roach out of the ashtray, Paul was suddenly alerted to the sound of air-horns. A semi-trailer was heading directly for him on the narrow driveway. He swerved off the road and onto a long-grassed verge that might have once been a garden bed. In the time it took to get back onto the drive the semi had all but disappeared into a cloud of yellow dust. Tom's on the case, he thought, must be an interested party.

As a courtesy to his fellow motorist, Dave Blainey had acknowledged the 'beetle driver' with a wave on the way past. But he shook his head and muttered 'Death traps' – cars like that shouldn't be on the road. He paused 'Viva Las Vegas' on the ten-stacker, then shunted through the gears until he reached the front yard. Then, in a mark of showmanship, he pulled up the *Lisa Marie* just short of the front verandah.

As the truck exhaled a long, slow hiss, Tom waved an envelope in the air and came down the stairs. 'Sorry to have missed you before, Dave,' he said. 'Been burning a hole in my pocket.'

'Waaaay back! Way back. Git in the back,' yelled Dave as the dog leapt from the cab to the ground then back up into the truck again. 'G'day, Tom,' he said as he accepted the envelope. 'No worries. Thought I'd better settle up now – won't be back this way for a while. We don't want these things draggin' on now, do we? "Takin' Care of Business" is what it's about.' He opened the envelope and silently counted the cash. 'How's the old fella doin'?'

'Fine, just fine.'

Emily came out and was about to ask him in for a cuppa, but Dave beat her to it with a 'gotta keep movin', it's a trucker's life' speech.

As he turned to climb back into the cab, Dave spotted the plane. 'Is that for real?'

'You bet.'

'Jeez, if I'd known that, I might have been a bit more careful,' Dave joked. 'Mind if I have a squizz?'

'Help yourself.' Tom joined him as they walked around the fuselage.

'She's a classic all right,' enthused Dave, as he checked his watch and headed back to the semi.

'Don't forget to give us a call if you need 'er moved again. I'll be seein' ya.'

Tom laughed. 'You never know,' he said and shooed the chooks away from the back wheels as Dave negotiated the tight turn that led to the driveway. 'Got some interesting theories on life, that bloke, Em.' He looked up to the verandah but Emily had disappeared.

Even before Dave had put the *Lisa Marie* tyres onto the bitumen, he was on the phone to Todd Davitt. 'Todd, remember that stuff I was telling you about, the war bric-a-brac? Well, it just got a lot bigger.'

'What are you talking about?' Todd slipped on his thongs and stepped out of his caravan. It was raining in Kiama, a kind of English drizzle that matched the surrounding countryside. He held the mobile hard to his ear as he walked towards the van park's shower block. 'A plane? What kind of plane?'

'I dunno, mate. An old plane. A propeller plane. You know, from the war.'

Todd thought back to the last time they spoke. 'What else did you say this bloke had?'

Dave pictured the stuff he'd loaded onto the semi from the warehouse. 'I dunno, everything – parachutes, old engine parts, gas masks, you name it.'

Todd stopped walking and started thinking. 'Was it all boxed up?'

'Might have been once. Some of it still is.' Dave held the phone with his shoulder as he pulled up the rig just short of Emily's letterbox. 'Lots of aeroplane bits, far as I could tell.'

Todd's mind began to race. Could it be? After all this time? It couldn't have all disappeared – it had to be somewhere.'Grenfell, you say?'

'Yeah. The Cowra side.' There was a silence on the other end as Dave pulled the semi onto the highway. 'Hey, Todd, ya still there?'

'Yeah, mate, just thinking what to do.' He looked back to the van. 'I'll see what Fran wants to do.' Fran Davitt was similar in age and stature to Todd, a little shorter maybe and perhaps a little more worn around the edges. She was sitting under the van's annexe with her arms tightly folded, looking more than a little irritated. 'Thanks, mate – I reckon we might be ready to move on. Grenfell could be just the thing.'

Evening fell on chump chops and Tom's sparkling wine. Emily retired early, suddenly feeling very weary, and hoping she hadn't shown too much bravado in her reassurances to Paul about Don staying on. She sat up in bed with a book on aphids and the rose, but it was another one that she was thinking of. One that dealt with the inner workings of the hydraulic pump, with header tanks and crank shafts to follow; one whose fold-out centre pages provided a detachable, fully detailed cross-section of an aircraft engine. She marked the chapter entitled 'Aphid Sprays? Yes or No' with a piece of ribbon, then spread the diagram of the V12 Merlin engine across her quilt.

Chapter Sixteen

The early morning light picked its way across the lawn in long stitches that ultimately led to the machinery shed. Inside, Emily ran her fingers along the underside of the aircraft fuselage and contemplated what lay within. Mountings. Engine bearers. Engine bearer attachments. Exhaust stubs.

She followed the engine cowling down to a gaping mouth that extruded from under the plane, and pictured pipes that force-fed air to ducts that led to carburettors. Out of curiosity she loosened an access panel that fell to the concrete floor. At first she thought she might have pulled it too hard, and blamed her arthritic fingers, but on closer inspection the hinges had corroded. She wondered with a sigh if this was an indication of how the rest of the plane might be. On the back of an old exercise book she began to make a list. A trip down to Wayne at the hardware store was in order.

*

Later, the three of them set off into Grenfell in Emily's red Laser. Ahead of them, on the eastern side of town, just before Hospital Hill, a sign came into view. Much thought, even a competition, had gone into its wording: *GRENFELL – a poet's home, a bushranger's haunt.*

Tom gazed at the words and tried to think of a Lawson poem, but none came to mind. 'I thought he came from Mudgee, Em.'

'Who?' came the reply.

'Henry Lawson. I thought he came from Mudgee.'

In the back of the car, a phrase popped into Don's mind about a bloke who 'went a-drovin'. He tried to remember where it came from, but only that phrase kept surfacing.

The insect legs that elevated the sign above the fence line disappeared behind the car.

'Lived in Mudgee,' Emily said. 'But born in Grenfell.' Her attention was still firmly on the highway. 'That's the important bit, Tom. You can live anywhere but you have to be *born* somewhere.' She emphasised that with a determined look and a little acceleration.

The tone of Emily's voice had left no room for discussion. He was obviously in Lawson country. Tom made a mental note to get a few of the great man's lines down in case somebody asked him.

Emily turned right where the old picture theatre used to be. She knew all the houses and their occupants, past and present. She could even tell you about the families whose names had been chiselled into the cenotaph on Main Street. It wasn't that she'd intended to spend most of her life in Grenfell when she moved back there with

Jock after the war – it just sort of happened that way. Anyway, she'd had as good a life with Jock as anybody could want, as she often pointed out.

The red Laser continued its journey, eventually passing the Catholic presbytery before pulling into the BP station.

'"We'll all be 'rooned" said Hanrahan,
In accents most forlorn,
Outside the church ere Mass began
One frosty Sunday morn.'

'There you go,' exclaimed Tom with a grin catching himself and Emily unawares. 'Lawson! Remembered that from school.'

Emily's mind flicked through the *Collected Works*. 'Are you sure?' she asked doubtfully. She stopped the car at a petrol pump and wound down the window.

'Afternoon, Em.' Gary Preston acknowledged her from his island of bowsers. 'Bit early in the day for you to be out.' He lowered himself down to the driver's window. 'And how are you, Tom? Gary.' He pointed to the name stitched onto his shirt. 'Remember? You came in for directions.'

'Oh, yeah. Yeah, that's right. How are you, Gary?'

Gary leant in to Emily and the conversation took on a more conspiratorial tone. He nodded towards the shop. 'I've put a couple of cans of that beef aside for you, Em. That brand you like. Special order.'

Emily took a deep breath, smiled tightly, then stepped

out of the car and opened the boot. 'I need a bit of work done on this.'

'What is it?'

'A radio access panel. You can see the hinges have just about given out.'

'Looks pretty old,' said Gary, picking it up. 'What's it off?'

'An aeroplane.'

'An aeroplane, eh?' Gary examined it more thoroughly. 'Can't say I've seen many of these before. In fact I can't say I've seen any.' He wanted to ask more about it, but could see Tom waiting inside by the cash register. 'No worries, Em – I'll have it ready in a coupla days.'

Emily tapped the side window as she returned to the car. 'How you goin' there, Don? Don't worry, we haven't forgotten you.'

Don paused to collect his bearings. 'Fine. Yep, I'm fine, thanks.' He sat as Jock might have sat, low and hunched forward with the seat belt holding him in position. 'How about you?'

Emily laughed. 'Yep. I'm fine too.' A one-way conversation continued via the rear-vision mirror. 'You know, I really hate the way he knows what I eat. It's only a little thing, but it can get you down – part of living in a small town, I guess. The moment you tell somebody something, everybody knows.'

'Here you go.' Tom appeared with a new pair of fluoros. Blue this time. He removed the packaging and passed the glasses back to Don.

'Very tasteful,' said Emily. 'Very Elton John.'

Don had forgotten exactly why he was waiting in the back of the car. His mind was all tied up with things. Nothing specific, nothing he could explain. He heard Emily's voice reassuring him that all was well. 'Goodo,' he replied, and as he did, his thoughts suddenly came together and he whispered to himself:

'He's left us in dejection now;
Our hearts with his are roving
It's dull on this selection now,
Since Andy's gone a-drovin'

They continued on to where the 'old part' of town turned into the new part. 'I thought I might have a bit of a fiddle with the plane,' Emily said casually, interrupting her own commentary on the sights around them. 'Just while you're sorting out your stuff . . . and that's the Post Office. And that's Margaret Prendergast with her three under-fives.' She waved a cheerio. 'Moved here from the city after her husband left her.' There were positive things about a country town, she acknowledged. The whole community had pitched in to get Margaret back onto her feet. 'Anyway, I thought the plane might be worth more if it looked a bit more together. What do you think?'

'Sure. If you can be bothered.' In his mind, Tom pictured Emily's front yard. It was full of people, all vying for the auctioneer's attention as his gavel hung poised in the air.

'And the Memorial Park, where we recirculate the water. Keeps the gardens fresh and alive.'

It was the town itself that was dying. It had been on its last legs since the gold ran out in 1890. Wheat and wool kept the district alive now, but the town was in decline. Giant monoliths that once were banks now held only curiosity value. The Western Stores, with its flash labels and uniformed staff, was now a Co-op. Even the town clock ran a few minutes behind the rest of the district. About the only thing left was the grain silo, but since the closure of the railway line, even that was under threat.

'Just need to grab a few things from the hardware,' said Emily as she pulled into the kerb. At least parking wasn't a problem here – except, of course, for the Lawson weekend. Emily took a list from her bag and disappeared behind a wall of lawnmowers on the footpath outside the shop.

The butchers shop was next door. In its window was a cardboard cut-out of Ginger Rogers and Fred Astaire gliding across a meat tray. Tom climbed out of the car to read the handwritten poster that accompanied them.

'G'day. How's it goin'?' The butcher put down the phone and waved him into the doorway. 'Tom, isn't it? Staying out at Emily's place?'

'Yeah, that's right, Tom. Tom Barton.' He stretched out his hand. 'Word gets around pretty quick.'

'No secrets in our town, Tom,' the smiling butcher replied. 'Merv. Merv Hughes. It's Dave actually, but everyone calls me Merv.' He clicked his tongue as he put imaginary bat to ball. 'Hear you're rebuilding an old plane out there. Good idea. A museum that'll put this place back on the map.'

A museum? Tom envisaged the aeroplane in Emily's shed, as tourist coaches filled the bottom paddock. The thought of an admission price brought him back to the poster. He stepped back to read it.

Olde Time Dance, first Tuesday of every month.
12.30 pm. Community Centre.
All Welcome. Admission Free.
Ladies, a plate.

He woke Don by giving the car door a good slam as he got back in. 'What's the date today, mate?' He placed a kilo of sausages on the dash and watched Em at the checkout. Under her arm was a socket set and a can of WD40.

The car knew its own way home. Usually, by the time Emily had got to the cenotaph her thoughts would have usually drifted into a game of bowls, or what she might wear to the next Red Cross meeting. Today, however, it was superchargers. The air-to-fuel ratio had to be exact, of course. And then there was the intercooler, and the lines that led from it – they would all need to be flushed. Which took her to the hydraulics, which naturally led to the undercarriage, and the air/oil shock absorbers. And mnemonics. E.R.R. – Examine, Repair and Replace – long-lost prompts that, once rediscovered, could not be erased.

The smell of sizzling sausages wafting down the hallway was overtaken by the smell of naphthalene. In one of the two empty bedrooms – Jane's old room – Emily held a pair of mechanic's overalls against her dress. They were old, but well preserved, rusty around the buckles, but the creases were still in the pants. Across one side of the front, faded military lettering made up her maiden name. She'd definitely put on weight since she'd last worn them. Still, that was what the buttons were for. She hung the overalls on a hanger then followed the smell of Tom's cooking back down the hall.

'What's Don doing?' she asked as she went into the kitchen. Through the screen door she could see him pacing the yard. 'It'll be dark in a minute.'

'Who knows?' Tom shrugged. 'Just got the wanders, I guess.'

With deliberate steps Don made his way around the fence line of the garden. It was his breathing that he was listening to. He'd never thought much about his body before. It was always there, it always worked. But now things were starting to fail. His memory was the most frustrating. He stopped in the middle of the yard and concentrated once more on listening to his body. But it was a piano that he heard. It filtered through the trees and entered his body with each breath. Schubert. A beautiful classical piece. A piece that Bernadette knew by heart.

Tom flipped the sausages, then leant out the window. 'Hey, Don, tea's up, mate! Your favourite!'

Don stood transfixed by the concerto. He waited for the final movement then looked towards the house. The shortest way back was to cut across the front of the shed. But the aeroplane was there and that would have meant crossing in front of it. He turned back to the fence and took the long way around.

By eight o'clock a cask of red had replaced the vase of flowers as the centrepiece of the table. Dinner had been a formal affair with Emily taking particular care with linen napkins, padded placemats, and silver cutlery from the 'good' drawer. On his fourth glass Tom had proclaimed himself to be a 'valuer of antiquity' and had suggested that the kitchen clock might be worth a bit – and that his associate might like to have a look at it. Don's skill as a watchmaker had come up as part of the evening's conversation.

Don simply nodded, as he had done for much of the evening, and on any given topic.

'No worries, Don. I might have a bit of a look at it myself.' Tom reached over and shook the cask.

'Don't worry, Don, he's not going near it. Not in his state.' Emily changed the subject. 'Let's play the other side.' She turned the record over and placed the needle onto the track. 'I don't know much about art – or in this case, music – but I do know what I like. Isn't that what they say?' A boxed set of classical favourites had been a gift from one of the girls. 'I really should play them more often. Don't you think?'

'Yeah, I'm always playin' mine. Got the same box.' Tom squeezed the last drops from the bag then helped himself to another sausage.

The music took Don into his other world. He closed his eyes for a time and listened to Bernadette playing in the next room. He looked down to see his old workbench, his tools of the trade, the small leather pillow he kept his 'bits' on, a clean polishing cloth. He reached over to his tools tray and removed a butter knife, then carefully inserted it into a crack that split the clock's housing. He removed his glasses and polished them with a napkin as his father and grandfather had done before him, then brought the clock's movement into focus. 'Fuse wire,' he said. 'A small piece of fuse wire will fix it.'

Emily dug around in a kitchen drawer and found some wire.

Don placed it beside the clock. He then did up the top button of his pyjamas and began shaping the piece of wire.

The next day began with an early start. It was going to be a big job – Emily knew that. A block and tackle would be required, and supports for the wings. There was now a purpose to the day, a chance to rediscover lost skills.

Inside the machinery shed, wiring diagrams and sketches of engine components covered a large desk that had arrived with the 'job lot'. At her feet was a case of her old engineering manuals, complete with margins full of notes she'd made half a century before. She rolled open a cutaway plan of longerons and frames and spread it across the table. Amid thoughts of retraction jacks and oil pipes, Emily thought about the kitchen clock. It had to have been ten years since that clock had stopped. Its hands had read a quarter to twelve since . . . Well, for as long as she could remember. And now it had been restarted. It was as though it had been given a second lease. Maybe it was the same with her. In her overalls she no longer felt seventy-whatevershewas. She didn't feel nineteen, but she felt pretty good.

Emily began a search for bolts that held wings to frames and clips that attached hoses to radiators. She'd worked on similar aircraft packed this way, aircraft that had been shipped from England, assembled for flight, then ferried to their final destinations. The reassembly wasn't that difficult; it was the making sure that everything still worked that required skill.

Outside the shed, Don remained in his own world, distancing himself from the plane and the slowly diminishing pile of surplus. Tom tried to encourage his involvement by pointing out an earlier discovery. 'There ya go, Don, why don't you see if you can get that going while I give Emily a hand?'

'It's rubbish,' Don replied, shaking his head and backing into the middle of the yard. 'It'll never work. We'll all be killed and the house'll burn down and I'll be back in the nursing home. It's a fire trap. An electrical fire trap.'

Tom remained optimistic. 'Don't be ridiculous, mate. You haven't even plugged it in yet. It looks hardly used.' The film projector sat in a metal box and, from the outside at least, it looked to be complete. Somewhere in the pile was the rest of it. Somewhere there were rusted cans and leather satchels.

Don wheelbarrowed the box to a shaded area beside the shed and for the rest of the morning fiddled around with electrical tape, pieces of cut-up extension cord and anything else he could find from Jock's old wiring collection.

'Whaddya reckon about Chinese for tea?' Tom reeled chains through pulleys in an effort to free up the rusted lifting system. 'We could grab some takeaway in town.'

The thing about the Chinese was it wasn't Chinese. Bruce and Gail Taylor ran it. They were retirees from Sydney, and it didn't much matter to them what the cuisine was. They were just interested in a small business that was out of the city.

'And I was just saying to Don that maybe we should take in a movie as well,' Tom continued. 'Chinese, then the flicks. We could all have a night out. One goes, all go.'

'A movie?' Emily hadn't been to a cinema in years.

'Yeah.'

'At Cowra, you mean.'

'Yeah . . . Cowra.'

'Umm . . . It's a bit of a drive, Tom.' Emily pictured the unlit miles of road between the two towns.

'It's supposed to be a good 'un – comedy. What was that film called, Don?'

'Hmmm?' Don replied.

'Anyway, it's supposed to be pretty funny.'

'Are you sure? We can always get a video.' Emily couldn't recall the last time she'd been to the movies. It would have been with Jock, of course, and it would have been a big deal, in the dress circle, with an ice cream and a car rug.

'No point sittin' at home, Em,' Tom said with a laugh. 'Time's a-tickin' away.'

At the BP garage Gary Preston flicked between the pages of *Penthouse* and the collected works of Henry Lawson. It was a big call: Cindy on page 37 or 'The Loaded Dog' on 29. The English teacher at the high school usually did the 'Birthplace readings', but this year Bob was giving the festival the flick and heading up north. So the duty had fallen to Gary. He consoled himself with the thought that he wouldn't have to be brilliant or anything; it was mostly a home crowd.

'Pump four, thanks, mate.'

Gary looked up to see an elderly man standing with his back to him. He wore a knitted cardigan and a faded cap and was showing particular interest in the part that Emily had dropped in for repair. 'You don't see many of them about. One for the enthusiast.' He punched pump four into the computer. 'That'll be fifty bucks or near enough.'

The man ran a finger around the metal frame.

'Belongs to an old girl on the Cowra Road,' Gary added. 'Gunna be part of a museum display. It'll put this town on the map for sure.'

'Really?' The man took a pair of reading glasses from his top pocket and examined the piece more carefully. He then pulled a wallet out of his back pocket and handed him a fifty. 'Is there a caravan park around here somewhere?'

'On the Forbes Road, west of town. You can't miss it. You'd be lucky to get a spot, mind. What with the festival and everything. Tell Barry that Gary sent you down. He'll find somethin' for you.'

'Thanks, mate.'

'No worries.' Gary returned the smile and thought no more about it. He switched on the driveway lights and turned his attention to page 37.

The moon crested over Emily's house. It wasn't quite full, but it wasn't far off it. In the kitchen, empty plastic containers told of Tom's early tea. All over by six. Sweet and sour pork, rice and something, and a market research tea. Perfect.

Emily stood on the front verandah and peered into the night. She'd taken longer to get ready then she normally did. She'd chosen a dress that her daughters had bought for her not long after Jock had died. And the comb she had in her hair was from a time before Jock. She looked at her watch, then stepped onto the lawn. The boys were nowhere to be seen. Even if they left now, they were going to miss the opening.

In the moonlight the aeroplane appeared to be almost airborne. The crate had been cleared away and the fuselage suspended by Tom's block and tackle. Wings sat on trestles stretched out across the entrance to the shed. Emily rested her handbag on the tailplane and retrieved her car keys.

'This way, Em!' Tom's voice came from the tennis court.

'We're going to be late,' she warned. Group travel – hopeless. She followed a waving torch to the wire gate.

'He made me do it.' Don stood at the gate, wearing an old military jacket. In the light he could have passed for an aging dictator of some tinpot republic. His bobbing torch eventually discovered Tom on centre court.

'It's . . . *Showtime*!' Tom stepped into the light. His arms opened in a grand gesture that encompassed a trio of decaying deckchairs, a pile of blankets and a maze of electrical cords that fed into a vintage film projector.

On cue the bulb burst into life. Belts travelled around pulleys, sprockets pulled film past the gate, and patriotic music crackled into the night. On a sheet secured to the court's wire fence came the opening credits: *Hell in the Pacific!*

'That romantic comedy,' Tom said with a grin, 'it didn't quite make it in time for the screening. But this is what it's all about, Em. A good sea drama.' He rubbed his hands together then motioned her to take a seat.

She looked to Don who'd taken up a position with the garden hose. 'Are you sure it's safe?'

'Absolutely. Don't worry about him, he worries about everything, don't you, Don.' Tom began distributing blankets onto the seats. 'Come on, mate,' he called to Don, patting the chair beside him, then turned to Emily. 'Malteser?'

The projector whirred away. Within the confines of the tennis court the Americans could do no wrong. Women waited and men fought. Black and white sea battles came to life with a breeze that whistled through the pines and rippled across the sheet that held the images.

By the end of the first reel Don was ready for bed. The film was hard to hear, made little sense to him and he realised it was now unlikely that the projector would blow up.

The second reel may well have come from another film. Not that it mattered. The stars sat low over the wire fence and the blankets kept out the cold.

Chapter Seventeen

In the light of day the tennis court had returned to its previous form. The cinema had vanished, as if it had all been an illusion. A trick of the night. Emily stood at Jock's old workbench and wondered if she'd been tricked into thinking the evening was something more than it was.

'Good as a bought one.' Tom's voice came from under the wing. A length of pipe gave extra leverage to a spanner that tightened wing spars to beams. 'No worries about that.'

Emily dismissed her thoughts as foolish and began thumbing her way through one of her old aircraft manuals as if it were a recipe book. Occasionally she'd write in a margin, then turn back to the index for something she might have forgotten.

'A couple more loads off to the tip and that's the end of the rubbish,' Tom said chirpily. Emily looked to the clothesline. Tom's definition of rubbish was obviously different from hers. 'You think?' She gathered up some loose pages and took them to the plane.

'Oh, yeah . . . Now, I hope you're still on for the dance this arvo, Em.' He crawled out from under the wing, grimaced in anticipation, then slowly straightened his back. 'Could be good.'

'It'll be a waste of time,' Emily replied as she made a closer inspection of the wheel bays. 'It's for older people.' She noted with satisfaction that the perished Dunlops still appeared to be holding air. 'Older than us, I mean.' And with that she released the landing gear, which dropped to a vertical position and locked into place.

Chains rattled through pulleys as the Spitfire began to settle under its own weight. The wings stretched across the entrance to the shed and the propeller reached high above them, but now it was beginning to look like the diagram on page 57. Emily dog-eared the page for future reference before standing back to admire their handiwork. 'Do you see the beauty in this, Tom? Or is it just me? The beauty in things mechanical, I mean.'

'The beauty in things mechanical? Jeez, Em, I reckon you might be spending a bit too much time with that festival crowd.' He ducked to avoid the oily rag she threw at him.

'You have to agree, it does have beautiful lines.'

For the first time Tom really looked at the plane and saw what Emily saw. 'Yep, it's definitely got something.' He thought about the line of the *Dolce Bella*. He was about to say, I had a boat like that once, but that seemed such a long time ago, and a part of another life.

'Beautiful lines means deep pockets' was what came out. 'But back to the dance . . . I still think we should go this arvo. It's just a one-off – Don and I'll be gone before the next one comes around.'

It was one o'clock in the afternoon and Emily found herself watching a man she didn't know playing 'Your Cheatin' Heart' on an electric organ. He wore a white shirt with a black tie and black trousers, and sometimes sang the lyrics to the song in a cheesy baritone. He looked hot. Between chords, one hand mopped a handkerchief across his brow. Scattered across the top of the organ were cardboard cards with the names 'Kia-Ora', 'Balmoral', and 'Traci Leigh'. With a suitable flourish of fingers he finished the song, shuffled back into the dance cards, then returned to the microphone. 'Gentlemen, take your partners for "The Vanity Waltz".'

'Hello, Emily.' Pat Mooney was the building's caretaker and, for the day's event, the doorman. His association with the Community Centre was purely geographic, as he lived opposite, and was always at home, so he was entrusted with the key. A man in his seventies, he had a lopsided smile that had become more so in his latter years. A white dust coat covered a suit and tie. 'Pretty good turn-out don't you reckon?' he said, looking around. 'Still, it all depends on the weather.' As he spoke, he produced a timetable and a fobwatch.

Emily placed her handbag on a chair and looked across the room. Couples regrouped, and soon perms and pearls, white shirts and pleated dresses, thin belts and gold shoes were setting off around the hall. She'd always imagined these afternoon dances were a prisoner's holiday for the residents of the local nursing home, but there were people she didn't know. People from Cowra, and maybe even Forbes. Some of them looked as though they could have danced competitively in their younger days.

'Nothin' now till 5.46.' Pat marked his timetable with a pencil. 'Got to sidetrack a goods train for the Coonamble express. Terrible mess if the line's not clear.'

Emily imagined the carnage. 'Indeed.' She beckoned Tom and Don over and introduced them. 'These are two friends of mine. Pat used to be the stationmaster, boys. Forty years of service.'

Pat's smile added another ten. 'Just sayin' to Em that the turn-out's pretty good.'

Everyone agreed.

Don missed Pat's last remark but picked up on Emily's mention of the number forty and figured it was a cue for something to do with his age. 'I'm seventy-seven,' he told the retired stationmaster.

'Ah, same age as me then. We're probably the youngsters here today,' Pat said, gently nudging Don. 'Come and meet Beatrice. She's ninety-two.' He took Don by the arm and led him across the dance floor.

Beatrice looked ninety-two. Behind her crumbling facade deep blue eyes followed his. 'I like to watch,' was her only comment.

On the road outside, Lynton McCabe was returning

from a successful sales meeting at the Caragabal County Club. He recognised Emily's car parked in the Community Centre car park and pulled over. The bonnet was still warm – she couldn't have been here more than ten minutes. He figured. He surveyed the building. It should have been pulled down years ago, but the council couldn't afford the demolition costs. Most of the town functions were now held in the school hall, which had heating. He straightened his tie in the side mirror of his Fairlane, then walked purposefully towards the front doors.

His outstretched hand preceded his voice. 'Paaat, maate. How ya doin'?'

'Oh, hello, Lynton,' said Pat, unable to hide his surprise. 'What brings you down here?'

'Well, I thought it was about time I dropped in to see how these dances were going. How you going, mate? You're lookin' good.'

'Feelin' good.' Pat swapped the timetable from one hand to the other. 'Opened a new branch line on the weekend.'

'Really?' Lynton feigned interest as he took in the new surroundings. Within the shabby exterior of the hall was an afternoon world of glamour and style. 'The Starlight Room' was written in sparkles across the front of the stage. Blacked-out windows allowed subdued lighting, as a mirror ball bounced tiny squares of light onto made-up faces and old dinner suits.

'Yeah, had to cut a tunnel through the living room skirting boards,' Pat continued. 'Joan's not too happy, mind. Still it'll cut the travel time by half, and I don't have to worry about not being able to shut the dining room door – terrible draught in winter. Besides, I picked up an XPT at a swap meet on Tuesday and that extra bit of track is going to be just the ticket.'

'Progress, Pat. Opening up new territories, that's what it's all about.' Lynton's eyes fell on Emily standing beside the supper room door. 'Remind me to tell you about my experiences on the *Scotsman*,' he added as he moved off in her direction.

Emily was in a dress that even she'd forgotten she owned. Her hair was smooth and wrapped in a bun. It used to be a tight perm, something her daughter Rosie had suggested, but she'd hated it. It made her feel old. She could see Lynton crossing the room. On his lapel was a pass to the previous year's Orange Field Day. His hair was slicked down around his shiny dome and, as he got closer, the smell of aftershave intensified. He wore a Pure Wool tie, its logo featuring heavily.

'Hello there, Emily,' he said smoothly. 'Fancy seeing you here.'

'Hello, Lynton. I didn't realise you were a bit of a dancer.'

'Oh yeah – rarely get time for it these days.' He took another look around the room. 'I think it's important local business gets behind these events. Thinking of putting a little sponsorship deal together actually. A corporate day, perhaps.'

Emily kept her amusement to herself and beckoned Tom away from the tea trolley. 'I'd like you to meet an old friend of mine, Tom Barton.'

'Lynton. Lynton McCabe. We bumped into each other at the pub.'

'Oh yeah, that's right. Lynton.'

'Heard you had guests staying on the property, Em. What brings you out here, Tom? Just passing through? A retirement trip perhaps?'

Tom straightened his tie and thought about what he was actually doing out there.

Emily answered for him. 'Tom works as a part-time safety consultant for the Department of Education. Crossings, that sort of thing.'

For a moment Lynton looked half-interested but his attention was taken by the tempo changing to a quickstep. 'How about it, Em? You don't mind, do you, Tom?' Without waiting for a reply he glided Emily onto the floor.

Tom followed for a bit, and watched from the side-line. Her shoulder disappeared behind another as couples swirled in front of them. Then there was a glimpse of her hair, followed by a brief moment as her dress brushed by again; in between, she would disappear altogether.

Beatrice watched too. She watched younger men in old dinner suits with bow ties and polished shoes. But Don noticed none of these things. He'd seen a watch edging from under a cuff – a watch cheaply manufactured and mass produced. There was a time when he'd had one in a tobacco tin. He could still tell you every detail of its case and where it was stamped, the font, the mainspring . . . each and every mechanism. He knew every tiny part of it. For most of his life it had been a terrible demon that had haunted him, one that could never be exorcised. Perhaps it had once been a gift, a recognition of some achievement, but a terrible force had been thrust upon it. Sinews of flesh had once impregnated the watch's casing, blood had stained its face. Its leather band had been sliced through in a cut so clean it could have been severed by a butcher's boning knife. And then he'd seen the owner's eyes piercing straight through him. Don quickly wrapped his fingers around his wrist as the watch slipped back into the crowd of dancers.

'Blue Stratos.' Beatrice said suddenly. She pointed towards Lynton as he and Emily passed in front of them.

Tom also watched them dipping back into the crowd. He envied Lynton's familiarity, his ease on the dance floor. He went to where he'd last seen Don, but only Beatrice remained.

'He's gone out for air,' she said. 'He was looking a little pale.'

Tom found him seated in the supper room. He pulled up a chair. 'I think maybe you should ask Emily for a dance. What do you think? She's still with Lynton, so you'd have to cut in.'

'Cut in?' Don pushed back his fluoros and looked to Tom. 'I don't know that I'm feeling that well. Why don't you cut in?'

'Don't be ridiculous, mate. You're a much better dancer than me. You look great. You'll be right – it's easy. You might even enjoy it.'

Suits and gowns, fast and slow, coupled around the floor. For Don it was a pinball game. The mirror ball bounced light around buffers of dancers that moved unpredictably and at some speed. Somewhere in there were Lynton and Emily.

'There. Near the fire extinguisher.' Tom guided him towards a break in the traffic. 'Off you go, mate.'

'Hello, Em,' Don said, grasping for the right words. 'Um . . . we have to go in a minute, and I was wondering if I might have the pleasure of this dance?'

Emily looked for Tom, but he was nowhere to be seen. 'Of course. I'm sure Lynton won't mind, will you, Lynton?'

Lynton combined his gracious smile with a pair of open palms.

Arm in arm and step by step, Don and Emily embarked on a slow circuit of the room.

'I can't recall exactly how long she's been gone.' The organ music covered much of what Don was saying. 'It's been a while now . . . still, the older I get . . . the closer we get. Not far away now.' He held Emily's hand as he meandered through thoughts of Bernadette. 'We've always been together. Since . . .' He tried to think of a time when they weren't. 'Since . . . always.'

'Well, you've been lucky, Don. Maybe we both have.'

Over in the supper room, Lynton joined Tom at the table. 'Hell of a mover, that one. She's got a great sense of rhythm, Tom. You know what I mean?'

Tom wasn't sure that he did, but he agreed anyway. And he thought about decking him.

Chapter Eighteen

Todd Davitt had been sitting in his caravan at the Grenfell Bushranger Caravan Park for two days, most of which had been spent thinking about Robbie Steele and Spitfire inspection panels. Could it be? He wouldn't have believed it possible, but he'd seen the panel with his own eyes at the BP servo down the road. As if to jog his memory, he mouthed the words again, then, in an effort to clear his thoughts, he opened the van door and took in the early morning air.

Considering their late arrival, they'd done well. Far enough off the highway so as not to be blown around by the semis and yet close enough to the amenities block for a dash in thongs and pyjamas.

A woman in her early seventies opened the caravan's side venetians and watched Todd brushing leaves from the Commodore. He looked a bit shabby, like he'd been living off the land, and she wondered if she looked the same. He wore a pair of Ugg boots that were generous enough in size to allow the bottoms of his pyjamas to be tucked into them, and a faded cap with 'Evinrude Outboards' stitched across the front.

'It's got to be it. I mean, what else could it be? It's not like those planes turn up every day.' Todd got back in the van and reached for his trousers. 'You carry on, I'll hitch up the van.'

Fran Davitt held onto a rope that looped from cupboard to cupboard. As the van rolled back on its bogeys, it brought to life small pennants that were pegged to the rope. She brushed aside Airlie Beach and Coober Pedy to get to the tea. She'd been relying on this trip. Something had to happen between them. It couldn't continue the way it was. 'It's because he's older' – that's what people said.

They'd been on the road now for nearly four months. It had been Fran's idea, to get them out of the rut they'd fallen into, she thought, give them a chance to rediscover each other. By week two, she'd realised her mistake.

With the Viscount in tow Todd headed towards the line of pines that led to Emily's house. As he approached the front yard he couldn't believe what he saw. Leaning against the front gate was what appeared to be the running gear of a torpedo. He parked the van on the grass and wound down his window. 'Hey Fran! Just look at that!'

'No more stuff, Todd,' said Fran, looking heavenward. 'I'm telling you. No more souvenirs!' He'd suddenly got old, and she'd only just realised. She had to force change or he'd go under. Talk of the van trip was being replaced with talk of a retirement village on the Central Coast – she had to nip that in the bud.

At the sight of the van pulling up, Tom had left his breakfast cereal on the verandah rail and taken to the stairs. 'That's for sale, if you're interested. 'Course you have to be a bit careful with it – it's likely to blow at any second.' He laughed. 'Only jokin', mate – make an offer.' He opened his arms to the yard. 'It's all for sale.' Tom had already picked over the yard for 'pieces of interest'. Anything that looked as if it might've been worth a few bob had been placed to the side. The box of altimeters lived in the house. There was an order to it now, but he wasn't expecting any visitors; he hadn't even had time to put ads in shop windows yet.

'For sale? I heard in town that you were opening a war museum out here or somethin'.'

'Ah, yes,' Tom blustered, a little embarrassed. 'Yes, there has been talk of a museum . . .' He left it at that, but was suddenly acutely aware of how vague his plans had been.

Todd skirted the pile, then introduced himself. 'The bloke at the garage, Gary. He had a part that I'm interested in.'

'Gary. Good bloke Gary, doing the Lawson readings this year.' Tom was getting into the small-town thing. 'Should prove very popular.'

'Right . . . well,' he said, 'I was wondering if you'd have the rest of it?'

'Right this way, Todd, step into our showroom,' said Tom grandly, pointing the way to the shed. 'Not too many of these about.' Tom revealed the aircraft and ran through a few of its features. ''Course it needs a bit of work, but it's all there. We've got our mechanic working on it at the moment. Come up beautiful when it's finished.' He lifted the engine cowling. 'Supercharged Rolls-Royce V12, well over a thousand horses, all the power you'd want.' Tom was in his element, thanks to Emily's coaching. 'Only so many made of this model . . . thinking of putting it up for auction, actually, unless we get an offer beforehand. If you know what I mean.'

Todd stared into the shed in disbelief. He started mumbling to himself, shaking his head as he looked over the plane.

'Yep, she's a beauty.' Tom continued his pitch. 'Have a closer look if you like.' A sign at the petrol station, he thought, that's the ticket. Most of what was in the job lot was rubbish, but passers-by might pay a few bob for some of it. 'Of course, if that's out of your price range, I can do you an excellent line in gas masks.'

Todd was working his way around the fuselage, trying to fathom what he was seeing. 'Where did you say you got it?'

'I didn't. It was part of a warehouse consignment, as a matter of fact. A job lot.'

'The radio access panel,' Todd said strangely, tapping the space where the panel belonged. 'It's got a patch on it.'

'Well, I'm not saying it's perfect. It's a pretty old

plane, you know?' There was no pleasing some people, Tom thought. Tyre kickers.

'No, no,' Todd said insistently. 'I mean, it's my patch. I was the one who riveted it.'

'I hope you don't mind me asking, but I was wondering if I might be able to use your shower?' Fran stood hesitantly at the back door of Emily's house. She wore a chenille bathrobe and a pair of thongs. In her hand was a bag of toiletries that she pointed toward the plane. 'The chap with my husband didn't think you'd mind.'

Emily looked out to see Tom chatting to a bloke in the yard. She turned back to the sound of Fran's voice, seeing a woman of her own age with a grey perm that had begun to fall.

Fran stepped back. 'Of course, if it's a problem?'

'No, no,' Emily assured her. 'Come in, come in.'

Fran introduced herself with the same breath. 'We've been staying at the van park.'

Emily opened the screen door and beckoned her into a seat. Fran rummaged through her toiletries bag in search of a comb. In the process, a plastic bag of tokens fell to the floor. 'I must look a fright,' she said. 'It's been a long trip.' Her fingers levered a coloured washer from the lino. 'Hervey Bay shower block . . . You name it, we've been there.' A sigh turned into a nod as she pulled herself into her chair and took in her surroundings. 'You've got a blender,' was all she could think to say. She sat for a while, collecting her thoughts. Thinking of her kitchen and the routine of her life back home. The garden. Her friends. The postman at three. 'I've got one at home,' she said. 'Similar but not the same.'

She looked through the window to see Todd talking to Tom. It was only a little thing but it was one more thing. As he'd gotten older Todd had turned into one of those types who just bailed people up. Innocent people. People minding their own business. He just never shut up. Maybe he'd always been like that. Maybe she'd never noticed or cared, or maybe she'd simply forgotten. She rubbed the token and wondered what he was going on about now. Without even hearing what Todd was saying, she willed him to get to the point.

'Talk about bein' up shit creek.' Todd stood in front of the aeroplane, his hands working the story, as Tom took it all in. This bloke was obviously here on a nostalgia trip of some sort. As Todd kept talking, Tom started thinking that this could work well for him – here was the key to the plane's history. That's what the punters would be interested in, and here was a man who'd actually worked on the plane during the war. Someone with stories of its grand past; of 'chocks away' and dogfights and lots of 'tally-ho' type stuff. Who could tell what that kind of background would add to the plane's value?

Todd was in full flight. 'Robbie Steele. Stainless. Stainless Steel. That's what we used to call him.'

'Strewth,' said Tom to himself as he pictured Don's

letter from the Public Trustee's Office. 'Robert Allen Steele . . .'

'Anyway,' continued Todd, regardless, 'Stainless acquired this boat, he needed the boat to get the plane, see. He was always acquirin' things, things that might come in handy, things that might be of value. It was all to do with supply and demand, and, for the right price, Stainless had the supply. Kept it all in a shed. Everything from ammo to . . .' He tried to think of something beginning with Z, '. . . girlie maga-*Zines*, from America. He had this idea about startin' an airline, or a trucking company, or a somethin' – he was always startin' something. But he was one of those blokes that never got it together. You know the sort. Fran's brother's the same, Christ, don't get me started on him. Talk about a dropkick . . . I remember it like it was yesterday. I got outta bed, took the old road down to the docks. I remember it was the old road 'cause I made a point of checking the air in the tyres, the road not being sealed and all. Not like today. Beautiful. Seventy kilometres all the way today. Always check the air in your tyres . . .' Todd walked and talked. He was on a roll.

'I remembered something.' Don appeared in the doorway of the kitchen. 'Something important.' As he spoke he began to crumble a little at the edges, like a sandcastle waiting for the tide. His fingers clutched at the bottom of his pyjama sleeves. 'I left the heater on,' he said. 'In the upstairs bedroom.'

'Hello, Don.' Emily ignored his confession and pulled out a chair. 'This is Fran. Would you like a cup of tea, Don? Fran? It's a new blend from . . .' She looked at the label. 'Malaysia.'

'I went upstairs.' Don gave no sign he'd heard Emily. 'I was having a shave and I can't remember turning it off.'

'I don't remember there being an upstairs here, Don.' Emily patted the chair next to her. 'Never mind, these things happen. Fran was just telling us about her holiday.'

Don sat down as Fran glanced out of the window to see Todd waving his arms at Tom as they walked towards the back verandah. 'There he goes, on and on with the same old stories.' She sighed. 'I guess if you hadn't heard them . . . I thought this trip might bring us closer together. Well, it has in that we're now living in close proximity. And now he's talking about selling the house and getting a unit in a retirement village. I am sorry, Emily,' she said, 'to be going on like this, but it's been a long week.' She wound a towel around her head, turban-style, and tucked in the edges while she looked at photographs of Emily's family. 'It's on the lake. We can fish, he says. Fish! Todd's never been fishing, or played golf or bowls, or any of the other things they reckon you can do.' She took a deep breath then composed herself for Don's benefit. 'Do you play golf, Don?'

Don looked startled. 'Um . . . no.' Did he?

'There you go. We'll be so far away from our friends. He's drifted into a bad crowd at the bowlie: "Past

Dwellers" I call them. I'm seventy-two and I'm looking to the future. Do you know what I mean, Don?'

'Absolutely.' Emily replied for him. She'd had moments like this. Moments when circumstances in life had pushed her into intimate conversations with strangers. Fran's eyes filled with tears, '. . . and the thought of another van park . . .'

'Well, you're more than welcome to stay for a few days.' The moment Emily said it she regretted it. 'We could run an extension lead from the house.' The woman was obviously distraught.

'Are you sure, Emily?' Fran wiped her face with the back of her hand. 'I really don't know where to turn. If it's not an imposition. Just the night would be great.' She reached for a tissue. 'We started out together with nothing and then we had everything and now we've got nothing again. Not material things, I don't mean that. Not that we had much.' She shook her head and stirred her tea. 'Now it's back to being just the two of us. Time's running out. Who cares about the past? There's no future in the past: I read that somewhere – it's so true, don't you think?'

'Yep. No question,' replied Don. 'That's what did it, that's what burnt the house down.'

'And back into your gearbox.' Todd began enhancing his stories with a stick in the dirt. 'Aaaaanyways, like I was sayin', Stainless, he gets this boat and up this creek we go . . .' He paused for a moment, then looked across to the kitchen window. 'Hey, Fran, what was that movie called, you know the one with Charlie Allnut?'

'Excuse me, Emily.' Fran gave an apologetic smile then leaned out the window. '*The African Queen*!' She returned to the table. 'He's up to the bit where he goes up the creek. You can appreciate my problem, Emily.'

Todd acknowledged her with a wave. 'Yeah, yeah, that's it. Did you ever see that movie?'

'Umm.'

'Weeell, it was nothin' like it, heaps worse. Up this creek with crocs, and currents like sideway waterfalls . . . Mind you, Stainless's drinkin' didn't help. 'Course he used to drink a bit then, well, all the time really. It was the heat. Lot hotter in Darwin then, we had to float in on the tide, pick up the plane, then float out on the next high . . . mind you, bigger tides then, too. Tides that grabbed ya round the ankles and dragged ya along the bottom like a sucker fish. Anyway, there was no turnin' back.'

'When was this?'

'I dunno. '45, maybe?' Tom's interruption caused him to lose his place. He picked it up a bit further down the track. 'Aaanywaaay, we get there and finds this plane sittin' in the mud, in pretty good nick, considerin'. Anyways, we pulled it apart and winched it onto the deck. Meanwhile, the tide was moving faster than we were, racin' us to the gate. So we end up stayin' the night. Talk about a stuff-up. Next day the tide lifts us like a kid's toy and hurtles us out to sea. Three days it took to get back. Three days. Ended up dumping the plane on the old flying-boat base.' He paused, then shook his head from side to side. 'That was his big mistake. Sat there for two days before he could get a truck. Questions got asked. It was hardly "finders keepers", if you know what I mean, what with the war and everything.'

Tom had almost given up on the idea of learning about the Spitfire's combat history, but this development was the last thing he'd expected.

'The time passed,' Todd went on, 'but what could he do with it? It was knocked off. What else could he do with it? I mean, he could hardly give it back, could he?'

'Give it back?' Tom was feeling increasingly uneasy. He shuffled his weight from one foot to the other.

'So Stainless had it sittin' on this bloke's property, in a shed, a bit outta town, a bit outta the way.' He looked around him and took in the house, the machinery shed and paddock. 'Funny how the wheel turns, eh?'

'The wheel? How d'you mean?' Tom asked.

'Well, you know . . .' He flicked his eyes around the yard. 'Anyway, he starts restorin' it, and that's when I did some work on it for him. Patchin' bullet holes mainly, like the one in the access door. Stainless did a rebuild on the donk. It was all coming together nicely. Then,' he looked to Tom for his reaction, 'wouldn't you know it, I turn up one day and he'd gone. Gone! The plane had gone – everything; the place had been stripped clean. Musta thought he had a buyer for it. Bit hard to move something like that without people noticing, though. Know what I mean?'

Tom looked at the plane. Images of the Gold Coast

slipped through his fingers and into the sand that led to the Surfers Hilton.

'Yep, funny how it all comes back. What goes around comes around, eh?'

Chapter Nineteen

Don couldn't remember if there'd always been an extension cord running out of his window or not. He reached for his fluoros, then followed the cord's path out of the window. At the edge of the verandah he saw that it joined another, and then a double adaptor took it through the window of a caravan that was parked on the edge of the lawn. It must have arrived during the night. Either that, or he'd somehow missed seeing it all morning. He watched a man securing an annexe to the van.

Don moved back behind the curtain. He tried to think who the man might be, but no one came to mind. He pulled on his dressing gown and beanie and shuffled towards the smell of breakfast.

Tom pulled out a chair for Don, at the same time catching a glimpse through the window of Emily working on the aircraft engine. He wondered if there was any truth in what Todd had said the night before. 'Ahh, Don . . . just harpin' back to the war for a moment.' He buttered a piece of toast. 'We're trying to piece together a bit of history on the plane. The bloke that left it to you, Robbie Steele. "Stainless", that's what they used to call him. According to Todd, he ran a black market during the war. What can you remember about Stainless, Don?'

Don followed Tom's conversation with random smiles that seemed to fall in the right places.

'If you can't remember Stainless, Don, maybe you can remember his black market caper?' His line of questioning had begun in a nonchalant kind of way but now an edge of frustration had crept into Tom's voice. 'Maybe you remember buying something? Like some cheap fags, or, I dunno, something? Anything!' He leant forward across the table and willed Don to remember. 'You can do this, Don. Our future depends on it.'

Todd rummaged around in the boot of the Commodore. It was a travelling workshop of tools and bits and pieces and anything else he thought might come in handy for the trip. Behind the spare and next to the bits of wire and tent pegs was the car-care section, and in it were his tins of cut and polish. Not that the Commodore needed it, but you never knew, a scratch here and there. He set himself up beside Emily and began work on the fuselage. 'What do you reckon, Emily, a number three, or a number four cut?'

'I'm sure you'll make the right decision, Todd,' Emily replied encouragingly.

'Number four, I'd say. Brings the cars up something beautiful.'

Emily was lost in rubber hoses and fuel lines. A trip to the wrecker's at Cowra was going to be necessary. As she worked on prying off perished parts she thought about Fran's loneliness, and Todd's obsession with the past. She'd never thought of herself as being lonely or living in the past, but maybe she was, and did. Her thoughts were cut short by an unexpected long, shallow breath. She leant over the engine and concentrated on her breathing. She suddenly felt very weary and made her way slowly down the ladder, where she sat quietly under the wing, waiting for the tightness in her chest to pass.

'Are you all right, Emily?' Todd asked gently.

Emily's shortness of breath had passed quickly but it was enough to have given her a scare. 'I'm fine, thanks, Todd. Just fine.' But she wasn't.

The Shearers Hotel in Grenfell was no longer the working man's pub it had once been. A brochure in the main bar showed off its new Bed and Breakfast appeal with photographs of wide verandahs and potted palms. The ritzy tiles of the Guests Only bathrooms on the second floor had not been seen by any of the locals and had now taken on a mythological quality. The cappuccino machine was real enough, though, as was the sit-down outdoor bistro with smart cane furniture. But the patrons hadn't changed. George Davies still sat at his stool as he'd done for the past twenty years. And the pub cockatoo still called for drinks in somewhat florid language as tick-tacking pokies galloped away in the back bar. And from somewhere came the sound of Race 4 from Doomben.

Trevor Styles paused as the horses approached the post, then turned back to the meeting. 'And so, Teddie, don't you worry, mate, you'll still be doin' your bushranger thing.' He ticked names from a list. 'Gavin, the guinea pig races; Gary, the Birthplace reading; and Tony, as usual, has pulled together a beaut cast and rehearsals are well under way for this year's production of *South Pacific*.' He repositioned himself on the barstool as he continued down the page.

'Now, you'll be aware from the minutes that George Tooney's idea about the Blessing of the Tractors has been carried, and we thank George for his contribution. Father Trimble will do the honours at the Showground.' After a murmur of approval, he continued with details of the menu for the official dinner.

Emily took a seat between mention of Helen's beef pockets and Dorothy's pears in brandy sauce. She opened her handbag and removed a small number of photocopied sheets of paper.

'Followed by port and coffee. And now to report on this year's guest attraction is Emily Marsden.'

'Thank you, Trevor,' Emily began. 'We have to be realistic. Since the passing of Leonard Teale, the quality of our "official guest" has been on the decline. However,' she added, 'this year I've managed to contact Craig Donnelly's agent, and Craig's agreed to do the honours.' She pushed her glasses up her nose and read from a biography of soap. 'Andrew' in *Passions*, 'Troy' from *Paradise Beach*, 'Dr Brixton' in *Neighbours* – and more recently, 'Camden' in *Home and Away*.

Camden. The name rang a bell, but no one could quite place him. The committee drifted into their own versions of what Craig might look like. Susan Edwards thought he might have been the alcoholic school counsellor in *Home and Away* who had an affair with Kylie, one of his students, and wondered as to his suitability.

'Anyway,' Emily said firmly, handing out copies of his resumé, 'I'm sure we'll all recognise him when we see him.'

'And give him a big Grenfell welcome. Thank you, Emily.' Trevor returned to his notes. 'Now, the statue of Ol' Henry has survived twelve months in the council lock-up and looks as good as new thanks to a good scrub. Lynton's given us the use of a crane to drop him in the roundabout first thing tomorrow. And a reminder to everyone – we still need marshals for the parade.'

'How's that plane coming along, Em?' Lynton leant over the back of her chair. 'I trust it doesn't have to pass any certification tests?'

'Why's that, Lynton?'

'Well, it takes a certain amount of expertise, you know. They're pretty complicated things, aeroplanes.'

'Is that right?' She returned the smile and with it a photograph of Craig.

'Meeting adjourned.' Trevor Styles signed off in time for the 6th at Doomben.

*

The following morning Emily had got herself organised for a trip to the wrecker's. It was located on the outskirts of Cowra, and, according to a sign that hung over the front gate, was under new management. Her mind was filled with the items remaining on her To Do List from the previous day's meeting. Thank God she didn't have to billet anyone this year, she thought. Some of those 'Festival Guests' were an absolute pain in the backside. The guy from the cooking show was the worst – all he'd talked about was himself and Sydney real estate. 'There are some truly nutty people in the world, Don,' she said to her passenger. 'People who just don't get it.'

'Exactly,' replied Don in a manner that implied he was following the conversation.

'Tom seemed a bit depressed when we left, you know,' said Emily. 'It's not at all like him to miss an outing. One goes, all go, isn't that what he says?'

Don nodded. Outside the window a paddock of rusting car bodies drifted by as the car slowed and stopped.

A long line of empty beer bottles led to a shed. In front of it were three piles of gearboxes marked *Jap*, *Holden*, *Ford*. *Brian Maynard Prop* was written on a sign that had recently been taped over the doorway, and, at the sound of Emily's car, he appeared underneath it. 'I'll give you three hundred bucks for it, and a cab into town.'

He was a man in his early fifties, softly spoken with sharp features brought on by early aging. He looked as though he'd once been a heavier man. A loose double chin of skin overlapped a weathered parka that had been zipped together to form the name of an American baseball team. In the shadows he looked businesslike. As he stepped into the sunlight he looked like a garden gone to seed.

'Sorry?' Emily asked, stepping over a long chain that disappeared into a dog kennel.

'If you can't hear what I'm sayin', just say so,' the man said. 'I had to have an operation on my collarbone – Jimmy Dancer. They got it all, but had to remove part of my throat, the speakin' part.' He continued in soft gravelly tones with a story about the miracles of modern medicine and this doctor who removed one of two arteries to his brain because the tumour had wrapped itself around the artery. 'So I'm only operatin' on one artery.' It was a story he'd told many times to explain his patterns of speech, and then, as if proof were somehow required to back up his story, he opened his parka to reveal a long scar. 'Saves any embarrassment,' he added. 'People don't like to ask, you know?'

Emily expressed her concern for him.

Having got that out of the way he got to the point. 'So, what can I do for you?'

'Got anything less perished than these?' She handed over a box of hoses. 'And a new fuel line'd be good. Perhaps you could make me up something? An early Morris or Leyland truck might do it.' She handed over the corroded piece.

'Right.' He stood there for a moment digesting what Emily had said. 'No worries.' He pitched his masonry tones towards Don, who'd wandered over to where they were. 'A woman who knows what she wants, can't be many of those around.' He grinned at Emily. 'It's lucky you caught me in the mornin', I'm not too good in the arvo.'

'Really?' Emily said. 'I'm the opposite.'

'Still, it's the early bird that catches the worm, eh?' He turned the fuel line in his fingers. 'What's it out of?'

'An old Roller.'

'A Roller, eh? Nice.' He lifted his eyebrows then just as quickly knotted them down. 'Nothin' like that in the yard.' He paused. 'Trouble not your soul about material things . . .' and he stopped there, as if thinking about where that was leading, then headed off into the junkyard.

'Sorry?' Emily said, to indicate that she hadn't quite followed, but it was too late, he'd taken his musings with him and disappeared into the shell of a truck.

CHAPTER TWENTY

Don sat on the verandah steps scattering his thoughts, sometimes audibly, to a squabble of chooks chasing breadcrumbs through the garden. Here was yet another development. Another stranger. It was late afternoon and now the junkyard man had turned up. At least, that's who he thought it was – he noticed the lettering on the man's jacket and wondered if he had anything to do with the police. That thought led him back to the house fire and the heater that sat on the bathroom floor. But the chooks didn't care. They followed his fingers and the pieces of bread that fell from them.

Over the engine cowling Emily could see Tom going through his 'to keep' boxes. Pieces that had just been thrown in were now being individually wrapped in old newspaper and carefully re-packed. Maybe it was fate with Tom, she mused, or maybe it was some grand plan that had been set in motion fifty years before. And maybe Don was part of it as well. She placed exhaust blankings to one side and looked in the manual for how many gallons of lube oil would be needed. The electrical system could only be tested under pressure. Either it worked or it didn't.

Brian Maynard came into the shed. 'Found a few more bits,' he said to Emily, walking to the base of the ladder. 'Shoulda told me you was workin' on a plane. There's somethin' that looks like it might have been a plane in my paddock – that or an old Galaxy.'

'That's so kind of you, Brian, thanks.' Emily looked down from her ladder.

'Let me know if you want any printing done,' Brian offered. Brian was looking pretty ordinary, she thought, more so than earlier that day. And his words were starting to slur. Her first impression was one of loneliness, as though he didn't have enough conversations, so let them all go at once when he did.

'Printing?'

'Yeah. I used to be a printer – printed all sorts of stuff, 'cept people don't need to get stuff printed anymore, 'cause they do it on their computer. So I got a computer. Then this happened.' He revisited his scar. As his scratchy tones continued he appeared to become agitated. 'I'll just grab those bits for ya.'

Emily watched him at the boot of his car. He rummaged around a few mechanical bits and pieces then produced a bottle of scotch and took a swig out of it. Then, to her surprise, he wandered off towards Don, bottle in hand.

Brian took a seat next to Don on the verandah steps.

'I tried everything,' he said, continuing the conversation he'd had that morning with Emily as though Don had also been part of it and it had just that second been interrupted. 'Well, you would, wouldn't you?'

Don found himself sitting next to the man from the junkyard. The step was small and he folded his arms to fit.

'Diets, Chinese medicine, acupuncture . . .' Brian paused to lubricate his throat with a short sharp swig. 'I tried everything, but things weren't gettin' any better, so I had surgery. And when I was on the operatin' table, that's when I started thinking about what happens at the end. Have you ever wondered about that?'

'The end?'

'Yeah, you know. Death. The transition. I can say it now – I couldn't say it before. After the chemo, I met this bloke from California. He had the answer. Spiritual serenity, that's the key. You have to find inner peace.' He turned the bottle in his hands. 'Got rid of most of my possessions. They're just a burden, if you know what I mean. One should float on eternal currents.'

'Eternal currents,' Don repeated.

'Yeah. Now you're gettin' it.' His sandpapered voice began slurring in half-whispers. 'You know, we're all transitory. But in us dwells the imperishable.' He put an arm around Don's shoulder. 'It'll all work out for the best. You'll see.'

Most of what Brian said was lost on Don, but he followed him with his eyes and mouthed the occasional word that seemed relevant.

'Anyway it's all here, all here,' Brian said, 'all in this little book.' He pulled out of his pocket a tattered little publication: *A Serene Life*. 'I found it very helpful, very helpful indeed. Some of those Californians are pretty smart, you know. You can borrow it if you like.' Using Don's fingers as wrapping paper, he pushed it into his palm. 'But, remember, if you hold onto something that moves away, it holds onto you.'

Don held the book. Nervous now as to whether or not he should be holding it.

Tom peered out of the shed window. Now someone else had turned up. The person had been talking to Emily first and was now talking to Don like they were old mates. Paranoia was beginning to set in. God only knew what Don had told him. News of the aeroplane was obviously getting around. The cops would be next. Then a government man with a contractor to take it all away. Just salvage what you can, he said to himself, just in case. Altimeters, compasses, wireless components, anything else that looked of value and was portable would need to be stored well away from prying eyes.

'Tom? Tom Barton?'

Tom turned from the window to see another stranger standing in the doorway. Unbelievable. The man removed a pair of spectacles and neatly placed them in the top pocket of his blazer. 'I'm Malcolm Parker.' He was small, orderly, methodical – a place-for-everything man, by the look of him. 'And this is my wife, Trudy.' A woman of similar stature appeared beside him.

'Um . . . hello. Yes?'

'We were wondering if there might be a kiosk?'

'A kiosk?'

'Yes. Postcards, that sort of thing. The chap at the BP told us about the museum. I was hoping someone might be able to take a photo of us, you know . . . in front of the aeroplane.'

As the day progressed more and more people arrived. Tom and Emily retired to the kitchen to watch the proceedings from the window. A kind of carnival atmosphere prevailed. It was almost as though the 'museum' at Duraminar was one of the festival attractions. There were whole families with grandparents in tow, toddlers in strollers, people taking photographs. The ladder to the Spitfire's cockpit was in constant use, with children sitting low in the seat machine-gunning an imaginary enemy. 'A part of aviation history here, folks,' spruiked Todd, who appeared to have taken over as tour guide. 'And I can tell you 'cause I was there. I personally led the recovery team. Me and this bloke called Stainless. Up this crocodile-infested creek. Crocs, tsetse flies, mosquitoes – not normal mosquitoes, but malaria-carryin' ones, big as all get out. Then we had to get it back. You know that movie, *The African Queen*? Weeell, I'm here to tell you . . .'

Tom stared blankly out the window. Well, that's that, he thought. It was out of his hands now. Sooner or later there was sure to be a knock at the door.

'Ever have that problem with a van . . .' Todd's voice droned on in the background. Sometimes he'd digress from the plane's history and onto unrelated matters that revolved around himself. 'I do a lot of travellin' these days.' He opened his hands to the big picture. 'Just being a part of it all. Have any of you ever been on the Yass Road? Not the new Yass Road, the old Yass Road.'

Feeling more sympathetic towards Fran by the minute, Emily closed the window and sank into a chair. Perhaps she had taken on too much; perhaps it was all getting out of hand. She felt so tired. She'd thought it beforehand and now she said it to herself again. Must give Megan a call. Must make a doctor's appointment. She lifted her eyes to the mantelpiece. 'The clock's stopped,' she said.

'She'll be right.' Tom placed a reassuring hand on her shoulder. 'Don'll get it going again.'

Fran appeared at the kitchen door with a bag of groceries. 'I really do think what you're doing is marvellous. It's just nice to stop for a while. With different people. When I say different, I mean, not Todd . . . you know, different people.' She hefted the bag onto the table. 'You know what I'm saying, Emily?'

Emily smiled and nodded. 'I think so.'

'Goodo. I'll put you and Tom down for my stir-fry.' And with that she opened the pantry door and began unloading the groceries.

Don sat on the verandah with a blanket over his knees and watched a small crowd peering into the engine bay of the aircraft. It was as if some family member had passed away and now they were viewing the open coffin. Timepieces began ticking through his head. He tried to distract himself with other thoughts but images of the watch kept coming back to him. Interlocking cogs turned tiny sprockets that led to a ship. The *Canberra*. Sydney to London. Ten ports of call.

Emily's farm seemed like a port, a harbour that protected him from storms and rough seas. And Tom was a mooring that secured him against the tide. He swung free from the line that tethered him and drifted into the past. He looked across the paddocks and saw an ocean that stretched to the horizon and found himself seated not on the verandah but at a card table that looked out over the stern of a ship. Passengers wondered about taking photographs and discussed their itineraries.

It was a postcard of the P&O liner the *Canberra* that convinced them they should take the trip. A retirement cruise. Then the brochure arrived: the cities looked so beautiful – Rabaul, Colombo, Naples, Lisbon. A cabin on the promenade deck. That was what Bernadette wanted and that was Bernadette got. It wasn't quite the *Normandy* or either of the *Queen*s but she still had a certain amount of style about her.

'The trick is staying together,' said Bertrand Bauer, who, with his wife Elsbeth, had joined the ship at Singapore. He reached out for Elsbeth's hand. 'Staying alive together. I don't know how long we would last without each other.'

Elsbeth replied with something in German that

brought them closer together. The Bauers were in their early eighties and had been together since school.

'The world is a dangerous place,' Bertie continued. 'When will it ever end?' The past twenty-four hours had brought with it a sobriety that had passed between the decks. Apart from pickpockets in Naples, news from the Falkland Islands told of a British warship that had been struck by a missile, and that the *Canberra* was to be requisitioned as a troop ship. 'We had a son,' he said, 'whose childhood dream was being able to fly. That was all he ever wanted to do. Life was laid out before him. He sat on the cusp of the earth. Peter was still a boy when he was shot down, in a war he never wanted to be part of. He came of age at the wrong time. And we are still here. That is the terrible thing. It's not right,' he said. 'It's just not right.'

Together with Don and Bernadette, the Bauers had shared the experience of passing through the Suez Canal en route to Southampton. They'd endured English comedians and Island nights, bingo, fancy dress and Victor Borge. It was a shipboard friendship – six weeks that might lead to other places, or might not. They'd worn masks of coloured card passed around by pursers in starched white. They'd sat and talked and strolled in dinner jackets and evening gowns. In the artificial time of cruising life, the minutes of longitude wound back the clocks and the sunsets hung on the horizon. And at each port of call, the four of them had enthusiastically taken in the local sights.

'Naples was founded by the Greeks and flourished

during the Roman Empire.' They were all standing outside the Museo Nazionale now, a tour group of accents working on phrases and place names. Another twenty minutes and they'd have the Castel Nuovo down pat, and twenty minutes after that, the Floridiana. All recorded in photographs and postcards.

'Come on, Don,' Bernadette called to him. 'We're going to miss the bus if we don't hurry.' There was always the worry of being left behind.

Don looked at his watch. He wound his fingers around the leather strap. 'Yes,' he replied. 'Yes, we don't want to miss the boat.'

Verandah shadows took the form of cell bars that crept across Don's blanket. He looked agitated. His eyes wandered across the yard but manacled thoughts brought him back to the plane.

'Hello, Don.' Emily pulled up a chair. She sat with him for a while, watching the flickering of his eyes and the turning of his fingers. 'Are you all right?'

'I'm fine,' he said softly. 'I'm tired. I'm very tired.'

'What are you reading?'

'I don't know.' He shrugged. 'Brian gave it to me.'

'Maybe you should have a lie-down, Don?'

'Yes. A lie-down.' He held the little book and rocked it gently against his chest.

'Let me help you.' Emily took his arm and helped him to his feet. 'I'm going to be late,' she said. 'But that's all right, they can wait.' Together they set off down the verandah.

*

It was the final committee meeting, and in a last-minute coup the district pipes and drums had agreed to lead the parade with their special rendition of 'Advance Australia Fair'. They would be followed by the historical motorcycle club and then, on the back of Stewie Procter's semi, would be the *pièce de résistance*, the Combined Schools Poetry Tableau. That was always a big crowd-pleaser. Many of the events had already begun – the guinea pig races, the bus tours, the clay pigeon shoot – and everything was now in place for the parade. Emily leant back in her chair and rubbed her eyes. She'd been 'feeling her bones' for the past few days, and even before the meeting began she'd decided to leave early.

It was late evening before she got home. The place was quiet. Festival programs and food wrappings the only reminder of the day's events. She parked the car and turned out the lights in unison with the light that spilt from Todd and Fran's van.

Tom was waiting for her in the kitchen. 'Saved you some tea, Em,' he said, taking a small casserole dish out of the oven and putting the contents into a bowl for her. 'Don's gone to bed. They all have. He's certainly taken to that book.'

Emily exhaled a long pent-up sigh as she collapsed onto a chair and took a forkful of food. 'Well, it's good he's interested in something.'

'How was the meeting?'

Emily rolled her eyes and finished her mouthful. 'Long. And I've got to pick up Craig tomorrow.'

'No worries, Em. I'll take you. I think I need to get out for a while.'

'Me too.'

Tom busied himself at the sink while she ate her dinner. 'I've been thinking about that aeroplane,' he said after a while. 'And I had a bit of a chat to Don this evening, and we thought it might not be a bad idea if we donated it to a museum.'

'Really? I thought you were going to sell it.' Emily had known there'd been something up over the last couple of days.

'Yeah, well, we were. And we still might. It's just an idea. I mean, it belongs to the people really. As a memorial. What do you think?'

Emily nodded. 'I think that's a decision for you and Don.' She gestured towards her now empty bowl. 'You know, Tom, it's not that bad, considering the state of Fran's mind. Her stir-fry's not bad at all.' She went to get up. 'Why don't I make us a cup of tea?'

Tom was immediately by her side to help her out of her chair, and it seemed neither of them was prepared for what happened next. They just kept holding hands. Not for very long – perhaps for a second or two longer than what might have felt comfortable. Both were aware of hands on hands.

It hadn't been the touch of relatives or grandchildren, but a touch of intimacy. One she hadn't experienced for a long time. It was not something she thought would ever happen again, or ever really wanted it to.

Emily spoke first. In an ordinary sort of way she

asked him if he'd like milk and sugar. Even though she knew full well how Tom took his tea.

'I wonder if Don would like one,' he replied.

'Go and see – he's probably asleep.' She placed cups on saucers. The kitchen window caught her reflection. Her face still looked like yesterday's face. Somehow she was expecting to see a younger person's face. Perhaps she was just an old fool tricked by thoughts of what might be, she thought. She was seventy-seven, not seventeen. She'd already lived a life and given life to others. Maybe Tom saw another person's face, she mused. A younger Emily – the person she'd been all those years ago. She studied her reflection, but it was still yesterday's face.

Down the hallway, Don lay in bed, drifting in and out of sleep as his mind wandered around the room like a weary traveller looking for directions. He stumbled across a lost path that led to an information board of photographs of the trip he and Bernadette had taken, of museums and cathedrals, of Elsbeth and Bertrand on the deck of the *Canberra*. He looked down to see his workbench and the photographs pinned on the wall behind it.

He bent down and opened the safe under the bench. Inside were his 'Work to be Done' boxes, a carryover from his father. He reached inside and removed a carefully wrapped watch case.

'It's getting late.' Bernadette appeared in the doorway. 'Come to bed.'

'I won't be long.' He unwrapped the string and gave the casing a final polish.

'What are you doing?'

'I'm sending this watch to Elsbeth and Bertie.'

Her eyes widened. 'But, Don, you've been so obsessive about it. You've spent so much time repairing it, and now you're going to give it away?'

He gestured wearily. 'It was never mine. You never know, it might even have been theirs. Their son's.' He wrote their address on the lid of a small box. 'And now it's finished. All finished. Thank God.'

In Emily's spare room he put his arms around Bernadette, lay back on the pillow and closed his eyes.

Emily spent the following afternoon with Tom in his ute. The regular plane service to Cowra had been terminated, which now meant a further hour's drive to the next airport.

Every town had something. For Orange, it was Mount Canobolas, so it was always colder than anywhere else. Tom made as if to turn on the heater but it had long died. 'All in the mind, Em,' he explained. 'I've moved the knob over to the red bit and it feels warmer already.' In a theatrical gesture, he undid his top button, ran a finger around the inside of his collar, and fanned his face.

Emily did feel warmer. Or maybe it was just being with Tom.

'Never this cold on the Gold Coast. That's where we're headin', Don and I. Get ourselves a little unit near the water. Close enough to smell the salt. I got some brochures there if you want to take a look.' He pointed to the glovebox.

Emily looked at the brochures. They were old and dog-eared, as if they'd been transferred from back pocket to back pocket. Some of the cars in them looked almost the same vintage as the vehicle they were travelling in. But the people looked young. Maybe that was how Tom saw himself.

They detoured via the fuel depot on the way, then returned to the airport car park. By the time they'd reached the arrival gate the plane's wheels had touched down on the strip.

With fingers clenched through the wire fence they watched the aeroplane swing to a halt. The draught from the propellers cartwheeled Tom's hat across the grass to the terminal, where it lay wedged against a baggage trolley. Emily got there first. She straightened it out then pulled it tight on his head, laughing at the sight of him.

'You know, Em, I just had this great idea.' Tom raised his voice over the dying turbines. 'Why don't you join us? You know, up at Surfers?'

'Surfers?'

'Yeah, Surfers. You've seen the brochures. There's the plane. What if we just got on it?'

Emily laughed. 'Apart from any other reason, I don't know that I even like Surfers.'

Tom rearranged his hat. 'What's not to like? How do you know? They sell gold chain up there by the metre, and those sunglasses with the roman coins on the side are as cheap as casino chips. Things happen, Em. Life is uncertain. If we knew what was going to happen then we wouldn't do anything. That's the great thing. *We don't know.*'

'I'm too old to not know, Tom,' Emily replied. 'I think I'd prefer to stick with the little I do know.'

'But Don and I'd be there. What could possibly happen?'

Another voice joined the conversation. 'Emily Marsden?'

The star turn of the festival had arrived. Craig Donnelly looked like his photograph, which was unusual. Most of the previous 'guests' had sent out publicity photographs that were clearly out of date. In some cases, they were barely recognisable.

The young man looked dubious as they arrived at the ute. 'Is this what we're travelling in?' He unplugged his Walkman and looked over at Tom. This was not what he was expecting. He looked about twenty, with sandy tips and good looks. 'I thought there was going to be a limo.'

'A limo?'

'Yeah, a limo.' He grimaced. 'Bad smell around here, isn't there? Kero or something? Seems to be coming from your car.'

Tom pointed to a 44-gallon drum sitting in the tray of the ute. 'High-octane fuel,' he explained, not noticing the look of horror that passed over the youngster's face. 'Been doin' a bit of work on the donk. Should be a quick trip.' He hefted the boy's bag into the tray. 'What do you know of Lawson, son?'

'Lawson? The pace bowler?'

Emily gave an audible sigh as she slid across the bench seat.

Tom pulled the column shift into gear. 'Nah. His brother, Henry. Played for New South Wales.'

Chapter Twenty-One

Everyone turned out for the parade. By the time the procession wheeled past the TAB on Main Street there would have been twenty floats. Decorated bicycles single-filed past women in period costume who drank Billy tea around a mobile campfire. 'Miss Henry Lawson' was towed along in Gavin Everett's speedboat, which had been cleverly camouflaged in wattle and eucalyptus. She wore a gold crown and waved to the crowd from a throne constructed over the Evinrude. Everything went as planned. Teddie did his bushranger thing, Craig spoke about himself from the back of a lorry, and the school tableau received tumultuous applause. Every year was better than the last one, and this year was no exception.

'Excellent turn-out, Emily,' said Lynton McCabe as he handed out flyers promoting his used machinery centre.

Emily slipped out of her shoes and felt the grass through her stockinged feet. 'As ever, Lynton,' she replied. The endless meetings and sandwich-making would soon be over. She told herself this was definitely her last year of serving tea and scones at the poetry reading comp.

'The Blessing of the Tractors couldn't have gone better,' Lynton crowed. 'Definite buyer interest there. That'll be a regular event from now on. I'm thinking about indirect sponsorship through the church. Maybe a sign on the pulpit: "You reap what you sow with a McCabe harvester". What do you reckon?'

'You've got a talent for it, Lynton,' she said, inwardly recoiling. She could see Tom and Don sitting on fold-ups supplied by the bowling club. They were listening to Jenny Davis pouring out her innermost turmoil. She was 'loose' at the best of times and now she had an audience. Modern poetry was her bag. Emotion and pain and terrible suffering were wrung through her fingers, then cast unedited into the crowd. There was much cheering. That was the great thing – everybody got a go.

Tom could hear Lynton holding forth in the background. He seemed to have everything. It might have been Jenny's poem but suddenly Tom felt heavy with depression. He'd accumulated a lifetime of nothing, nothing material anyway. In his eyes, a flat on the Gold Coast was a castle. In Emily's, it was probably a bad holiday.

Lynton's voice punctuated Jenny's inner grief. 'Hayman Island, Em. Got a conference there next month, annnd, if you don't mind me saying, you're looking a bit tired. Treat yourself to a break . . . No strings . . .

relax . . . let someone else do the cooking. Offer's on the table, Em.'

A cheer went up as Jenny brought her poem to an end.

Tom let out a deep sigh, then picked over the last of his sandwich.

'Batteries.' Emily wiped her hands with an oily rag. There was a no-nonsense professionalism in her voice that brought the crowd of onlookers together. 'We need batteries. Lots of 'em. And we need to get the old girl into the yard.'

It was time. They'd done as much to the aircraft as they could. The battery from Todd's Commodore was first to come out. Then the Laser. In all there were four, all interconnected from a pallet placed on the wheelbarrow. A heavy lead led to the starter motor. House bricks chocked the wheels, and the garden hose was put on standby.

Emily lowered herself into the cockpit. For a moment there she thought about Jock and the old airbase Avro. But it had been her Uncle George who'd got her interested in mechanics.

'She's all yours, Em. Wind 'er up.' Tom gave her the thumbs-up. The crowd fell back behind the clothesline.

'Here's to you, Uncle George,' Emily proclaimed. She adjusted the Spitfire's rear-vision mirror as though it were the Laser, then pressed the starter button with one hand and engaged the supercharger with the other.

The propeller slowly began to turn. Lubricants flowed around the engine. The whine of the starter increased with each revolution. Air was sucked into the pistons and mixed with the fuel. Smoke lifted from the exhausts. It took a short, sharp breath, then combusted to life.

The noise was deafening. Birds took to the air as soundwaves ricocheted through the gums. A powerful stream of turbulent air rocked the aircraft forward against the bricks and sent Emily's notes racing across the lawn.

The curtains in Rosie's old room fishtailed in a gentle breeze across the glass-topped dresser and onto the patchwork quilt. Between the sheets, Don lay dozing. Fingers subconsciously scrubbed watch components, quotes from *A Serene Life*, voices passing the window, all moved in and out of Don's consciousness.

Suddenly, the roar of the engine bursting into life ripped through Don's body like an intruder violently forcing a lock. He blocked his ears, but the sound kept screaming through his mind.

Angels fifteen. Vector one three zero. Adrenalin coursed through Don Cameron's body. In the middle of an English winter he began to sweat. Hot air expanded as the exhausts of his Spitfire left a long con-trail across the London sky. Fifteen seconds straight and level.

He'd seen pilots come and go, the Kid, all blokes his own age. And now he chose not to get to know the new recruits. It was one of his survival tactics. Where others went to the pub and drank away their fears, the Kid stayed in the barracks and ran manoeuvres over the backs of cigarette packs and rehearsed them until thought was no longer necessary. Until they were just a reflex. He knew the enemy's every weakness; studied the performance details of their aircraft. He knew that they were just as young and just as tired as he was. He was riding on seven kills and two probables and all the laurels that went with them. No one knew how the Kid had survived this long.

Twenty seconds, change course. He was climbing now, towards fifteen thousand. Ahead and below was an easy target: a straggler, crippled by shrapnel and unable to stay with the flock. The bomber spat oil and smoke across the fingertips of clouds that reached up to hide it. He trailed the arc of smoke down to seven thousand feet, then fell in behind it. The gap closed rapidly. His airspeed indicator climbed past 400 miles per hour. Vibrations shuddered through the airframe. Time was measured in fractions of a second. Turbulence from the stricken plane buffeted him in his seat. He held his position and slid the safety catch off the trigger. The bomber's dorsal turret fell into frame. Frantic efforts by the gunner distracted him. His arms were in the air, his head shaking wildly from side to side. The Kid blinked out the reality of the moment and squeezed the trigger; bullets ripped open the belly of the Heinkel. The turret was torn apart, as shattered glass and metal edges fell towards the earth.

The sky was filled with debris. The Kid recovered

from a blackout turn only to find himself again under the torn-away fuselage of the other plane. Through acrid smoke, the German airman fell. His glass coffin smashed through the canopy of the Spitfire. The windscreen turned red as the gunner's body was impaled on its metal frame. As the airstream washed away the blood, the Kid saw the gunner's eyes staring through the shattered glass. They looked like anybody's eyes – they looked like his eyes. Time stopped. Over the engine noise he could hear the sound of the airman's arm buffeting wildly against the broken screen. A butcher's blade of glass sliced through sinews and bone until the arm was no longer attached to his body.

He couldn't remember the wing-over that cast the body free. He was flying straight and level now, on the approach to RAF Biggin Hill. Vomit filled his oxygen mask. The cockpit was a slaughterhouse of guts and human tissue. He wiped the blood from his goggles and looked down to his lap. On it lay the gunner's arm.

Below, the other world waited, then arrived. Silent drizzle, grey skies and sodden fields, and slivers of frosted grass that snapped under foot. He stumbled onto the wing then fell to the tarmac.

'Are you all right, sir?' The mechanic looked on in shock. 'Oh, Christ.' Not waiting for a reply, he raced back to the ambulance station.

Don looked down at himself. It was his body and somebody else's body, all mixed up. Blood and guts soaked through his uniform and into the pores of his skin. He ripped off his gloves and started frantically brushing and clawing at himself to get rid of it but the harder he scrubbed the more ingrained it became. His knees gave way. On the grass in front of him was the gunner's watch. The bloodied casing had been ripped apart to reveal cogs still beating. Don's cries were lost to the sound of spinning propellers arcing to a halt.

The engine ran for just a minute. Then there was silence.

'Oh my God.' Fran broke the stillness. 'It works.'

Todd's case of Lion's Club Port was one he'd been saving for a special occasion. He pulled the cork on yet another bottle then slid back the screen door to his van. 'Who's for a refill? What about you, Ellis, and . . .' He brought Sam into focus. 'I dunno that you're old enough, son, but what the hell.' The numbers had dwindled, but half a dozen hangers-on had lingered for a celebratory drink that had gone long into the evening.

'Hey, Tom,' Todd yelled out across the garden. 'I've been doing some thinking. Where are ya?' He shaded his eyes from a spotlight that hung from the verandah.

'Be there in a sec – just tidying up a few loose ends.' Tom taped up the last of his boxes and threw a tarp over them. As he passed under the wing of the plane he picked up a beer he'd placed on the tailplane. Todd's cut and polish had taken the plane just about back to metal, and in the moonlight it shone like a 'Ride of your Life' carnival attraction. Had it been another time, he might have been standing there with a hat and cane spruiking the thrills and spills. He might even have coaxed Emily from the crowd for a free demo. Through the windows of the van he could see her in a one-sided conversation with Fran.

'Heeey, Tom.' Todd had been drinking for some time. He gave himself yet another refill, then motioned Tom to sit down. 'I remembered about that bloke. The pilot.' He waved his glass towards the house. 'It was Don. Had to be. How else would he end up with it? The more I'm thinkin', the more I'm rememberin'. It was like yesterday. It was hot, bloody hot, and not a dry heat neither, not like today. No sireee.' He paused to quench his Darwin thirst. For a brief moment he thought about where this story was headed and, as a mark of respect, attempted sobriety. 'He was a hero. I mean, a real hero. A war hero. Wiped out half the Luftwaffe! His name's there, under the paint: "The Kid" – that's what they used to call him.' He raised his glass towards Don's bedroom, downed it, then fell backwards in his chair.

Tom and Emily found Don in his room, collapsed on the floor.

'Oh, Jesus,' muttered Tom, as he slid his arms under Don's back and gently lifted him onto the bed. 'Don, can you hear me? Can you hear me, mate?' In helping him up, he felt his hand being squeezed, and heard Don say, almost imperceptibly, that he was just tired. Very tired. 'It's OK, mate, I'm here. You just take it easy.' He straightened the blankets across Don's chest and listened to his breathing.

'Ayy, Tom – how good's this!' Todd's voice penetrated the closed window. '*Hits of the Blitz*, mate! Appropriate or what?' From the Commodore's cassette player came the voice of Vera Lynn.

Emily threw Tom a look and charged out into the hallway to tell them to shut up. Tom drew the curtains and returned to Don's bedside. 'Silly old prick,' he said. 'What's he rabbitin' on about, eh, mate?'

But Don had fallen into a deep sleep.

Tom sat with him for a few minutes before returning to the verandah. Outside, at Emily's insistence, the party had moved to the far side of Todd's van, away from the house. A chorus of voices sang along with Vera Lynn.

'It's true, mate.' Todd turned up the volume, but lowered it again when he saw Tom's face. 'True as I'm standing here. He was the Kid – a legend! And a real nice fella, I mean, as much as anybody was. He was the sorta bloke that'd do anything for ya. Seen it all, he had. Weell, who hadn't? Mind you, thinkin' about it now, he might've been a bit shell-shocked. Chrissst, who wasn't?' The more famous the Kid became, the closer their friendship was. 'We were like brothers . . . then he cops it himself . . . shot down savin' one of his mates.' He digressed for a moment into 'Never have so many owed so much to so few . . .' He straightened himself up against the van and nodded solemnly to himself.

'Shot down?' Tom joined him by the van as he continued his reverie.

'Yep . . . and that's when Stainless gets the idea about

retrievin' his plane, gunna be worth a mint one day, he reckoned. Weeell, he got that bit right, eh?' He pointed his glass to the plane. 'If ya still don't believe me, check out the cockpit. His girl at the time, well, her initials are scratched into the instrument panel. It's faint, but it's there.'

Tom was guided by a string of party lights that hung over the cockpit. He slid back the canopy and peered inside. They were faint but they were still there. The initials 'BW' had been scratched into the paint. He couldn't remember Bernadette's maiden name, but the 'B' was there and a heart surrounded it. Tom fell into a state of confusion. Todd seemed to know more about Don than he did. But he'd known Don for twenty years – he was his best mate. He climbed down from the wing and joined Emily on the verandah steps.

'How is he? How's Don?' Emily slid along to make room.

'Not lookin' too brilliant.' He sat down and quietly thought over what Todd had said. 'Don't worry, he always seems to come good.'

Tom looked over to the van and then back to the aeroplane. It was all starting to fit. Stainless, the plane, Don being a pilot.

'Tom?' said Emily softly. 'Are you going to tell me what's going on? Because I think I've worked it out anyway.'

He looked at Emily and shook his head. 'He should've told me, Em. He should've said something. Christ, I've been living on my stories for years, of being torpedoed in the Pacific and spending a coupla days on a life raft. Had drinks lined up at the bar for me, even had Don toast my exploits.'

'Maybe he didn't want you to know.'

'Maybe that was it. Maybe by then it was all too late. I mean, what was he going to say. "Oh, by the way, Tom, I forgot to tell you, I was a fighter pilot during the war, bit of a hero actually." '

Emily took his hand. 'Maybe he *couldn't* tell you. The thing about being a hero is, you have to live with whatever heroic deed you did, and in wartime that might be something you don't want to remember.'

Tom thought about his own circumstances. It was easy being a victim – you didn't really have to do anything. All he ever thought about was his own survival. He never had to instigate anything.

'That's the price you pay, Tom. That's why they make you a hero. That's why they give you a medal. I suspect he was just in the wrong place at the wrong time.'

He sat for there for a while, punctuating his thoughts with what had happened over the past month or so. 'I honestly thought all this was going to set us up.' He was addressing himself more than Emily. 'I was going to look after him. And now all this has come out.' He shook his head again. 'How naive am I?'

'Come on, you can't think like that. It's a swansong for all of us, Tom. I think we should celebrate it. Would you care to dance?' She held him close, then guided him into a slow waltz around the yard. 'You know, I haven't been too honest with you, either.'

'What are you talkin' about, Em?'

'I've been a bit crook over the past few weeks.'

'Crook?' He looked stricken.

She squeezed his hand as they danced. 'I'm going into hospital tomorrow. Just for a few tests. It's all arranged. My daughter's coming down.'

'Tests? What sort of tests?'

'Just a check-up, Tom. Nothing to worry about. Something I've been avoiding for a while. I'm good at that. And there's something else.' She carefully worked through what it was she was trying to say. 'I'm having a bit of trouble working us out,' she said, as gently as she could. 'I can't see a future in us, Tom. I know you do. But I'm too . . .' She thought about the word 'old', but that wasn't right. 'Settled. The trouble is, you've made me feel sixteen again. I'm just a vain old woman flattered to discover that somebody can see past this aging body.'

Tom started a reply, but Emily put a finger to his lips.

'You don't have to say anything. It might be better if you didn't. Ever since you arrived, you've made me feel as if I could start over. A second chance. An opportunity to share whatever was left over. The spirit's willing, but the body's, well . . . getting on. Let's just have a dance. Vera Lynn in the moonlight – perfect, as you would say.'

A drunken Todd leant out of the van window. 'How's your dance card lookin', Em?'

Tom replied for her. 'Sorry, Todd. I've had a long-standing booking that's going to last the night.' He lowered his voice and turned back to face Emily. 'You know it's taken me a lifetime to get here, Em. And now you're telling me I'm too late. But it's like you said, it's how you *feel.*' He withdrew a hand from hers and tapped his heart. 'How you feel on the inside. You're not old there. Neither of us is. We can do it.' He took hand again, pulled her closer, then gently kissed her.

She closed her eyes, and, from some place within, and just for the moment, she was sixteen. In shorts and a top that might have doubled as swimmers. Her hair, still wet from the sea, flowed straight down her back. A peeling nose blistered between freckles and her blue eyes. With her hand in his, she held the spell for as long as the moment would last.

Much fuss was made the following morning about Emily's trip to the hospital, but she insisted that everything was fine. There was no panic, no sense of urgency, just a leisurely drive to town. They'd even stopped at the library on the way to borrow some books.

The hospital was small. Made out of brick and stone, it had been completed at the end of the last century. It was a community hospital, a long way from St Vincent's.

'I'll be all right,' she said in a stoic, drover's wife kind of way. She gave Tom an awkward hug and then presented herself at the reception desk with her small case.

Tom made an early return the next day. He hadn't known what to expect. He fussed about with newspapers and flowers. 'You'll probably recognise these,' he said. 'Fran picked them for you.' He stripped the lower leaves and placed the roses in a vase. 'What did the doctor say?'

'Aphids, that's what I recognise,' she said at first. 'Not much. Plenty of rest. And a lifetime of pills.' She pushed herself up against the pillows. 'I'm a bit of a disappointment to him, I think. He looked like the operating sort. Never mind. How's Don?'

'He's good – sort of. I spoke to Paul last night, he's coming down today. Seems he was planning on coming anyway; he's taken a few days off school. I guess it's all for the best.' All for the best. That was the best he could do to sum up how he was feeling. He knew it was the beginning of the end for Don.

'I don't know if you can help him anymore, Tom.'

Tom placed his hand on hers and looked to the window. The sun was shining gold onto the Weddin Ranges. He reached down and picked up a cane basket. 'Now, I know it's a bit early and we're not exactly outside, but I brought you in a picnic. It's just a sandwich and a thermos of tea. It's a new brand,' he said. 'Try it. You might like it.' He placed the basket on the bedside table and began unpacking it.

Megan Morris was a no-nonsense woman and her husband, David, fitted in with her. 'Marry a man with a town job, the country's too hard.' That was her mother's advice, and that was exactly what she'd done.

They turned off the highway and drove down the line of pencil pines that led to Emily's farm. It was the place in which she'd grown up, a place she knew intimately. Indeed, as a three-year-old she'd helped Jock and Emily plant the row of pines. 'To give the place a sense of grandeur,' that was the plan. Now, almost fifty years later, long-neglected branches dropped drifts of needles across the road.

It must have been a month since she was last there. That was the usual timing. They would normally have stopped at a couple of antique shops along the way, but with Mum going into hospital, Megan was keen to spend the time with her. 'We've got to fix these trees,' she said. She always said that.

In some ways she still looked like the childhood photos of herself under the glass-topped dressing table. Her hair was shorter now and cut to a bob, and her face a little fuller perhaps, with a few more lines, but only if you really looked. She was still telling people she was forty-something and could probably hold out for a bit longer. As the car came to a halt she leant forward in her seat belt. 'Oh my God! What's going on? What's with that van?'

'The van?' David pointed to the front lawn. 'What about the *plane*?'

'Greetings, folks. Come for an inspection?' Todd appeared on the verandah. 'Just park 'er next to the shed. Fran's just put the jug on.'

Don rested on the stairs. An outsider was approaching. He wasn't sure if he knew her or not. He straightened his dressing gown, then pulled himself up on the balustrade. 'The indweller is invulnerable and indestructible,' he said. 'Therefore you should not grieve.'

'Grieve?' Megan stopped in her tracks. 'Oh my God, nothing's happened, has it?'

'Happened?' Don asked, puzzled.

'To Mum. Emily.'

'I don't think so. It's from the book.'

'What book? What are you talking about? Who are you?'

'Brian gave it to me.'

'Brian?' This was going nowhere.

'Oh, don't mind Don.' Fran appeared in the doorway. 'Emily's at the hospital. She was feeling poorly so Tom took her in yesterday. You must be Megan – she mentioned you'd be coming down. I'm Fran and this is my husband, Todd.' Todd got up and gave them a wave from the kitchen table. 'And this is Don.'

Todd came to the door. 'Your mum'll be right. She's just gone in for a bit of a kick-start. Had the same thing happen to Fran here. Didn't we, love.'

Fran looked unimpressed. Megan just looked aghast.

Don had insisted on going to the hospital. He had vital information to impart. A lively discussion on the merits of him going, or otherwise, had continued all the way to the back seat of the Morrises' car. In the end it seemed easier for everyone if he just went.

'I just need the toilet,' Don said as soon as they arrived. The receptionist pointed him to the end of the corridor. There was a clarity to his thinking this morning. An order was surfacing from somewhere within. He removed his beanie and pushed on down the aisle.

The door to Emily's room was open. Megan sat close to the bed. 'Well, thank God you're all right, that's all I can say. I mean, Mum, you should have rung last night. Anything could have happened.'

Emily patted her hand. 'Nothing happened, it wasn't an emergency. And I'm fine.'

Megan grabbed Emily's hand as she was withdrawing it. 'It's a warning, Mum. *De-stress*. You've got to start taking it easy.' She threw up her hands. 'There are people camped in your front yard, for God's sake. You can't take on every stray. I mean, really. Is there a problem with the van park? Apart from anything else, think of your own security. I'm stressed just thinking about it.'

Emily drew breath. 'Yes, yes, I can see you'd think things aren't quite as they should be.'

'And I had no idea we owned a plane. I suppose it's just in for a service?' Her hand went to her forehead. 'It's time to start thinking about priorities, Mum. About yourself.'

Emily looked up from the bed. 'Hello, Tom.' She beckoned him into the room. 'This is my daughter, Megan and her husband, David. We were just discussing my state of health. This is my old friend, Tom Barton.'

'Hello, Megan.' Tom reached out his hand. 'We've

met before. It was a very long time ago – you were a little girl.' He'd had a story prepared, but was interrupted by Don, who continued a conversation he'd begun somewhere in the hallway.

'The point is there is no . . . point.' He looked up to see who he was talking to. 'It shouldn't be this hard. Revelations, Emily. It's been a day of revelations. It's all here, all in the little book.' He could have been talking to any one of them, really, but Megan was in his line of sight. Words bumped against each other as he confronted her. 'It's just . . . too hard . . . all too hard.'

Megan looked at the others before turning back to her mother. 'I really think a self-contained unit is the go, Mum, like the ones near the church.' She paused, waiting for Don's next move. A white coat passed the door. 'Doctor Kirk?'

David joined her outside the ward. Mitchell Kirk seemed very young for the responsibilities he held. 'She's had a mild myocardial infarction. A heart attack, if you like. We'll need to do more tests, to find out the extent of the damage, but her blood pressure is good and I've put her on prescription tablets for starters – that should reduce the chance of re-occurrence.' He softened his diagnosis with a reassuring smile. 'Just part of growing old, I guess. Unless you want to go down the surgery road, there's not much we can do.'

'Surgery?'

'We could do a bypass. At your mum's age, it's risky, but it's within acceptable parameters. It's a good option. Then again, given proper medication and not too much stress, who knows? She could keep going for years.'

Megan hung onto the words 'heart attack' and 'stress'. Oh my God, she thought. Megan was probably not the best of Emily's children to be dealing with the current situation. She was simply the closest.

'Well, that settles it,' she told her husband. 'She's moving into town. She should have done it when Dad died. It's ridiculous. That, or we take her on.' In an effort to keep up with her thinking she began to pace. 'We need a family meeting. A *crisis* meeting. Maybe Cath can do it. She's got that downstairs area she doesn't use. Rosie's overseas; she'll have to be contacted.' She thought about Jane, but she was plain hopeless. 'She needs to be near people. I mean, real people. Not, you know . . .' She tilted her head towards the door.

Emily listened to her future being shuffled around the family like a loose card in the pack. She closed her eyes and rested back into the pillow. 'I'm sorry, Tom,' she said with a sigh, 'they mean well. They're trying to work out what's best for me. And I guess I'm trying to work out what's best for them. It's how families work. I really am getting too old for . . .'

Megan came back into the room. 'Mum, we really need to discuss this operation.'

'Yes, I know.' Emily reached out for her daughter's hand. 'I've been meaning to discuss it with you for a while.' She looked towards the door. 'Now, I'm sure that nice young man out there is very good at his job, but I've really thought about this and I've decided to put my faith in the man upstairs. I'll be fine.'

'No, you won't, Mum. You won't be fine at all.' She looked across to David and Tom. 'We'll discuss it later. I think it might be easier if we book into a hotel for the night.' Megan gave Emily a hug as David picked up her bag. 'We'll just get ourselves organised and be back after lunch. Can we get you anything, Mum?'

'No thanks, darling. I'm fine. Truly.'

'OK. Remember: de-stress.' She kissed her on the cheek, then followed David to the door.

'Your children rule your life right to the end, Tom,' Emily said, continuing the conversation as though the interruption had never occurred. 'All I've ever wanted is their happiness. That's all. They don't come with any guarantees. Maybe it's time I did move off the farm. I have been thinking about it for a while.'

'Well, what's stopping you, Em?' Tom asked.

'There's just so much stuff there. Emotional baggage. Suitcases of it. More than you could fit in a flat, put it that way.' She gave a long sigh. Now the garden seemed so much bigger, and her friends were in town, and sooner or later she'd lose her nerve in the car. A townie. That would be about the level of change she could deal with. It was probably now or never.

'Don't be silly, Em. A holiday. That's what you need. We could get a flat at Terrigal maybe. The salt air will give you a second wind. You might even have another think about having that operation.'

Emily took his hand. 'You're a good man, Tom. But I don't think I can do it. I guess I'm not brave enough.'

*

Paul had arrived at the farm earlier that afternoon, while his father and Tom were at the hospital. He'd been subjected to a long dissertation from Todd on the merits of night driving before he heard the welcome sound of Tom's ute making its way up the drive. A warm reunion had taken place between father and son, and Paul was relieved to find Don so lucid and calm. 'Yes, Pop,' he'd replied with a laugh, 'I got the Beetle serviced and she's running like a dream.'

Later he sat in the kitchen with Tom and discussed when he should head back to the city with Don.

'After lunch tomorrow might be the best time to head off. Pop can have a sleep and hopefully the traffic would have died down.' He picked up his beer and followed Tom onto the verandah. 'Looks like everybody's packing up anyway.'

'Yep. She's all over.' Tom descended the stairs and walked across to the ute. All over. All too late. Fifty years too late. One more visit to the hospital to say goodbye to Emily, one more night at the farm, and then he'd be off first thing in the morning.

As he filled the radiator, Tom went over a little speech he'd been working on. 'That Gold Coast plan, Em . . . I really think we could make a go of it. Take a chance and really live the life that we have left . . . C'mon, Em – you're a brilliant mechanic, you can coax anything back to life. I can be brave enough for both of us.' He took a deep breath. 'Or maybe I could pop back and see you here. Tea at the bowlie, that sort of thing. Take in a movie – a real movie – over at Cowra.' He looked up to find Don standing beside him. 'Don! How ya doin'?'

'Good, good,' he replied. Everything suddenly seemed very clear to Don. Serenity. That was the key. Release and be released. Let all things troubling you pass as lightly as ripples on a stream. 'Yeah, I'm good. You?'

Tom closed the bonnet. 'Yeah, I'm good. I'm good too.'

'Don't worry, Tom.' Don put his arm around Tom's shoulder. 'It'll be all right. It's all for the best.'

Emily was asleep when he got to the hospital. With a stillness that you might expect in a photograph. She looked beautiful. She looked like the girl from Terrigal. He pulled a chair close to the bed and sat with her. A breeze gently picked away at the curtains. Afternoon light began to fade.

He couldn't say how long he'd been there. There didn't appear to be set visiting hours, but he was slowly made aware of people moving towards the door. He held her image for a last time, then quietly closed the door.

The pencil pines fell into line. There was now an end to it all. In the following days everyone would go. The plane would go to a museum. Don would be back in the nursing home, and Tom would be stuck in the lift to Tierra del Fuego being bored to death by his neighbours.

It began to rain. He switched on the windscreen wipers and thought of what might have been.

Chapter Twenty-Two

Don wasn't sure who woke him. An anonymous knock on the door brought him back to life. He opened his eyes and looked around the room. The single iron-framed bed had been placed as far away from the window as possible. It could have been any time of the day. A metal trunk and a matching wardrobe broke up the room.

His hand wiped the condensation from the window to reveal another day of bad weather. Outside, bodies in heavy greatcoats appeared as phantoms in the mist, apparitions that fed hoses and cartridge belts into his aircraft. In the background, hangars and runways disappeared into morning drizzle.

His movements seemed restricted. Joints in his body had to be prompted into action and his uniform seemed to hang loose on his body. He sat back on the bed and washed his face with his hands.

A middle-aged man with a Yorkshire accent and a mug of tea appeared in the doorway.

'Cuppa for you, sir. Briefing in twenty minutes. I don't think anyone's going up today – including Jerry.' He gestured towards the window. 'Not unless the weather lifts.' He placed the mug on the dresser, then headed off down the corridor.

The weather would lift. The fog would burn off and he would be in the air again before lunch. He knew that. That was how it had been all week.

He pulled on his boots and lifted the collar of his flying jacket around his ears. In his hand he held his flying cap.

The wardrobe mirror caught his reflection as he closed the door. Long pyjamas hung over plaid slippers. The collar of his dressing gown had been lifted up around his ears. In his hand he held his green beanie.

He shuffled towards the front door of Emily's house and wondered what the outcome of the day would be. At the verandah rails he watched the rain silently falling across the open hangar. A siren triggered shadows that brushed past him. He tried to catch them but his slippers sank into the mud. Hurried half-steps took him across the yard where diaphanous figures waited to help him onto the wing of his aircraft. The rain fell in sheets. It saturated his dressing gown and flowed unimpeded against his skin.

He lost his place for a minute. The tarmac was all wrong, and he couldn't remember going to the briefing. But the aircraft was real, and so was the rain that swept across its wing and stung his face. He half-fell, half-stepped into the cockpit and slid the canopy across his head, locking it into position. He felt cold. He wrapped a scarf of fingers around a hand, then turned his attention to the yard. The rest of the squadron must have left without him. He began to panic. There must have been a mechanical problem. He looked into the clouds for familiar shadows but saw only the gunner's eyes. Terrified, half-green, half-blue, they pushed him back into his seat. He tried to shut them out with his hands, but they flashed past him in an entanglement of flesh and twisted metal.

A flare burst over the cockpit. At the same time the sun rose into his eyes. The silent explosion of white light marked the beginning of his journey. It shone brightly over the runway, then fragmented into daytime stars that drifted back to earth. That was the signal. It was time. He remembered his watch and reached into his dressing gown pocket to retrieve it, but it was gone. He must have left it on the dresser, he thought, beside his letters from home and the photograph of Bernadette.

The supercharger forced air into the engine as the propeller blades slowly begin to revolve. The engine fired.

He leant forward in the cockpit and tapped the gauges. Some of them worked, some didn't. As the engine settled into a steady drone, he waved off the battery cart. With the rising heat came the smell of burning oil. He released the brakes and opened the throttle. The plane rocked forward over the bricks. The lead to the batteries snapped.

The sound of the engine sent Tom stumbling to the window. Through drizzling rain he could see Don in dressing gown and beanie as he taxied the Spitfire down the side of the house. 'Shit . . . Ohhh, shit!' He held his hand against the vibrating glass then fumbled with his jacket buttons.

At the door he collided with Paul. 'I just took him in a cup of tea. Like just then. Quick, we've got to stop him.'

Paul was half asleep. 'Stop who? What's going on?'

'Don!'

Paul took the verandah stairs two at a time. Ahead, Fran and Todd were running towards the back paddock in their pyjamas.

Don couldn't see the end of the runway. He'd passed the marshalling point, he knew that much. He swung the nose into the wind and ran through a checklist. Wing surfaces rose and fell. Instruments were scanned. From the tower he picked out two figures hurrying through the shadows of others. One of them gave him a distinct wave. He returned the acknowledgment, then opened the throttle.

The propeller bit into the air. It pulled the aeroplane along a dirt track that ran away to the boundary gate. He was moving quickly now. For luck, his fingers traced Bernadette's initials. The tail lifted off the ground. The noise of the engine filled the cockpit.

Adrenalin pushed Tom on. At the gate, he fell, then pulled himself up against the railings and shouted for Don to stop. 'Oh my God, the fence. He's gonna hit the fence!'

Boundary markers raced towards him. He must have overshot the runway. Don increased power to the supercharger and concentrated on his airspeed. He was committed now. At ninety knots, he drew back on the stick, and fence posts disappeared below in a blur of lantana and barbed wire. He retracted the gear and began climbing into the dawn.

Todd stood open-mouthed. 'Just like the good old days.' Before he knew what he was doing, he punched the air, then cupped his hands around his mouth, 'Give 'em one for me, Kiddo!'

In less than a minute he'd gone, swallowed up by cloud and fog. Whispered voices strained to hear the engine, but there was only the sound of the bush. The paddock closed in around them. Somewhere from the tall timbers a crow gave a mournful cry, then there was silence.

Tom didn't know what to do. He had to call someone. 'An ambulance! Call an ambulance!' Whatever the outcome, an ambulance was probably a safe bet.

Paul raced back to the house. Tom tried to keep up, but age slowed him. He looked behind to see Todd and Fran following in his footsteps. Surely someone from the neighbouring properties had seen or heard the plane – there had to be someone who had seen where he was heading.

The sound of the engine knocked him off his feet. The noise was deafening. The plane passed directly overhead. It came from nowhere. Tom looked up to see the tail of the aircraft heading down the line of pines. A hundred feet above the roadway, it banked sharply towards town.

Tom got to the ute first. He crunched it into gear and skidded off down the drive, searching the sky for any sign of the plane.

Don straightened up on his new course. The fog was beginning to lift, but there was still no sign of the others. He tried the radio but there was nothing. His flight plan was missing. He looked for landmarks but nothing was recognisable. Then a town appeared. He came in low. Houses, roofs, back yards, roads, people pointing . . . It all became a blur. He banked over wheat silos then lined up the main street. Shops, banks, lamp posts, cars, pubs, more people . . . Then, on the hill, the hospital. A landmark he knew.

Windows shook in their frames as the aircraft passed low overhead. Emily woke from a deep sleep; indeed, had it not been for the commotion in the hall she might not have woken at all. In an orderly manner, she gathered her robe and proceeded down the corridor. A small group had gathered by a window. Someone was on the phone to the police, it seemed. Others spoke of an aeroplane.

She walked towards the foyer and arrived at the main entrance as a whistle of silver flashed past the window. She hurried out to the porch, but the aircraft had gone. It was the sound left behind that she recognised.

Don began a tight turn back to the hospital. It was an imposing building, familiar only in that he knew that was where he had to be. He tapped the gauge again, but the needle remained unchanged. He was losing fuel. He tried a mental calculation to determine how many minutes he had left in the air, but he couldn't make the equation work. His mind jumped in and out of flight school, to Henry the fat instructor, to Bernadette, to emergency procedures. But there were only flashes; nothing stuck.

In front of the hospital, he saw a ground vehicle arriving. It was the one from the air base. Open-trayed with cannabilised aircraft parts and a forty-four of fuel. That was it, no question. Someone got out of the car and began waving to him.

Down below, Tom ran from the car park up the hospital stairs. Ahead he could see Emily breaking through the group of spectators. 'It's Don . . .' he told her, before doubling over with his hands to his knees to catch his breath. His jacket and pyjamas were soaked, and mud stained his cuffs. 'We've got to get him down.' He measured his breathing and concentrated on what he had to say. 'The airport. We've got to get him to the airport.'

The noise of the propeller cutting a tight turn began to drown his words. He staggered clear and pointed to the east. 'That way! *That way*!' The aircraft swept by. It might have been Don acknowledging him in a low pass. Or it might not.

The ute had never travelled so fast. Wind cleaned out the crevices as the speedo nudged eighty on the straight. The whole thing shook as he urged more speed.

'There. There he is!' Tom pointed to a spot through the windscreen. The Spitfire sat momentarily between this year's rego sticker and a parking permit, in and out of cloud, sometimes at altitude, sometimes above the trees. At least Don was heading in the right direction, towards the local airstrip. 'How long do you reckon he's got?'

Emily looked through the window, but he was gone. 'Not long. Five or six minutes at the most.'

Tom put his foot down. It would take them at least another twenty.

From his cockpit seat Don could see the world. Its beauty, its imperfections. It was another place, the 'below', a place where he'd once lived a life. Everything appeared in minute detail – trees, birds, blades of grass, even the individual drops of morning dew. He felt a clarity he'd never experienced before. Everything seemed so simple. So obvious. So serene.

Then a whiteout of cloud moved over, covering the windscreen like a hospital sheet.

The engine began to falter. An airstrip came into view. The real world raced at him.

As the wheels touched the 'below' he let go. His body crumpled like a piece of paper. His last breath was a sigh of relief. From some other place, he watched his aeroplane cartwheeling down the tarmac.

EPILOGUE

It was a number four lure that Tom chose. 'Old Faithful', the one Ted the fish diviner used to swear by. Slowly, slowly, he let it drift through the water, then gave it a quick tug to propel it up through the depths.

Tom let the line settle across his fingers and sat back on the rocks. A seasonal life, that's what it had been. He thought about the time he'd worked the Snowy, and when he'd been a farmer and a fisherman. And all the other jobs he'd done. That was how it was, that was how life turned out. Some people got it together early, others took a lifetime. If ever.

Most of the town had gone to Don's funeral. That was the great thing about living in a country town, he'd realised. Stan wheeled out the LTD and everybody showed. The *Grenfell Record* even put in an obituary, as a follow up to its 'War Hero Death Plunge' story from the week before. The RSL were there. An Australian flag. Rows of campaign medals. There had been talk of holding the service at the Eastern Suburbs Crematorium but it seemed easier for Paul to come to Don, and in his eulogy Paul had said his Pop would have wanted it that way. Brian read from *A Serene Life*. Fran cut a morning's worth of sandwiches, while Todd cracked a bottle of Lions Club Port, and they both talked about heading home to see their old friends. It was a day to remember.

The wreck of the aeroplane remained on the tarmac for a week after the crash. Air safety regulators came and went. Eventually a long corridor was cordoned off as historians from the aviation museum at Nowra sifted through the wreckage. Individual components were identified, tagged, then carefully placed onto the back of a truck.

Tom looked around him. Terrigal had changed. The holiday houses were now duplexes. What was once Mullet's old boatshed, where fish were gutted and thrown to the pelicans, was now a fashionable eatery. The Terrigal of his past had become a world of smart cafes and flash resorts, surf shops and kids in sporty cars.

He reeled in his line. 'Nothin' here, or I would have caught it by now,' he said. 'What we need is a boat. A tinny.'

'A tinny?' Emily looked up from her book.

But the sea hadn't changed, the salt still permeated the air, and the rocks that had formed imaginary whales in his childhood still breached along the point.

Hand in hand, the two of them walked across the sand. He with his bucket and rod, she with her folding chair and book.

ACKNOWLEDGMENTS

Many thanks to the people of Grenfell who perpetuate the spirit of Henry Lawson; to my family and friends, Fiona Johnson, Martin Daley, Rose Creswell and Annette Hughes, Jane Cameron and Leslie McFadzean, Virginia Bell and Ron Sinclair. Thanks, as well, to the staff at the Matthew Talbot Hostel, the RRMYC, and the Australian Museum of Flight at Nowra. My gratitude to Jane Palfreyman at Random House, who never gave up on me. And finally, to Spitfire enthusiasts, I beg your indulgence.